# SOLOMON'S RING

Also in the Daughters of Light series

*Finding Jade*

# SOLOMON'S RING

## MARY JENNIFER PAYNE

Daughters of Light

**DUNDURN**
TORONTO

Cover image: 123RF.com/Karel Miragaya
Printer: Webcom

**Library and Archives Canada Cataloguing in Publication**

Payne, Mary Jennifer, author
    Solomon's ring / Mary Jennifer Payne.

(Daughters of light)
Issued in print and electronic formats.
ISBN 978-1-4597-3783-9 (softcover).--ISBN 978-1-4597-3784-6 (PDF).--
ISBN 978-1-4597-3785-3 (EPUB)

    I. Title.  II. Series: Payne, Mary Jennifer.  Daughters of light.

PS8631.A9543S65 2018          jC813'.6          C2017-903397-2
                                                C2017-903398-0

1   2   3   4   5      22   21   20   19   18

We acknowledge the support of the **Canada Council for the Arts**, which last year invested $153 million to bring the arts to Canadians throughout the country, and the **Ontario Arts Council** for our publishing program. We also acknowledge the financial support of the **Government of Ontario**, through the **Ontario Book Publishing Tax Credit** and the **Ontario Media Development Corporation**, and the **Government of Canada**.

Nous remercions le Conseil des arts du Canada de son soutien. L'an dernier, le Conseil a investi 153 millions de dollars pour mettre de l'art dans la vie des Canadiennes et des Canadiens de tout le pays.

Care has been taken to trace the ownership of copyright material used in this book. The author and the publisher welcome any information enabling them to rectify any references or credits in subsequent editions.
— *J. Kirk Howard, President*

The publisher is not responsible for websites or their content unless they are owned by the publisher.

Printed and bound in Canada.

VISIT US AT

dundurn.com | @dundurnpress | dundurnpress | dundurnpress

Dundurn
3 Church Street, Suite 500
Toronto, Ontario, Canada
M5E 1M2

Solomon's Ring *is dedicated to my niece, Olive Payne. May we leave an environmental legacy that allows her generation to live in peace and harmony with our natural world.*

# JASMINE

We hear the sounds at the same time. Jade and I don't say a word; instead, we start walking faster. The footsteps behind us speed up as well, keeping pace. Whoever — or whatever — is following us clearly doesn't feel the need to keep their presence secret.

My stomach does a nervous somersault. This isn't good. During the last few months of training with our Protectors, we've been taught to recognize when a situation may be dangerous. And at this moment, every cell in my body is screaming that this is a code-red situation. My gut feeling is that Jade and I are not just being followed. We're being hunted.

There are still four full city blocks to go before we'll reach a lit street lamp, before we can turn off the tiny flashlight we're carrying. Right now, other than the pathetically anorexic beam cast by our flashlight, we're walking in complete darkness and the street is empty. Rolling electricity cuts are to blame for the lack of lighting; only a small number of street lamps are now turned on at night, and those are found almost exclusively on the city's main streets or in the wealthiest neighbourhoods.

"Stop," Jade whispers, and we stop walking at the exact same moment. We're naturally synchronized like this; it's a twin thing.

The footsteps stop too. And though I try not to, I can't help thinking about the recent rash of abductions and murders in our city. Local news websites post daily updates and photos of the missing ... and those found. Thing is, not many people fall under the found category. And those that have been found are not found alive ... or in one piece. It's a modern-day Jack the Ripper sort of thing. Or at least that's what the media and police would like us to believe.

But as Seers we know better. We're at war.

Jade and I begin walking again, this time more quickly. The night air is only slightly cooler than it was during the day, and the humidity, along with the adrenaline surging through me, makes my face slick with sweat. Instinctively, my hand moves to the oversized knapsack on my back. I run my fingers over the smooth surface of my bamboo pole. Though any sort of strong, pole-like structure will do, I made this pole in class at Beaconsfield. The bamboo is light but strong, which makes it easy to carry. We're only supposed to use our poles in the most serious of circumstances, when we believe our lives are under immediate threat.

I listen. The footsteps are definitely closing in. This seems as good a time as any to use my pole.

Jade nods at me, her dark eyes solemn. "One, two …" she whispers.

At the count of three we swing around to confront our stalker. In one fluid motion, I pull my pole out of my knapsack. It slices through the air, making a sharp whistling sound as it moves. Ready to strike, I hold it across my body like a shield.

A wiry male figure stands less than five feet away. Jade directs the beam of the flashlight at his face, and even though it doesn't illuminate much, I am startled by the chalky, grey-white colour of his skin and the cavernous, dark circles that frame his eyes.

Great. Some strung-out junkie thinks he's going to mug us. I flex my arms, tightening the grip on my pole.

"Back off," I say, keeping my voice low and even.

He doesn't move or say a word in response. I feel Jade tense beside me. We're like two cats, coiled and ready to spring. My newly developed muscles, the result of hours of daily training at Beaconsfield, give me confidence. This guy is likely high as a kite. That might make him less fearful, but he's still nothing for two Seers to take on.

Jade shines the flashlight beam at his face again. I see it before she says anything.

"Jazz. His eyes." Her voice is barely a whisper, but the demon hears. In response it draws back its concrete-coloured lips. Razor-sharp teeth glisten at us. The smell of rust and decay hits my nostrils like a tsunami.

There's only one. This means it will be a minor challenge for us, especially as I'm already armed. If anyone told me a year ago that I'd be killing demons, I'd have thought they were crazy. But after travelling to the Place-in-Between and seeing the armies of demons that reside down there for myself, there's nothing I won't believe. Tell me I've been signed up for riding lessons on a unicorn and I'll ask if pulling on its horn will make it stop galloping.

Without any warning, the demon rushes at Jade. She scurries backward, moving just out of its reach as it lunges for her face.

I dart forward, keeping my centre of gravity low, and swing my pole, throwing my entire body weight behind it while aiming for the soft part of the demon's neck. The only way to destroy one of these creatures is to behead it. I wait for the satisfying impact of rattan against flesh.

This demon is fast, though, much faster than the ones I encountered in the Place-in-Between. And as it grabs my pole and tries to wrench it out of my grasp, I discover it's also much stronger.

Jade is beside me in an instant. The sticky, humid air is causing my hands to sweat, making my grip on the pole even more tenuous.

"You're not armed. Get back," I shout at her. I'm not willing to lose her again. I already spent nearly half my life believing she was dead and that it was my fault, so I'm not going to risk having it happen for real now.

The demon takes advantage of the split second I shift my focus to Jade and gives the pole another hard tug. This time it slips through my fingers like water.

I immediately backflip away from the demon, but it still manages to catch my lower legs with the pole. The wood smashes against my shins, causing me to scream with pain. Flickering stars fill my vision, and my legs give out from under me as I land.

Jade drags me out of the demon's reach as it lunges again. This time the pole comes within centimetres of my ear. A little closer and my head would've cracked open like a sun-ripened melon, brains spilling onto the pavement.

I jump back to my feet, trying to force down the sickening nausea sweeping over me. There's no way I can let myself faint. Not now. It would be a death sentence for both of us.

Jade runs at the demon, veering off sharply to the left at the last moment. She's fast, but not fast enough. The demon catches her shoulder with its long claws, ripping open the back of her T-shirt.

The diversion works just long enough. I spring toward the demon and kick it squarely in the soft area between its hip and groin. The creature bellows in surprise and drops my pole. I hear it bounce along the cracked pavement of the sidewalk and onto the road.

Without thinking, I dash toward the sound. There's no way I can lose my pole. I've trained for hundreds of hours with it in my hands over the last few months. It's become an extension of me, like another appendage. Besides, Mr. Khan would kill me.

"Jazz!" Jade screams as I crouch at the concrete lip of the sidewalk to retrieve it.

I turn in her direction and immediately see why she's screaming.

Three more figures have emerged from the shadows of a nearby alleyway and are making their way toward us. I'm almost certain they're not human.

My fingers scurry, crab-like, along the warm skin of the street until they hit my pole. I snatch it up and run toward Jade.

"We have to get out of here," I say, grabbing her by the arm. She nods. Trying to fight would be crazy. Not only are the odds now stacked against us, but this seems to be a new breed of demon: stronger, more cunning than any we've encountered before.

I begin to run without thinking. I know the demons are close behind us. I can hear their laboured breathing and smell the rusty odour of blood from their exhalations.

Jade's a few feet ahead of me. Speed is her strength; a deadly and accurate aim with the pole is mine.

I keep my eyes locked firmly on the glimmering street lamp ahead. The small orb of light illuminates one of the city's busiest streets — surely the demons won't risk chasing us out in the open. There'd be too many witnesses.

Not that these demons seem too worried about being discovered. After all, they've left over a dozen dismembered bodies strewn around the downtown core of the city over the last few weeks.

Jade is nearly at the intersection. The light from the street lamp glows around her, giving her an angelic aura. I watch a police car roll past the intersection. Maybe Jade can flag them down. If they give us a ride home, we'll be safe for sure — safe for tonight, at least.

Something grabs hold of my knapsack, and for a brief moment, I'm suspended in mid-air, caught between the force of me moving forward and the demon pulling me back.

I shout out as my feet slip out from under me. Jade turns, her face a mask of panic.

"Keep going!" I yell, reaching for my pole. One of us needs to make it out of this situation; it will be a disaster if the demons kill both of us. If that happens, the demons will be able to unify our soul — and steal our powers.

Jade knows this. Pain washes across her face. She needs to let me try to battle them alone.

"Go!" I scream as the demon pulls me down.

She turns and runs, her dark ponytail disappearing into the darkness.

I hit the ground with such force, my elbows feel shattered. They've taken most of the impact of my fall. The demon is on me instantly. The smell of dried blood and rotting flesh fills my nostrils, making me gag.

I use my right leg to kick out at it, hitting it in the abdomen. The creature barely flinches.

"We've been looking for you, Jasmine," it whispers, placing its cold hands around my neck. The voice is gravelly and hoarse. "Easy to find you after your sister's story."

An icy finger of fear travels up my spine.

*Me?*

My airway is closing … I'm like a fish out of water … gasping.

*Why me?*

I can't die. Not now. I need to be with Jade, with the rest of the Seers. I need to be alive to protect Mom … and Jade won't be strong enough to do that if I'm dead.

The pressure around my neck is growing. Small stars dance across my vision.

"Why?" I manage to choke out. Darkness is speeding toward me like an express train. I wonder if Jade is home yet. I wonder if she's safe….

"Because you're *elegido*," the demon hisses as it lowers its face closer to mine. And that's when I notice. Even though the face in front of me is grey and pallid, the resemblance is unmistakable.

I saw this face on an evening news broadcast about a week ago. I can't remember the name. I think it was Tim or Jim or Jamie or something normal and boring like that. Nineteen years old. Worked as a bartender at one of the busiest clubs downtown. Disappeared on his way home from work late at night.

And now he's somehow no longer human but demon — and not just any demon. He's the demon that's likely going to end my life.

# JADE

Blood-red light floods my face. I squint, my hand instinctively shielding my eyes, though this motion obscures my vision and puts me in greater danger.

The window of the police car slides down, and I freeze like a doe in the headlights. I'm unarmed. The line between human and demon is so unpredictable now that every situation is cause to be on high alert.

"Where are you heading?" an officer asks, leaning his head out the window. I can't see his eyes. The brim of his hat casts long shadows down his face. He smiles. Straight white teeth shine out at me. Seemingly human. Relief washes over me.

I walk over to the cruiser. I'm shaking with worry about Jasmine but can't risk telling the police anything. Besides, what could they do? Their guns are useless against demons. And they'd send me straight to a psychiatric hospital if I tried to explain the Place-in-Between to them, or the fact that climate-change terrorists should be the least of our worries right now.

"One Oak Street," I reply, glancing back over my shoulder into the darkness beyond the street lamp. No sign of Jasmine. In fact, there's no sign of life at all. My throat tightens and tears spring to my eyes. I'm finding it hard to get any air into my lungs. It's as though someone's just hauled off and given me a strong punch to the abdomen, knocking the wind out of me.

"Are you okay?" the officer asks, his face full of concern. "Is One Oak your home address?"

"Yes, I live there. And I'm fine," I say, forcing a smile. It's difficult to speak. "Just a little spooked by the dark, that's all. I lost track of time at a friend's place studying for exams."

The officer shakes his head, his brown eyes darkening. A shiny film of perspiration covers his cheeks. He takes a well-used handkerchief out of his pocket and wipes the sweat away as he speaks. "Your friend's parents should know better than to let you stay this late if they aren't going to provide a safe way home. There's a reason for curfews." He nods toward the back of the cruiser. "Hop in. There's no way a young woman like yourself should be out here with less than twenty minutes to go before curfew. I'm PC Parks, by the way, and my partner is PC Edwards. We'll get you home safely, but don't let this happen again. You know the situation we're dealing with in our city."

I open the back door and slide across the seat. Curfew for anyone under eighteen starts at eight o'clock sharp.

Mom is going to lose it when I arrive home without Jasmine. I knew we shouldn't have done that final hill with Cassandra tonight, but they were both so intent on pushing us beyond our normal training schedule. Without Lily there, my warnings about the time of sunset were completely ignored. Two first-born, risk-loving, and very stubborn Seers against me. It was a no-win situation. By the time we managed to scramble up the steep embankment, the shadows cast by the sparse bushes and rocks had lengthened, and the sky was top-heavy and as dark as ink. The setting sun's blood-red light screamed at me like a warning. And we still needed to get Cassandra home. One of the most important rules we've been taught at Beaconsfield is that no Seer is ever to be left on her own.

The thing is, none of this should've even happened tonight. All of us could have already been safe in our respective homes. Anger swells up in my chest as I think about how Cassandra and Jasmine ignored me when I said we needed to leave, that it was not safe to do another run. They know better than to take risks like that. We're always being warned about our strengths and weaknesses as Seers. Their rashness and need for adrenaline as first-born Seers is their Achilles heel. It can put them, and others, in incredible danger.

But my being angry isn't going to help the situation now, and it is a dangerous emotion, so I stare out the window, practice deep breathing, and try to visualize Jasmine safe. It would be the best thing ever if she were already home when I arrived, though I know that is about as likely as me suddenly sprouting a third head.

The streets are nearly empty. Two other patrol cars pass by us, the officers inside giving a quick wave of acknowledgment to Parks and Edwards. Regular crime updates come in over the video screen on the front dash from police headquarters. No bodies found yet tonight in Toronto, but reports of riots and fires all over New York City for the second night in a row. Fire is a real danger now with the water restrictions. It's been a worry in large cities since Los Angeles was pretty much completely destroyed a little less than a year ago. An army of homeless people, desperate for water and food, rose up and basically burned the city to the ground. Considering the fact that the majority of the remaining population in the City of Angels was homeless and had been basically left to die in the streets, it shouldn't have come as a big surprise. In fact, pretty much the entire state of California sits empty now, with most people having fled years ago to either San Francisco or somewhere even farther north in search of water, food, and medicine after more than a decade of drought and wildfires — not to mention a series of powerful earthquakes.

A streetcar dotted with less than a handful of passengers slides past us in the darkness with the grace of a serpent just before we turn onto Oak Street.

"Is there a parent or guardian at home?" PC Edwards asks, her thin lips pursed tightly. She stares hard at me, trying to keep her dark-green eyes neutral to cover the prejudice she's feeling. But I can read her thoughts.

*Hispanic-looking teen living in one of Toronto's poor areas and out at curfew. Likely being brought up by a drug-using single mother who is out at night selling herself. Might even end up as one of the bodies we've been finding scattered all over the city like dog shit on the sidewalks....*

I nod, trying not to let it get to me. She's right about the single mother part, but that's it.

"My mom is definitely home. I contacted her as I left my friend's place. It's just that she has lupus, so she's pretty sick most of the time. That's why she couldn't come and get me." It's not a total lie. Mom suffered from lupus for many years, and it nearly killed her. In fact, she'd likely be dead right now if Raphael hadn't come along.

"Well, we'll wait here until you're in the building," she says. "Don't let this happen again. You're getting in with only a minute or two to spare. Any later and we'd be issuing a Teen Anti-Social Behaviour Order."

I really am not in the mood for a lecture from this woman, who is so sure she's responsible for keeping the city safe, when I know the truth. A blindfolded Seer could crack her in half like a walnut. And police guns and bullets are as about as useful as feathers when it comes to dealing with demons. The truth would deflate her bloated ego in a heartbeat.

"I'll be sure to remember that," I say as I leave the cruiser, making sure to close the door just a little too hard on my way out.

On my way up the stairwell (the elevator in our building only runs for about an hour a day), I try to think of what to tell Mom about why Jasmine isn't with me. I could say my sister is staying the night at Cassandra and Lily's, but Mom will hit the roof if she's hearing that from me rather than Jasmine asking for permission herself. It could even result in Mom calling Cassandra and Lily's parents, which would complicate things way too much. But I can't see any other story that would be even slightly believable.

The thing is, Mom doesn't know what Jasmine and I are … or about the true purpose of our high school, Beaconsfield. I often think she suspects something is up, especially since we've become uber-fit over the last year or so, and most of our close friends are identical twins. I hope she never needs to find out, because if she knew the whole truth, she'd be scared to death every waking second. In fact, the entire world would be terrified if they knew what was actually happening.

I finally reach the front door of our apartment. Before I can even get my key into the lock, the door flies open. Mom stands on the other side, her face flushed with emotion.

"Where have you been? Do you know what time it is?" she asks as she pulls on my sister's red high-top Converses and twists her long, dark hair back in a pony-tail. Her face is a mask of concern.

I open my mouth, but no words come out, because I don't want to lie to her. After all the heartache and suffering she went through because of my abduction when I was younger, I just can't do that.

"You need to come with me," Mom says, grabbing her purse. I open my mouth again to remind her about the curfew but immediately close it. If she's leaving the safety of our apartment, there's no way I'm not going with her. An Anti-Social Behaviour Order is nothing compared to Mom being at the mercy of roaming demons.

"Where are we going?" I ask.

Mom stands and looks straight at me, her bottom lip quivering. "Your sister's been attacked. She's at St. Michael's Hospital. With Mr. Khan."

# JASMINE

Searing pain spreads across my throat. I can barely breathe. My airway is closing, the soft tissue crushed between the cold hands around my neck. I'm dying.

First Mom loses Jade for five years and has to live that entire time with the heart-wrenching belief that her daughter's dead, having been taken from the front lawn of our house by a stranger in the middle of the day. And now she's going to lose me. Except this time there will be no miracle reappearance. I'm going to be die … and likely be reported as just another victim of our city's serial killers (who are supposedly part of organized climate-change terrorism).

Tears leak down the sides of my face. I'm not crying for me, but rather for Mom and Jade. My heart twists as I think of Raphael as well. The thought of never seeing him again makes me ache with sorrow. No matter how hard I try, I can't help but be frightened. And I know that's making the demon stronger.

I manage to open my eyes and look at its face, which looms above mine like a helium balloon.

I'm not ready to surrender yet.

"Jamie?" I ask. My voice is barely more than a squeak.

It's a long shot, and I'm not even sure I've got the name right, but I figure it's worth a try.

A flicker. It's brief, like the passing of a shadow, but some part of his humanity is still in there. I can see it in his eyes. He's thinking about his mother. He's not completely demon. Jamie's not dead. Not yet.

I think about the tear-soaked, deflated face of Jamie's mother as she was broadcast across the city last week, pleading for news about her son's whereabouts and for his safe return. He was definitely loved during his lifetime, and some memory of that clearly remains in what's left of his soul.

Besides, that glimmer is the only chance I have of survival.

"Jamie, your mother told the whole city how much she loves you and misses you…. How proud she was of you." My voice is barely a croak now. In the distance, I can see a light. And, though the lack of oxygen might be causing me to hallucinate, I swear I see my father and grandmother standing in the light, motioning for me to come to them.

I move my gaze back to the demon. "She clearly loved you very much. You were special to people…. You made a difference while you were here."

Something shifts in its eyes. The blackness starts to

break apart like oil doused with dish soap. A few moments later, hazel eyes filled with deep sadness are staring back at me rather than the flat, black pupils of a demon.

The pressure around my throat loosens for a second. It's only a second, but it's enough.

I stretch my right arm out and touch my pole. As the lips above me mouth the word "Mom," I bring my knees up in one fluid motion, propelling the thing off me, and roll out from under it. It reacts with a surprised and angry growl, and the demonic darkness is back. But I'm already scrambling to my feet. Seconds later, I bring my pole down across the back of its neck.

The pole slices cleanly through flesh and cracks the bone of the spine in two. Then there's that familiar gurgling sound, and the smell of copper washes over me like a tsunami. But this time the feeling is different. This time it feels a little like murder. And as I look down at the head lying at my feet, a stream of putrid blood flowing from the jagged cut my pole made, I don't see a demon. Instead I see the face of Jamie, the young bartender who'd had something happen to him that shouldn't be possible in our world. Something beyond terrible.

I stagger backward, my hand covering my mouth. Vomit fills my throat. The world spins around me, and I try to steady myself, but there's nothing to grab hold of. I'm falling. My face slams against the concrete of the sidewalk, pain reverberating along my left cheekbone and temple.

Tendrils of grey smoke linger around Jamie's body for a moment. It's the demon. Now without a vessel, it will leave in search of another to possess. Right now it's like a snail without a shell.

I'm a Seer. I can't lie here for long. Those who are hunting us will sniff me out like a lion stalking its prey. Fear washes over me, causing beads of perspiration to erupt on my upper lip and forehead. I lick my dry lips, tasting the saltiness of my skin, and try to push the fear away. Negative emotions, especially fear, will only make the demons stronger and lead them straight to me. It's critical that I get back up and to a main street.

Thing is, every time I try to lift my head, it feels like hot knives are being thrust into the left side of my face. Waves of nausea and dizziness wash over me and the world tilts dangerously. It's like I'm on an amusement ride.

Clutching my pole in my right hand, I drag myself forward like a dog that's been hit by a car. Each tiny movement is excruciating. There's no way I'm going to be able to get anywhere like this.

I roll over onto my back and stare into the blackness. There used to be so much more light pollution at night, but now you can see the stars above Toronto. I'm beginning to swim in and out of consciousness. I won't be able to fight if I'm attacked. I'm spent.

*You came back to save me from the fire. Sometimes I swear I feel like you're still with me. I need you now. Please save me again. I don't want to die.*

He wasn't supposed to save me. According to Ms. Samson, that's something he's forbidden to do. And yet he did it all the same.

My eyes are closing. I try to force them open, but they feel so heavy, as though they're made of lead.

What does it mean to be *elegido*? And why did he use the Spanish word for chosen? Does it mean I'm the next Seer chosen to die? If that's the case, it seems the job has been done.

Footsteps. My blood runs cold. I hold my breath and listen. The footsteps stop, and I wait, holding my breath. I know I'm not imagining things. There's definitely someone, or *something*, out here with me. My heart thrums loudly in my chest.

"Jasmine?"

The voice is instantly recognizable. It's Mr. Khan. My Protector. I press my free hand over my mouth to keep from shouting out in relief. It's too dangerous. Instead I give a low whistle.

A video phone flashlight clicks on, its beam of light casting a ghostly shadow on the sidewalk to my right, by the alleyway between two darkened houses. Mr. Khan's slender silhouette is visible against a backdrop of brick.

I whistle again, and the beam slowly moves toward me, hugging the ground in its search.

The light washes over my Converse-clad feet, then up my body to my face. I smile weakly and try to wave. Mr. Khan turns off the beam, rushes over, and kneels down beside me.

"Are you badly hurt?" he asks, pushing his dark hair back from his forehead and peering down at me.

"Well, I don't think I can walk on my own, which probably qualifies as 'I've been a lot better during my relatively short life.'"

Mr. Khan looks around and briefly turns on the flashlight again to scour the alleyway adjacent to us. He frowns before quickly turning it off and putting it into his bag.

"We've got to get you out of here," he says, his voice thick with concern.

"Really? Tell me something I don't know," I reply.

"Jasmine, this is no time to be a wiseass. You're in immediate danger. *We're* in immediate danger."

I want to tell him to be careful with his emotions; his fear is so strong, I can almost taste it.

"The city is becoming more heavily populated with demonic entities. There seems to be a nightly rise in the population. The rift must be wide open. I'm getting us an ambulance." He turns on his video phone.

In less than ten seconds, a concerned-looking dispatcher appears on the screen. Mr. Khan tells her our location and then pulls a gym towel out of his bag.

"It's used," he says apologetically as he folds it into a makeshift pillow and gently eases it under my head. Every centimetre of my throat screams with pain at the tiniest motion. I'm definitely injured.

"Not all the demons are getting here through the rift," I say. "Go take a look at the one I just killed. Look at its face."

Mr. Khan gets up and switches on the flashlight again. He walks over to the decapitated head lying a few feet away from us. I can't turn my head enough to see his expression, but I know he's closely examining it.

He walks back over and crouches down beside me.

"What happened here, Jasmine?" he asks, his voice low. I can read his thoughts.

*That's a human head. She's murdered a human. Don't tell me Jasmine is losing her mind. Don't let her end up like Fatimah. Please. Not Jasmine.*

"But it wasn't human," I say. "Well, not entirely. He … it presented as demon. And I'm not losing my mind." There's a long pause. I don't want to tell Mr. Khan that I appealed to the glimmer of humanity still there to save myself, though I don't know why it feels like something I need to keep secret. The faint sound of sirens in the distance reaches us. I breathe a sigh of relief.

"Well, it's certainly human now," he says, sitting back heavily onto the sidewalk and wrapping his arms around his knees.

I frown. "The thing was definitely a demon when I killed it," I say, trying to pull myself up onto my elbows. The pain is too much and I collapse back against the towel. "And it was trying to kill me. Kept saying I was *elegido*, chosen, whatever that means."

There's a sharp intake of breath from Mr. Khan. "It called you the Chosen One?" he asks, his voice low.

"Yeah. And said they've been looking for me. But the demons are looking for all of us, aren't they? All the Seers?"

The ambulance is louder now. It's close. Hopefully closer than any demons.

"Jasmine, you mustn't tell anyone else what you've just told me. Not yet."

There's deep fear in Mr. Khan's voice, but now I can't read his thoughts. I'm not always able to tap into that ability. Sometimes the connection works, sometimes it doesn't. Except I think he's now deliberately trying to block me from knowing what he's thinking. I open my mouth to ask why, but don't have the energy to say a word. As the ambulance swings toward us, its lights bathing us in a scarlet glow, I slip into unconsciousness.

# JADE

It takes Mom over twenty minutes to get a private cab hired via her video phone account.

"This is madness," she says, frowning at the screen. "Hardly any drivers are working, so the fees are four times higher than usual. And the connection keeps cutting out."

I stare out the glass doors of our building into the inky blackness, trying not to think about the things lurking out there. If I really think about it, I'll be scared, and that will only make them stronger. My throat feels really sore now, and I wonder if I'm coming down with strep or something, since every time I swallow it feels like glass is mixed with my saliva.

"It's because of the curfew and abductions," I say, turning around. "No one wants to be out at night. Hired drivers keep getting questioned by the police about every disappearance. You couldn't pay me enough to be driving at night right now."

Mom gets up off the torn fake leather sofa in our front lobby and begins to pace back and forth beside a palm that stoops over in its pot like an elderly man. Worry is etched between her eyebrows.

"I'm going to have to pay the extra because we really need to get to your sister as soon as possible." She stops pacing and shakes her head. "It's times like this when I really miss … I really …" Her voice wavers. Unable to continue, she takes a tissue out of her purse and dabs at her eyes. "Sorry, it's just sometimes I can't believe she's gone."

I go over and throw my arms around her. "I know you miss Lola hugely. Please don't cry. We'll just cut back on spending next week to make up for the ride to the hospital."

Mom nods and hugs me back. "My wise girl. Sometimes I feel that you are the *madre* and I am the child. However, I don't know how we can possibly cut back any further this month unless we eat dust. *Dios*! No wonder people are thieving so much these days. It's simply to put food in their mouths."

I walk back to the window and wait for Mom to tell me the name of the driver and the make of the car that's coming to pick us up. Lola. I was careful not to say *we* miss her. And that's because Jasmine and I don't. We don't miss her even one tiny bit. I mean, it's not like we're celebrating the fact that she's dead, but Mom has no idea that her so-called best friend was the reason I was abducted. Lola's betrayal was the reason I spent five long years living in a place that is literally one small step away from Hell. It would kill Mom if she ever discovered the truth about what Lola did to me — to our family. Or the truth about where I was. All I've ever told her, the swarms of media that descended on us when I reappeared, and anyone else who asked was that I couldn't remember anything, or was so traumatized by my experience that I'd completely suppressed it. If only they knew....

"It should be a red Honda. Our driver's name is Jordan."

Mom's video phone beeps.

"The car's here already," she says. "Can you see it?"

I lean my forehead against the glass, cup my hands on either side of my eyes, and look out. The car is just pulling into the drive in front of the building. The yellow beams from the headlights illuminate the scraggle of bushes in our unkempt courtyard.

Someone is standing near the bushes. Or is it just a shadow? I narrow my eyes, straining to see. I'm positive there was movement when the car rounded the drive. It looked as though someone, or something, ducked behind one of the clumps of bush just before being exposed by the light.

"Jade? Do you see the car?" Mom's beside me now. "Come, he's here," she says, pointing out the window.

Taking a deep breath, I link my arm through hers. I want her close to me, because I'm pretty sure our driver is not the only one waiting for us out there.

# JASMINE

I'm wheeled out of the ambulance by the paramedics. A misty curtain of rain falls on my face as we move toward the emergency entrance. Mr. Khan pulls the hood of his sweatshirt up over his head. Hair is important to him, even at a time like this. I smile through the pain. My throat feels really swollen, and each breath I take is excruciating.

"How are you doing, Ms. Guzman?" one of the paramedics asks, his thick eyebrows drawn together with concern. He's built like a Lego figure, a compilation of different square shapes stuck together. His biceps are so overdeveloped, the cotton sleeve of his uniform looks like it's about to burst.

I give him a thumbs-up as we enter the foyer. He looks at me dubiously.

"Your neck is pretty bruised up," he says. "Emergency is packed, but we'll try to get you looked at as soon as we can. The city's homeless have been making every excuse to pack in here at night now, with the murders happening. It's hard for us to turn them away when we know they might end up disappearing ... or dead."

I want to tell him I get it, that I wouldn't send anyone out there until the sun was up either, especially after what I saw tonight.

"I'm going to grab a quick chicory and video message your mum to see if she's been able to secure a ride," Mr. Khan says, leaning over me. His dark eyes radiate worry. "I want to be sure Jade's coming with her ... that they're getting here safely."

I give him a thumbs-up too. The thought of Mom and Jade heading here in the dark makes my blood run cold.

I'm wheeled past a marble statue of a winged man. One of his pale arms points at the sky, a chipped index finger stretching heavenward. The other hand holds a sword that's stuck into what looks like a demon at its feet. The statue is doing the job of a Seer.

I try to turn my head to get a better look, but the pain radiating through my throat drags me back down onto the pillow of the gurney.

"That statue ... what's it about?" My voice sounds more frog than human.

The muscular paramedic cocks his head in the direction of the statue. "The one back there? That's St. Michael. He's the patron saint of the hospital. Reckon he's looking after everyone who comes in and out of here."

I stare at him, my heart beating harder in my chest. St. Michael?

"He's an angel, right?"

The paramedic stares hard at me. He's wondering if I'm crazy or if I somehow missed the newsflash that angels have wings. Nice. Sometimes being able to read minds is a pain in the ass.

"Yeah, yeah, I know, angels have wings." The paramedic glances at me, surprised. I ignore his reaction, knowing Mr. Khan would kill me if he knew I what I just did. Seers are supposed to keep their abilities under wraps at all times. "What's at his feet?" I ask. "The thing with the sword sticking out of its back?"

"It's a demon. Looks like some sort of dragon to me," he replies with a shrug. "Supposed to be St. Michael, the archangel, killing the devil, Lucifer, in the last battle. At least that's what I was told when I was a young lad. Grew up Irish Catholic." A faint blush rises to his cheeks. "Learned about all this stuff as though it were truth when I was in school."

I can't help but wonder what he'd say if I told him I used to live in the same apartment building as St. Michael and even kissed his brother. Would probably be a good way to get myself a one-way ticket to the psych ward.

The paramedics wheel my gurney against the wall of a long hallway filled with at least a dozen other gurneys. The hall is painted a dreary, gunmetal grey, its walls mottled with dents and scuff marks. Talk about depressing. To top it off, most of the people parked here are elderly. Some lie moaning quietly to themselves with no one attending to them, tufts of cotton-like white hair peeking out from over their pillows. I feel bad that so many of them are here alone.

Mr. Khan arrives, a cup of steaming chicory in his hand. He's walking so quickly that brown liquid sloshes over the side of the cup.

"What's going on?" he asks, glancing around the hallway. "Why are we just sitting here? We need to see a doctor ASAP. She could have internal injuries to her throat."

"Jasmine's going to be seen shortly," one of the paramedics replies. "The ER doctors are tending to the patients out here. We're part of the overflow. Every hospital is bursting at the seams. There's nowhere for ambulances to be diverted to, because every emergency room in Toronto is in the same situation."

I wave at Mr. Khan. "I'm right here." There's nothing I hate more than being spoken about as though I'm not even present. He should know that. "Are Jade and Mom coming?" My voice is still more of a croak.

He nods. "They're on their way. I told Jade to message when they're close so I can go out and meet them." Taking a sip of his chicory, he leans against the wall. "I imagine the emergency rooms will be filling even more than this tonight. The hospital cafe was just broadcasting a breaking news story when I was there. That's why it took me so long. Seems the police found a body in the downtown core about half an hour ago. This one's been decapitated. Head taken clean off. Turns out he's the young bartender that disappeared a few weeks back. Was struggling with a pretty severe cocaine addiction, so it seems the mother was holding out hope he was hopped up in some crackhouse or something." Mr. Khan pauses and stares at me hard. "The police are hunting a new killer now. And Sandra Smith is holding a press conference about it in about fifteen minutes."

His words hit me like a sack of bricks. "Do they have any leads?" I think about the security cameras dotted all over the city. You can't pick your nose without being caught on film. Thousands of cameras went up overnight just a few months ago as part of the government's antiterror action plan.

Mr. Khan shrugs and sips at his chicory again. I know he's trying to act as casual as he can because of the paramedics being with us. "But I think I should definitely try to get back to the cafe to watch that news conference, if your mom and Jade are here by that time."

I lie back in my gurney and watch a frazzled-looking doctor stride toward us. Sandra Smith. A knot of worry begins to form in my stomach. Lola's friend and Toronto's esteemed mayor. And someone I suspect knows a lot more about Seers and what's going on in our city than she lets on.

# JADE

It's hard for me to really see anything beyond the street because of the speed we're travelling and the dimmed street lights (another energy-saving initiative), but I can't help but try anyhow. I have a deep-seated feeling that we're being followed, that something out there in the inky blackness is tracking us, even though I know that's crazy. There are no headlights behind us, and no one except Mr. Khan and Jasmine know we're on our way to St. Mike's. Still …

"It took a long time for us to get a ride," Mom says to our driver as she turns on her video phone. "Thank you for taking our … *solicitud* …" She look over at me. This happens to her a lot when she's stressed. English words disappear from her vocabulary.

"Our request," I say. "We're glad you picked us up. Have you been very busy tonight?"

The driver eyes me through the rear-view mirror. He's surprisingly young, with a strong, chiselled jaw and deep-blue eyes. His black hair is short and unkempt.

Beneath his relaxed appearance, a nervous energy seethes. He's scared. Fear rolls off him in waves.

"You're my first customers," he says. "I just came on. A lot of drivers aren't working tonight. I wasn't going to either, considering what just happened, but …"

"What's just happened?" I ask, knowing Mom is going to be really upset that I've interrupted the driver midsentence. Good manners are something she's rabid about.

"You haven't heard?" He glances at us in the mirror again. "There's been a killing already this evening. A body's been found in the downtown core. Head taken clean off. Apparently it's some bartender that disappeared a few weeks back. Honestly, if you were men, I wouldn't have accepted the drive request. But when I saw your profile, I figured you two aren't exactly the decapitating type." He laughs nervously.

I laugh as well, hoping it sounds sincere. Little does he know I could take the head off a demon in less than five seconds flat, and his even faster than that.

"Do you mind if I turn on the news?" he asks, unwrapping a stick of gum with one hand. He folds it in half and pops it into his mouth. "I feel safer knowing what's going on."

"I'd like to know what's happening as well," Mom says, leaning forward in her seat. "Please, go ahead."

"Toronto city news," he says. The video screens on the backs of the headrests in front of Mom and me blossom into life.

Bright lights shine down on a middle-aged reporter with a gleaming scalp and bleached white teeth. He's standing in the foyer of City Hall. From the colour of his skin, he's familiar with the inside of a tanning bed. He lifts the microphone to speak, his face serious.

"We're waiting just inside City Hall for Toronto mayor Sandra Smith, who has called an emergency media conference tonight in the wake of yet another murder. It's highly unusual for the mayor to comment on a homicide so soon after the discovery of a body, but the victim's next-of-kin has already been notified, and Mayor Smith says the situation has reached a crisis point."

A photograph of the victim fills the screen. He's young and cute, with blond hair that flops over one eye. In the photo he's smiling widely, standing behind a bar, a bottle of expensive vodka in his hand.

I've seen him before. Recognition hits me with the force of a sucker-punch to the stomach. The blue eyes were black and the face deathly pale, but it's definitely the same person that attacked Jasmine and me tonight. Or thing.

Taking a deep breath, I try to steady myself.

That's impossible, though. Demons are from the Place-in-Between and originate from a place even darker than that. This bartender was alive just a few weeks ago.

"Bless his family," Mom says, wiping at her eyes. "Such a handsome young man. I hope Ms. Smith finds the psychopaths who are doing this and makes an example of them. It's time to get tough with those climate-change terrorists as well."

"Some people say she's going to bring in the death penalty," our driver says. "Apparently there are a few cities thinking that it might help put a stop to some of the violence that's happening. I don't think it will work, since a lot of these people don't seem to mind blowing themselves up at the same time as they're killing innocent people."

"What I don't understand is what the climate-change terrorists think bombing subways and killing people is going to change. It doesn't make sense," I say.

"They feel the Canadian, American, and UK governments, amongst others, haven't done enough to combat climate change. Remember that these terrorists are originally from countries that have been decimated by environmental disasters. They don't like that so much power has been given to cities like Toronto and New York to create laws and govern themselves. And they certainly don't believe in closing borders to climate-change refugees." His words are like machine gun fire, rapid and forceful. It's clearly a subject about which he's passionate and more than just a little angry. "I'm not sure why they don't fess up to the bombings either. But I don't doubt they're behind some of these disappearances and kill- ings as well. Dishonest bastards. I think they just want to create chaos, to bring the establishment down. It's not our fault we have more resources than their home countries."

I think about the videos from the terrorists that get posted almost weekly on various news feeds. Their faces are always fully hidden behind balaclavas and scarves. And their voices are altered, so it's hard to tell much, if anything, about them. The broadcasters and government keep linking them to a variety of different countries, but I wonder how they can even know where the terrorists are from when they keep their identities so well hidden.

"I agree with you completely," Mom says to the driver. "Let them hang. I'm tired of having to be terrified every time my girls step outside the door. On top of everything else our governments have to deal with, this is too much. And we certainly don't need more of *them* coming here."

My mouth drops open. Mom is an immigrant herself. Doesn't she remember why she came here? Where would the three of us be today if she hadn't been able to leave South America when she was young?

"The mayor's about to join us now," the reporter says. The camera pans away from him and over to a podium. Sandra Smith strides toward it, dressed in a form-fitting red dress and dark heels, her hair cut short and bleached almost white. She's flanked by two sunglasses-wearing security guards in dark uniforms and a short, heavy-set man with a patch over one eye.

"Why are they wearing those stupid mirrored sunglasses when it's night?" Mom says, her face scrunching into a frown.

"And who's the chubby pirate with her?" our driver asks. "Never seen him before, but he doesn't look like he could offer up much protection."

Smith walks up to the microphone, scans the crowd of reporters in front of her, and holds up a hand. The room falls silent.

"This evening between six thirty and seven thirty p.m., Jamie Linnekar, a twenty-two-year-old Torontonian, was found dead near the intersection of Sackville and King Street East. Mr. Linnekar, who was not known to police, was reported missing on September twenty-eighth." Smith stops speaking and looks directly into the camera. "The victim died due to massive blood loss following his beheading. This is a marked departure from the state that the previous bodies found in the Toronto area over the last month were in. Forensics officers on the scene found the insignia of the climate-change terrorists on the sidewalk beside Mr. Linnekar's body. The insignia was painted with the victim's blood. It's an act of shocking barbarism."

There's an audible gasp from the crowd as a large screen lowers behind Mayor Smith's head. She steps to one side and points to the roughly drawn crimson C enclosed in a circle that's projected on the screen.

"Clearly the climate-change terrorists want us to know they're behind Linnekar's abduction and murder. The police are now investigating the dozens of missing persons reports received over the last few weeks with the view that it might not be the work of one or two serial murderers, but rather the climate-change terrorists, whom we will refer to as the CCT from here on in for the sake of simplicity at this conference."

Our driver lets out a low whistle. I just hope he's focusing his attention more on the road than the conference. We're nearly at the hospital, so I text Mr. Khan, sure to keep one eye on the screen in front of me.

"As such, I've decided to implement several new initiatives and laws aimed at bringing greater security to the people of Toronto. Tomorrow, city council will be voting to support the prime minister's decision to close our country's borders to climate-change refugees and, indeed, to any future immigration at all. I realize this decision is controversial, but we simply do not have the resources to properly sustain those of us living here now."

Several of the reporters begin to shout questions at the mayor, who holds up her hand again. The reporters fall silent like a pack of well-trained dogs.

"For the last month, my new head of public works and safety, Mr. Sajid Jawad, and I have been developing a work scheme that will benefit our city enormously." The man with the patch over his eye waddles forward and gives a brief wave. He's almost as wide as he is tall, and just that little bit of movement causes beads of sweat to sprout on his red face.

"Mr. Jawad and myself are starting a work-for-welfare-and-rehab program. Again, I know this is controversial. However, our city needs repairs to much of its infrastructure, and we know that the world's economic situation is increasingly grim. There simply is not the money to put into projects like solar panel repair and rainwater system maintenance. This program will allow struggling individuals living off the government and/or accessing expensive medical programs such as drug rehabilitation treatment to feel worthwhile and validated. More importantly, since these programs will be run at night, they may act as a deterrent to the terrorists."

She stops speaking and smiles at the reporters, her white teeth gleaming. As she runs a hand through her hair, the ring on her right hand glitters, caught in the beam of one of the lights. I remember that ring. She was wearing it last year when we went to her house up north. It was a strange silvery metal with a sort of Star of David on it. Definitely not a good match with her outfit tonight. It seems a bit unbelievable that we were at her house at all, but Sandra Smith was a good friend of Lola's. As soon as Lola died, she'd have nothing to do with Mom or us. I guess she blames us for what happened, though the cause of the fire that destroyed her home and killed Lola and Mina was never discovered.

"Now that's leadership," our driver says, turning the car toward the front entrance to the hospital. "You two be safe tonight and watch your backs. You never know when or where these terrorists are going to strike."

"Same to you," Mom says as she opens her door. "Wish we could stay to watch the rest of the news conference, but I trust that whatever Smith does, it will benefit us in the long run." She steps out the door, and I slide out after her.

There are security guards flanking either side of the hospital's entrance.

"Identification and reason for coming to St. Mike's," one of them says, putting an arm out to block us from moving farther forward as soon as we approach. He's cold and emotionless. Not the nicest welcome for families whose loved ones are injured and sick. They might as well get a robot to do his job.

Mom taps her video watch and brings up her driver's license. "This is my daughter, Jade. My other daughter, her twin sister, is here in emergency. She was attacked by a terrorist tonight."

"How old is she?" the guard asks, jerking his head toward me like I'm mute.

"She's sixteen. I know it's past curfew, but I don't feel safe leaving her at home either. We have no one else. Her father is dead."

"Exceptional circumstances," the other guard says. He's equally as robotic as the first. Where do they get these guys? "Let them through."

After Mom and I place our fingers against a tablet that records our fingerprints, and after we have a scan of our irises recorded, we're let into the building.

"We don't know who or *what* attacked Jasmine," I say as soon as the sliding doors close behind us. "You can't just go around saying it was terrorists."

Mom raises an eyebrow at me. "You heard Mayor Smith. We're at war."

*If only you knew*, I think.

Mr. Khan is waiting for us at the information desk. His fashionable striped shirt is rumpled and dark circles frame his eyes. Mom rushes toward him, gives him a hug, and kisses him on both cheeks.

"Where is my angel? Is she okay? What did they do to her?"

Mr. Khan nods. "She's going to be fine. A bit sore and swollen for a while, but they don't suspect any permanent damage has been done. They're doing a scan right now to be sure."

I give him a hug and lift onto the balls of my feet so I can lean in close to his ear. He smells of chicory and faded cologne. "We need to talk. Jamie Linnekar wasn't killed by a CCT. And I highly doubt a CCT left that insignia on the sidewalk using his blood."

"I know," Mr. Khan whispers back. "I'm the one that found Jasmine with the body. I don't know who or what arrived on the scene after us. But one thing's for certain, they must've worked fast, because the police would've been there within minutes. The paramedics contacted them before even getting Jasmine into the ambulance."

As we walk toward the emergency room, I watch Mr. Khan's face. His jaw is clenched tight and there's a look in his eyes I've never seen before. He's terrified.

# JASMINE

I don't want to be left alone. Even though I'm in the hospital under achingly bright fluorescent lights, what happened earlier tonight makes me wonder if I'm safe anywhere now. If demons aren't just crossing over from the Place-in-Between but are somehow actually inhabiting people's bodies in the here and now, who's to say they won't pop up anywhere, at any time? Will I be met by a smile full of razors for teeth and dead black eyes at the corner store?

As I'm wheeled away for an MRI of my neck, I glance over at Mr. Khan. I must look like a rabbit caught in a snare, because he comes back over to me and leans in close.

"Don't be afraid," he says, his breath warm on my ear. "I don't exactly know what's going on, but you're strong ... stronger than the others. I'm going to watch the news conference and meet your mum and Jade."

I nod, knowing he's right. I need to lasso in my fear. It's just I was always under the impression that the demons somehow belonged to the night, to the darkness. That, having come from a place beneath, they somehow needed the cloak of night to attack. Daylight felt safe. Now I'm not so sure that's true.

The scan doesn't take long, and then I'm wheeled back to the hallway by a porter who unceremoniously drops me off like a bag of trash and then walks away. The hall is even fuller than it was before and buzzing with conversation. I listen to two women that look to be about Mom's age, one on a gurney with her hand wrapped in a mountain of white gauze that's turning red with each passing second, and the other leaning over her.

"She's not letting any refugees into Toronto and is voting to completely close Canada's borders. And junkies and welfare recipients will be repairing the roads and water systems," the uninjured woman says. She's staring down at her video phone. I'm guessing Sandra Smith's news conference is on.

"If it will make the streets safer and save money, then I'm all for it," the injured woman says, lifting her hand above her head. "This is crazy. How long do they want me to keep it like this?"

"Keeping your hand above your heart is going to help slow the blood flow," her friend says. "Do you really think closing the borders will keep the terrorists from striking? Won't it just make things worse? I mean, we'll be dooming people across the world to death. Think of how many have died just since aid programs stopped." She frowns down at her watch. "Oh my god, she wants to bring in the death penalty."

"Might not be a bad thing. After all, part of the reason we're in this mess is all the people in those countries having so many children," the woman on they gurney says. "And I'd like to see some of these terrorists and psychopaths who are going around kidnapping and killing people get some of their own back."

The other woman shakes her head. "That's terrible to say. Remember, an eye for an eye makes the world go blind. I think this is dangerous. And making some of the most vulnerable people in our society virtual slaves, working all night long? What's next, dragging the elderly out to work for their pensions?"

"We'll have to just agree to disagree, Marsha," the injured woman says as a doctor comes to look at her hand. "'Cause I think they're finally here to sew me up."

I lie against my pillow, trying to swallow as little as possible to avoid feeling like shards of glass are being thrust down my throat. My stomach rumbles uneasily, and I realize I haven't eaten since noon. I'd kill for a milkshake.

The death penalty. It's so barbaric. How would the government kill people they found guilty? Hanging? Electrocution? Lethal injection? Just the thought of it sends chills through me. What if the person is wrongly convicted?

Then it hits me. What if a security camera caught my fight with the demon tonight? Caught me killing the demon that was Jamie Linnekar? The body didn't remain in demonic form. For all I know, the police are searching through surveillance tape right now, zooming in on images of my face as my pole took off his head. *Its* head.

Panic grips my chest, squeezing it like a fist. I need to get out of here. What if they're coming for me right now? I kick off the sheet covering me and swing my legs over the side of the stretcher.

A hand clamps down on my shoulder. I cry out in fear.

"Stay right where you are, Jasmine."

# JADE

"She's still in, having the scan," Mr. Khan says. Mom and I are standing near the back of the emergency room, which is heaving with bodies. It's hot and humid, and the smell of sweat, stale cigarette smoke, and various types of food hangs in the air like a wet blanket, coating everything. I feel sick.

"How will they find us when she's done? This," Mom says, sweeping her arm out, "is absolute *locura*."

"Alejandra, let Jade and I go and get you a chicory or tea. We may be in for a bit of a stay. I'll try to see if I can get someone to give us more answers and let them know where you are so they can bring Jasmine to you when she's done."

I look over at Mr. Khan. He wants us to leave Mom on her own in here? Seriously?

He nods at me. *We need to talk.* His lips don't move, but his thought is crystal clear.

"We'll be right back, Mama," I say, leaning in and

giving her a kiss. "There's probably a wait on scans since it's been so packed tonight."

As soon as we're in the hall, Mr. Khan moves closer to me. "What exactly happened earlier tonight? Why were you out so late?"

"Jasmine and Cassandra wanted to do more training after school," I say, careful to keep my voice low. "We went to do hills at the beach. I told them I didn't think it was a good idea."

The muscles in Mr. Khan's lower jaw tighten. "You're supposed to go straight home after classes. There's enough training being done at Beaconsfield. That was a defiant and irresponsible act, especially considering the circumstances right now."

"I agree," I say. "But if I'd left, I would've been on my own. The two of them can be pretty stubborn, you know. What was I supposed to do?"

Mr. Khan nods. "They're first-borns. You were put in a bad position. Sorry." He runs a hand through his hair. "What's more critical here are the events that followed. Did you see Jamie?"

I glance around. The halls are full of people: white-coated doctors rushing back and forth, relatives leaning against walls, patients and family members crumpled over in pain and sorrow on chairs.

"Can't we just say *him* or Bob or something?" I ask. "Is it really safe to talk here? About that?" Considering his name is plastered all over the media tonight as breaking news, I'm thinking the answer should be a big no. The fact that Mr. Khan even said the name out loud makes me realize just how tired and stressed he must be.

"The cafeteria. It's just up here. I need to find out more about exactly what happened with *Bob*."

Once we're in the cafeteria, I take a seat while he grabs another two chicories for himself and Mom and a mint tea for me.

"Okay, we dropped Cassandra off at her place and were heading home. It took us a bit longer than we'd thought, and it got dark pretty fast."

Mr. Khan takes a sip of his chicory. "Yeah, it tends to get dark fairly early in October. That's why we've been telling all Seers to go straight home after school unless there are extenuating circumstances. Going off to train at a remote beach at the foot of the city does not qualify."

"You're preaching to the converted, remember?" I say. "It was stupid. Agreed. Anyway, we were only about ten minutes from home when it became obvious someone or something was following us. When he got closer, we could see it was one of them." I'm not about to start whispering about demons in public, no matter how much privacy we have in our corner of the cafe.

"Did you actually see him? I mean, really see him? Which one of you decided he was … *different*?" Mr. Khan places his elbows on the table and leans forward. "Because I saw him after … everything. And he didn't look one bit different. He looked like a normal young *man*. And like you said, it was pretty dark."

I pause, letting the steam from the tea waft over my

face, the minty scent soothing me, and think back over the events. Everything happened so fast. But I've been trained to be observant, to be diligent in my awareness of my environment.

"It was me," I finally say. "Definitely. I noticed his eyes first and warned Jazz. Then it, I mean he … he kind of snarled, and that's when we saw his teeth. Like pointed razor blades. He attacked us, not the other way around. Bob was definitely one of them."

Mr. Khan sits back heavily in his chair and regards me silently for a few seconds. "What I tell you right now must not be broadcast amongst the Seers. Not until I talk to the Protectors about it, because I believe Bob wasn't fully one of them. He couldn't have been. He was still alive in terms of consciousness, but being used as a vessel, which means the demons that are among us are stronger than we thought … and more numerous. The less time a demon's spent in a human body, the more likely that person's spirit is still present and fighting to come forward. The demons in the Place-in-Between are inhabiting vessels that have been down there for decades and decades, and there is nothing left of the soul or consciousness of the original inhabitant of the body. When demons are on Earth, they need to feed, because here the tissues will disintegrate quickly. However, demons like the one that attacked you tonight are possessing bodies that are … fresher. To do that, the demons must be very strong." He pauses and looks out the row of cafe windows into the blackness of a park across the street.

"How come I was able to exist down there? If my soul was up here, trapped in the Ibeji, how was I down there and able to survive for so long?" I ask.

Mr. Khan looks thoughtful. "I'm not certain. Likely it was because your soul was still alive, though in the doll, and there was some sort of transference of consciousness and energy because of that between you and Jasmine. Just as she could reach you and open up the gateway to the Place-in-Between when she touched it. We've never had anything like that happen with a Seer before. All things considered, it's probably best that you don't dwell on that time. What matters is that you are now back here — with us."

I'm not sure if his explanation makes me feel better, but I can tell from his tone that we're done talking about it. Perhaps that's why I have no real memories from the Place-in-Between, or at least I didn't until Jasmine touched the doll.

"It's pretty worrying that some kind of super-strong demon is after us, isn't it?" I ask.

He nods. "That's not our only concern, though. It's highly likely all that happened between the three of you was captured on security footage, considering the amount of security cameras and patrolling drones around. You're positive he attacked first?"

I nod. "One hundred percent sure. He lunged at me, and Jasmine intervened."

"We better head back," Mr. Khan says, rising. "If that's the case, and the two you were attacked first, the police will see that Jasmine acted in self-defence. The hard thing is going to be explaining how a five-foot-three, sixteen-year-old girl was able to decapitate a grown man with a single blow from a bamboo pole. I'm pretty sure that falls just a little outside the boundaries of reasonable force."

"You don't think she'll be charged, do you?" I ask, pushing in my chair. A knot of worry grips my stomach.

"Nothing's certain anymore, Jade. What I do know is, the less attention drawn to the Seers and Beaconsfield, the better. Unfortunately, I have a feeling what happened tonight is going to put us directly in the spotlight."

# JASMINE

"Get a hold of your fear, Jazz," Raphael says beside me.

I sit up and stare at him, slack-jawed and wide-eyed like some sort of guppy. He's dressed in a worn army fatigue jacket and faded jeans with a grey cotton toque pulled down low over his ebony, shoulder-length hair.

"Are you back?" I ask, holding my breath, half afraid of his answer. "There's so much going on. I went by your apartment loads of times after we got back, but there was never any answer. The super said it had been empty for weeks…. My video messages were never returned. It's been over six months."

He puts a finger to his lips. "I've been around. Even when I'm not right here, I'm still helping you, guiding you." He gives me a lopsided smile, his deep-brown eyes changing to a vibrant green. There's something he's not telling me about his absence, though. I can sense it. Something to do with me. The lighthearted banter is a cover, but I can't fully read his thoughts. It's exhausting just to try. "And by the way, you're a lot of hard work to help. What were you thinking, training at Cherry Beach after school?"

A curtain of silence falls between us. I've missed him so much. That familiar energy is building between us again. We're like the opposite poles of a magnet; our attraction is that strong. Raphael removes his hand from my shoulder. I know he feels it as well.

"Yeah, well ... I nearly died tonight," I finally say, the words sticking in my throat. "I honestly thought that demon's face was going to be that last thing I ever saw ... not Mom, not Jade ..." *Not you*, I want to say, but stop myself. Tears spring to my eyes, but they're tears of anger. I'm angry with myself because Raphael's right. It was stupid of Cassandra and I to push ourselves by training more today. And if I'm really truthful, I did it partially because I wanted the opportunity to fight, to take on the demons, to test my training and newfound strength. It was ego and the prospect of excitement that drove me to the beach today.

"Well, you didn't die, and you need to get your emotions in check, because there's a lot happening. In fact, that's part of the reason why I can't stay long." He glances over his shoulder. "There are entities here controlling the dark forces via humans. They need to be stopped."

"What entities? What are you talking about?" How can there possibly be more for me to learn? Isn't it enough to have been a normal teenage girl one minute (albeit with a twin sister abducted and assumed dead), only to have found out in the span of a few months that I am a being with special powers, that demons not only exist but can be destroyed by yours truly, and that there is another plane of existence that houses lost souls?

"When the time is right, you will discover more. The world is changing irreversibly, and changing fast." He pauses. "You're going to have to be prepared for challenges you never dreamed possible. There will be losses. Terrible losses that will bring you to your knees. But you need to be strong, Jazz. Strong and smart. We need *you* to survive. The human race needs you to survive."

"I'm trying," I say. "This demon was so much stronger than the ones I fought last year in the Place-in-Between."

Raphael nods. "The Place-in-Between is like a holding ground for demons, as well as the lost souls. They gather their strength from negative energy, but here they get stronger from devouring souls and blood, the life source of all living beings, as well as negative emotion. They're vampiric here. And that is what makes them much, much more powerful."

A chill falls over me like a shadow. "The demon said they were looking for me. Not Jade, not other Seers. *Me.* It said I was *elegido*. In Spanish, that means chosen. Do you know what that means? Why is he saying that? What have I been chosen for?"

Raphael looks away, his eyes darkening.

"*Muy preciosista!*" Mom shouts. I turn and see her rushing down the hall toward me. She descends, vulture-like, and envelops me in a huge hug. "Are you okay? What happened? Who did this to you?" The barrage of questions is dizzying. She holds me tighter, her perfume, a mixture of vanilla and anise, washing over me.

Mr. Khan and Jade come up behind her. I look over at them, unsure of how to answer. We haven't talked about what to tell people when they ask what happened tonight. All I know is that demons aren't supposed to be part of the narrative.

"I don't remember," I say. "One minute I was walking back from Cassandra's, and the next I was waking up here."

Mom's eyes narrow. She straightens and turns to Jade. "Why weren't you together?"

Jade opens her mouth, then closes it again.

"Cassandra and I went to Cherry Beach," I say. "Jade thought it was a bad idea. I told her if she didn't want to come, she could stay at school to work on her project, and that I'd come back to walk home with her afterward."

Biting nervously at my lip, I stop and glance at Mr. Khan. He's impossible to read right now. His face is neutral, emotionless.

"Except I didn't make it back. I guess that's when Jade sounded the alarm, told Mr. Khan, and he came to look for me. Thank goodness for video phone tracking devices, right?"

Mom stares at me, her face transforming into a mask of fury. "With everything going on, you left your sister and went to the beach after classes? Are you trying to kill me?"

Mr. Khan steps forward and puts his hand on Mom's shoulder to calm her. "What's done is done. The most important thing to focus on is that Jasmine's okay, other than being bruised and having some internal swelling. Dr. Sullivan is on her way to give us more details, but the scan seemed clear. It could've been so much worse. We just need to watch that no further swelling happens over the next twenty-four to forty-eight hours."

"Where's Raphael?" I ask.

Everyone looks at me, worry creeping back across their faces.

"Raphael?" Mr. Khan says.

"He was just here with me … he was beside me when you got here." I look around. "How did you not see him?"

"Maybe we do need the doctor — right now," Mom says.

"I don't need a doctor; he was here with me." My voice is rising like lava, which is not helping the situation. "I'm not imagining things. Where did he go?" Panic claws at my chest. He can't be gone. Not again.

"Here comes Dr. Sullivan now," Mr. Khan says, looking behind me. His eyes darken with concern.

I turn to see what he's looking at.

The doctor is flanked by two police officers. And from the looks on their faces, they mean business.

# JADE

"Mrs. Guzman?" the doctor asks, extending her hand to Mom. Her white coat is crisply ironed and spotless, in contrast with the stained and rumpled appearance of most of the doctors at the hospital, and she looks like she's not much older than Jade and I. "I'm Dr. Sullivan, one of the doctors that's been looking after Jasmine this evening. I had the chance to look over her scans a few minutes ago, and I have to say this young lady is very lucky." She smiles at Jasmine, revealing a set of very white but (thankfully) slightly crooked teeth. It's good to see a flaw; I was starting to feel like my sister's being taken care of by Superwoman. "But attempted suffocation can cause complex injuries. There doesn't seem to be any serious esophageal damage or soft tissue damage showing on the scan. That being said, it's not unheard of for swelling to occur hours or even days after this sort of injury, so we need her to be monitored closely."

Mom nods. "I'm at home full-time, so I can make sure nothing worsens. Thank you for taking such good care of her."

Dr. Sullivan smiles. "You're most welcome. Despite the challenges we're facing here, especially on the nights when our generators don't kick in and we're packed to the gills, we still try to keep things functioning well. It's not always easy." She pauses and looks at Jasmine. "How are you feeling?" she asks.

Jasmine gives Dr. Sullivan two thumbs up. Dark marks cover the circumference of her neck like tattoos. Instinctively, my hand flies to my throat. That's why I'd felt like I was suffocating in the police cruiser earlier. A shiver travels up my spine. If anything happened to Jasmine, I'd be left with half a soul.

"Do you think you're well enough to speak with these officers for a few moments?" Dr. Sullivan asks. "Feel free to say no. We've given you some pretty hefty pain meds this evening."

Jasmine's brows draw together in concern. I'm not sure my sister is up to being questioned, especially considering she was just yelling her head off about Raphael being here when she hasn't seen him for nearly a year.

One of the police officers turns to me. "Were you with your sister this evening when the altercation with Jamie Linnekar took place?"

I look from Jasmine to Mr. Khan and then to Mom. The world is white light and silence, except for the sound of my heart thumping in my ears. I wish there was a way for the floor to open and swallow me whole.

"Yes." My voice seems very tiny and far away. "I was with her."

There's a sharp intake of breath from Mom as her eyebrows rise in surprise. "What exactly is going on here?"

What do I say? Jasmine, who so easily and quickly lied to Mom with her intricate little narrative, is now conveniently silent. I feel like I've been thrown under a subway train. And if I don't come up with something fast, Mr. Khan is going to be stuck here with me. We can't let Mom think he lied to her. It's ultra important she doesn't lose trust in him. He's our Protector.

"Um … after telling Mr. Khan that Jasmine was missing, I went out to find her as well. I know I shouldn't have." I pause, my face burning. "She was heading back to the school to get me when I found her, so we decided to just head home."

"And you left Mr. Khan out in the streets alone, with everything that's going on, all the disappearances, to search for you? Then you leave your sister to be attacked by some psychopathic man? She could've been raped; she could've been murdered." Mom's voice is razor sharp.

Each word lands like hot acid on my conscience, because I did leave Jasmine alone to fight the demon. Even if it's what I needed to do to ensure the demon couldn't fully take our soul, I didn't want to abandon her. God, how could Mom think I'd ever choose to do that?

Crossing her arms, Mom glares at me. "If there's *anyone* who should know better than to do that, it's you."

"We were going to video message him as soon as we got in," Jasmine interjects. "It was getting dark, and we just wanted to get home before curfew. I guess we weren't thinking. Jade ran to get help when I was attacked."

Mom raises an eyebrow at Jasmine. "You just said you didn't remember anything about the attack."

Mr. Khan steps forward. "Alejandra, the girls are both tired. You and I are beyond exhausted as well. Let's wait to discuss all of this. The girls seem to realize they both acted imprudently."

Mom turns to Mr. Khan. "I'm so sorry. You're right. Thank goodness you found Jasmine when you did. I don't know how I can ever repay you. The girls need to recognize how you have gone above a professor's duty."

One of the officers clears his throat. "We do need to get an initial statement from Jasmine," he says apologetically. "The surveillance video was somehow leaked to the media. "We will certainly wait and send officers over to do a more detailed questioning of the girls in the next day or two. It's just that, with everything that's been going on, Jamie Linnekar's death has already garnered a lot of media attention."

"Thanks to our esteemed mayor," Mr. Khan says, his voice tinged with sarcasm. "I thought it seemed a little trigger-happy for her to be on the news declaring this was the work of the CCT."

"We can't comment on that," the other officer says. "Except to say that the mayor's office has been very supportive of the antiterrorism squad's work." I don't like the way he looks Mr. Khan up and down like he's some sort of criminal as he says this, before walking away to record something in his video phone.

"Well, if the footage from tonight has already been seen, it's pretty obvious that Jamie, I mean Mr. Linnekar, attacked my sister and me. He was choking me. I was going to die, so I hit him in self-defence," Jasmine says to the other officer.

He puts out his hand to her, palm forward.

"Hold on. I'm just going to start recording now, if you don't mind repeating that," he says. "And can you also tell me where the weapon ... the pole ... that you used against Mr. Linnekar is right now?"

Jasmine pauses. I try really hard not to look at Mr. Khan. Her pole. Not that it's anything more than a simple bamboo pole in anyone else's hands, but it's the pole my sister's been training with for over a year.

"I don't know," she says with a shrug. "Sorry."

"And the insignia that was found at the scene. Do you know anything about that?"

Confusion clouds Jasmine's face. "Insignia?"

"What did you do directly after Jamie Linnekar died?" the officer asks.

"I tried to leave but was too weak. I couldn't breathe right. That's when Mr. Khan came. Isn't this all on the video?" Jasmine asks.

The officer nods. "Most of it, yes. Part of the video was lost, however, due to an apparent technological malfunction. We have footage until your friend comes into view. After that, the video is lost until about nine o'clock."

"If you're implying," Mr. Khan interjects, his voice slightly shaky, "that either Jasmine or I would do something as abhorrent as using a dead man's blood to write with, then perhaps we need to have legal counsel here. And I find it more than convenient that the video is missing."

"I would highly recommend you do obtain a lawyer," the officer answers. "We'll need to question anyone involved in the events that transpired this evening with regards to Mr. Linnekar's death."

The officer stops recording and turns back to Jasmine. "We'll send officers in the next day or so to do more in-depth questioning. By the way, I have no idea how you did what you did tonight. It took some guts and super strength. You must be some kind of Wondergirl."

Despite being totally exhausted when we finally get back from the hospital, my brain won't shut off once I'm in bed. Or to be more specific, the part of my brain that's responsible for memories won't let me sleep. Sometimes I feel like Jasmine, and even Mom, forget that I've been away, that things aren't a hundred percent normal for me here. Not yet, anyway.

I can't help but be angry with Mr. Khan. He had no right to go off on me tonight. Despite his apology, I'm still resenting the fact that I got a lecture because of Jasmine's bad decision-making. He knows just how stubborn my sister can get. She's impossible to reason with when she's made up her mind about something. It drives me crazy.

Don't get me wrong, I love being back with Jasmine. And with Mom. But sometimes it's just really hard for me to believe I'm actually here. At night I'm often afraid to close my eyes in case I wake up back down there. The strange thing is, since Lola's Ibeji doll was destroyed, all those years I spent in the Place-in-Between are becoming more and more blurry. I don't know if they were ever clear. It's like a nightmare where everything seems real when you're dreaming it, and even directly upon waking, but then progressively fades with each passing daylight hour. I now only remember my time down there from when Jasmine touched the doll and I could see her. That's why Mr. Khan's uncertain answer as to how I survived all those years with my half soul trapped in the Ibeji doll has left me uneasy.

The ceiling of the bedroom stretches out above me like a desert. I do vaguely remember sleeping in the Place-in-Between, mainly because it was something no one else around me ever seemed to do. I never questioned that fact … it just was. Everything down there just was. The reason I didn't question anything was probably because shortly after arriving there, the memory of my life before, of Mom and Jade, of Dad and his passing, of Toronto, of my friends, began to evaporate. Everything in my memory bank became more and more translucent and hazy. And yet there was always a deep feeling that something crucial was missing. Now I know that something was the part of my soul I share with Jasmine.

Every once in a while during the four years I spent there I'd suddenly remember a song or a smell, or a vision would pop into my head. Once I remembered singing in a restaurant with a girl that looked remarkably like me. It confused me so much, because I didn't even remember I was a twin. Most of the time I had no memories at all.

Or at least, I didn't remember until the day I saw Jasmine again. I was walking down a cobbled street when her image suddenly appeared like a projection against the low-hanging grey sky, her face filled with shock. She was holding a wooden doll in one hand, and there were wooden cupboards behind her. At first the vision terrified me, and I tried to run from it.

And that's when I was able to remember everything about my life before being abducted.

# JASMINE

Three events have happened over the last few weeks that changed everything.

First, simultaneous attacks with battery acid and bombs took place on the subways of New York, Tokyo, and London. Thousands of commuters were killed or maimed. Official newscasts contrasted images of passengers, limbs blown off and faces melted beyond recognition, with those of balaclava-clad CCT members pumping their arms in the air and claiming victory while threatening further attacks if countries closed their borders to the ships packed with climate-change refugees currently afloat on the world's oceans, including three ships packed with Australians. There were rumours of other videos, ones with climate-change advocates asserting they weren't responsible for the attacks, insisting they would not physically hurt civilians, that theirs was a moral war with the governments of those countries and cities, not the people, but those were quickly blocked by the government.

Second, Sandra Smith's work-for-welfare-and-rehab program rolled into action. Anyone sleeping rough was mandatorily enrolled in the program as well, and there was an immediate stop to the murders and disappearances. Images were broadcast every morning throughout the city, showing rows of mostly men dressed in grey jumpsuits with the words *To Serve and Protect Toronto* emblazoned on their backs, working on the roadways, fixing solar panels, and checking transport trucks at the tolls to stop immigrants from coming into the city. To ensure the dignity of the workers, their faces weren't shown. I found that a bit weird, since they were supposed to be doing such a great thing for the city. Smith also declared she will not allow Toronto to be destroyed like LA. If it comes to it, she said, she'll impose martial law, and anyone rioting or inciting terror will be locked away immediately, and she'll seek the death penalty for any CCT terrorists if attacks happen. "Inciting terror" includes any media sites broadcasting CCT videos that haven't been authenticated by government officials. Her ratings have soared.

In the wake of all of that, while I recovered from the attack and tried to figure out whether seeing Raphael had been real or I was actually losing my mind, the video of the battle between me and Jamie Linnekar went viral, and the media descended on us like a flock of hungry vultures. Not only was I being touted as some kind of teen superhero, but they'd also managed to dig up last year's coverage of Jade's reappearance five years after her initial abduction from our front yard. We were quickly dubbed the "miracle twins."

"They're camped out in front again," Jade says. She's sitting on a stool at the living room window of our apartment, staring down at the entrance. "I wish I could drop something on their heads."

Mom sighs. She's curled up on the opposite end of the sofa from me. A cup of chicory she's been nursing for the last hour is balanced beside her on the worn fabric of the sofa arm. The skin under her eyes is puffy and discoloured. I haven't seen her look this exhausted since her last lupus flare.

"We're going to have to speak with them eventually. You've missed nearly a week and a half of school because of this nonsense, and Jasmine, you're well enough to go to school now as well. And I'm sick of feeling like a prisoner in my own home."

My video phone pings.

"Mr. Khan's on his way here now," I say, reading the message. Mom's right. We are going to have to face the media at some point. Mr. Khan's brought us food for the last two weeks, allowing me to recuperate in peace and buying us time. Behind the scenes, he's told me the Protectors are meeting daily, trying to come up with something to say to the media that will hopefully both satisfy them and make them leave us alone.

There's a knock at the door. Jade rushes over to let Mr. Khan in.

He enters, fabric grocery bags in hand, tiny rivers of sweat rolling down his face. Dark patches stain the underarms of his shirt. "One of them nearly got in with me. Honestly, those parasites don't give a toss about privacy or trespass. Unbelievable." He puts down the bags, wipes a hand across his forehead, and gives us a lopsided smile. "You need to move to a lower floor. The stairs are too much in this heat. I'm not as fit as I was when I was a young woman."

"The only place we could move to is a cardboard box on the streets," Mom says. "I'm barely able to make the rent as it is."

So much for Mr. Khan's attempt to lighten the mood with a playful nod to his gender reassignment.

"All that really matters," I say, sitting up, my stomach rumbling uncomfortably, "is that breakfast is here. I'm starving."

Mom gets up. "I'm going to change and freshen up before we eat." She's stayed in her kimono since showering. More and more, she's acting like she did when she was sick. It's worrying. Even the way she moves is slower, more deliberate.

Mr. Khan kicks off his shoes and comes into the apartment. "Don't get too optimistic. The shelves are pretty sparse at the shops, and prices have jumped again. I managed to get us some bread and a few fresh tomatoes and a dozen eggs."

"Chicken eggs?" Jade says, her voice thick with hope.

"Not unless you're a lot wealthier than me," Mr. Khan says. "Wild pigeon. Apparently, according to the shop employee, these were freshly gathered by Sandra Smith's little night army last evening. Jade, if you'd be so kind as to help me in the kitchen, we'll whip up a little feast and then the four of us will discuss our strategy for facing the media today. Jasmine, I need you to go get ready."

"Should I change into my Supergirl outfit, cape and all?"

Mr. Khan grimaces as he glances toward the closed door to Mom's room. "This is going to be tricky. No matter what, we need to divert their attention away from Beaconsfield. If the media discovers how many twins are with us, and that gets out to the wider public, it could have consequences beyond our imagination. Especially if they investigate further."

About fifteen minutes later, the four of us sit down to eat. Mom brings out a fresh pot of chicory and the last of our honey.

"I think it would be wise to keep the story as uncomplicated as possible," Mr. Khan says as he pours himself a cup of steaming hot chicory. "Simply put, many people experience what happened to you. Life-threatening situations have often brought on adrenaline and cortisol surges that have allowed people to do something beyond their usual capabilities. That's our story for the media. I mean, that's what must've happened, right?"

Jade sneaks a sideways glance at Mom. I wish we could just tell her the truth that it had nothing to do with adrenaline — well, maybe a little — and a whole lot more to do with being a Seer.

"Yeah, must've been," I say. "Don't really remember much. Think I was on survival mode. I was carrying that pole because it was a prop for a play at school. I was going to decorate it at home."

Mr. Khan nods approvingly as he tears off a wad of bread and stuffs it into his mouth. "Really incredible what you did, Jasmine. Just tell it like it is, and hopefully another story will come along and knock you out of the spotlight sooner rather than later."

# JADE

As soon as we open the front door of our apartment building, we're bombarded. Questions are thrown at us like hand grenades. Reporters move forward en masse, leaving little physical space to move or breathe. In an instant I feel claustrophobic. Panicked.

"Jasmine, how are you feeling? How did you manage to defend yourself? Have you thought about meeting Jamie Linnekar's grieving mother?"

I look over at Jasmine. Her eyes are steely and her lips are set. She moves a hand to shield her eyes from the bright sun. I'm worried she's going to say something she shouldn't.

A reporter moves toward me. He's so close, I can smell his sweat. It's a pungent mix of onions and earth.

"Jade, you and your sister seem to be miracle twins. First you reappear as if from the dead, no worse for wear, and then your sister single-handedly saves you from death a second time."

I nod, not knowing what to say. The heat is intense. I wish I'd brought my sunhat.

"Where were you for those five years? You must remember something," another reporter chimes in.

I feel as though ice water has just been intravenously dumped into my veins, rendering me mute with shock. I shake my head, knowing I must look like the biggest idiot on Earth.

Thankfully, Jasmine steps forward. "My sister has always said she doesn't remember what happened during the years she was missing. She's told the police, her doctors, and us, her family, that she doesn't remember. And I didn't do anything out of the ordinary when my sister was attacked by Mr. Linnekar. Anyone would defend their family members, their loved ones, in the same way. And I don't remember much about what happened … just like my sister doesn't remember her ordeal. I guess adrenaline took over and allowed me to do what I needed to in order to save her and myself. Like people who can lift cars when there's been a bad accident with someone they love." She smiles widely. Several cameras snap photos. The reporters are eating this up like chocolate cake. I inwardly sigh with relief, glad to be off the hook.

"What about the CCT insignia? Do you have any affiliation with them?"

"I'm sixteen years old. Do you really think I'd be a terrorist?" Jasmine snaps. She's losing her cool.

"Less than twenty years ago, thousands of teens joined

terrorist armies in Syria, Pakistan, and other places in the Middle East," one of the reporters shouts out. "And how do we know you didn't tamper with the security cameras in order to make sure there was no evidence of you leaving the CCT marking on the sidewalk?"

Jasmine's eyes narrow. "Because they are at the top of posts thirty feet above the ground, and I'd just been nearly strangled to death. I couldn't even walk. It doesn't take a brain surgeon ..."

Mr. Khan steps forward and places his hand firmly on Jasmine's arm. "Toronto Police at 51 Division assure us that they've got forensic evidence from the scene that points to at least one other person being there shortly after Jasmine and I left in the ambulance. At no time have either of us been suspected of leaving that insignia. I'd recommend you direct your questions with regard to that part of the investigation to the police," he says.

And that's when I notice a long black car trying to pull into the semicircular drive in front of our apartment building. Sunlight casts a reflection over shiny paint that shimmers like water. The windows are darkly tinted. There aren't many cars on the streets these days, let alone luxury cars like this one.

Mr. Khan has noticed it as well. He stops speaking, his brows drawing together into a scowl. Curious murmurs spread through the crowd of reporters. They part like water as the car moves slowly up the drive toward us.

"What the...?" Jasmine says.

The car comes to a complete stop almost directly in front of us. Mom tenses beside me.

A uniformed driver gets out, walks around to the rear of the car, and opens one of the back doors. A set of tanned, toned legs appears. There's an audible hush as Sandra Smith steps out, smooths down the front of her white dress, and smiles widely at Jasmine.

"I've been waiting for this moment since I saw the video the other night," she says, moving forward and extending her hand to my sister. Her nails are painted silver and sparkle in the sun. She does a quarter turn and smiles toward the cameras as she grasps Jasmine's hand, giving it exactly three firm pumps.

To say Jasmine's return shake showed a lack of enthusiasm would be an understatement. I want to tell my sister to be careful, that she needs to hide her emotions. After all, Mayor Smith is a very powerful woman. And this entire exchange is being caught on video.

"This young woman represents the kind of fighting spirit Toronto, and indeed the nation, needs. She shows fearlessness and exercised the right to defend herself, despite the fact that in doing so she needed to make a difficult and perhaps unpopular decision."

The media continues to snap photos as Smith speaks. I watch Mr. Khan's expression darken, and Jasmine begins to look nervous as well as angry. Mom is beaming away, oblivious. I'm watching Smith's every move. Where exactly is she going with this?

"And if I may say so myself, Jasmine certainly inspired

me to add another few pounds and an extra repetition or ten to my strength-training regimen last evening." Smith flexes a well-toned bicep, resulting in a chorus of laughter from the reporters.

Then her face grows serious. She pauses, regarding the crowd of media silently, and places her hand on Jasmine's arm. I hold my breath in case my sister, who's now as tense as a tightly wound spring and sporting a look as dark as storm clouds, hauls off and hits her.

"These are uncertain, dangerous times. The events of the last few weeks in New York, Tokyo, and London demonstrate the need for constant vigilance. Climate change is an unfortunate reality, and our world has passed the tipping point. None of us wants to see the suffering and misery happening in places like India, South Africa, and Australia. We may have friends and family abroad. But there is nothing we can do. The situation is beyond salvageable. England closed her borders several years ago, knowing that there weren't enough resources to sustain the hordes of asylum seekers from Northern Africa and the Mediterranean regions. It's been a godsend having commercial flights stopped in terms of preventing new climate-change refugees from coming into Canada, but now we need to find ways to *strongly discourage* new immigration to Toronto and Montreal. Vigilance is required on all our waterways. We need to conserve what we have for those who are already here. And weed out those amongst us who might be threats to our safety and security."

There are murmurs that mostly sound like agreement from all around us.

"The kidnappings in Toronto have ceased for now, and thankfully there has not been a bombing for nearly a year. However, we can be assured that this will merely be the calm before the storm if we do not stay one step ahead of the terrorists. Our youth, particularly those who are disaffected, are vulnerable to recruitment by organizations such as the CCT. As such, I feel it is imperative that they have representation in leading Toronto, in helping to make this city the safest metropolis on the planet. And I can think of no one more suitable to lead our city's new youth advisory than Jasmine Guzman."

# JASMINE

Bitch.

I plaster on a smile for the cameras clicking every few seconds in front of my face like a tap dancer on crack. I'd rather pull out every one of my fingernails with my teeth than join her youth committee. I don't want to join anything associated with her. She's dangerous. I can smell it like a rabbit smells a wolf.

And that's because there's a lot more to this than meets the eye. I can read Smith's thoughts, though fuzzily, and there's a sinister side to her plan. She wants me to distract from the bad news, to stir up patriotic feelings, to get people to agree to her crazy plans about closing off Toronto to new residents and imposing the death penalty for terrorists, especially members of the CCT.

She holds up her hand, palm forward, in that annoying way she has. "I'd like to invite Jasmine and Mr. Khan, her advisor, to join me at City Hall right now for a lunch to discuss next steps. I'd like to see our youth, since they are our future, involved as soon as possible."

I glance over at Mr. Khan and raise an eyebrow. What about Jade? From the look on my sister's face, she's thinking the same thing.

The questions burst forth like a tidal wave. I'm grateful that most of them are directed at Mayor Smith.

"What powers will this youth advisory have? Will you appoint all the members? Can you ensure a diverse cross-section of Toronto's youth will be represented?"

"Why do you think the kidnappings and killings have stopped so suddenly? What do you attribute this to?"

"Can you share with us any information you have regarding the identity or whereabouts of any of the CCT members? Is there a reason so few of them have been brought to justice?"

Smith nods in the direction of each question. "Let me just say," she begins, "that your questions are ones I've asked myself. First, I think the diligence of our new night work crews and the extra eyes they provide have helped to quell the activities of the CCT for now. For that, I commend the men and women who are giving back in the program. Let me just remind everyone that the CCT is a highly structured, complex organization. It is also difficult to ID people who've blown themselves into small bits. Though it can be and has been done, we often have no suspects and would need the DNA of close relatives to make a match. I don't want to give away any classified information, but we suspect there are different levels or cells within the organization that we have yet to identify. Those individuals who are chosen, or who volunteer to embark on these heinous suicide missions seem to have been absent from society for a prolonged period. We believe individuals in the other cells are given the task of banking, shopping, et cetera, to enable this to happen. In fact, we can't be sure that some of those Torontonians who have been reported as missing aren't actually CCT recruits."

"How do we know that Jade Guzman, the young woman who disappeared from society for five years, isn't actually involved with the CCT?" one of the reporters shouts.

"Because she was ten at the time she was abducted, stupid," I snap, my face turning ember red. My hands are shaking from the adrenaline surging through my body, so I clench them into tight fists at my side as I turn to Mayor Smith. "Thanks so much for the offer. Tempting, but I'm going to have to pass. Really busy with my schoolwork this year. You know, grade eleven and everything, and I've just missed two weeks of classes because of my injuries. I'm sure the committee will be great."

Smith's impossibly white smile becomes even brighter in the intense sun. She leans over and whispers into my ear.

"Lola told me all about you and what you and your sister are. If you don't want to put your family, your loved ones, and all your little Seer classmates in immense danger, you'll join me. I need you, and believe me, you need me much more than you realize."

What she means by immense danger is that my family, Mr. Khan, anyone I love and care about, will disappear. Disappear and be killed. Her thought ricochets inside my head like a gunshot. Does she realize I'm reading her mind?

She straightens and smiles. "What do you think of that offer, Jasmine?" she says, more to the reporters than to me.

For a moment I can't speak. I wish I could talk to Mr. Khan privately, to tell him what just happened, what was just said to me, but know there isn't time. I get the feeling that Smith, like a cobra, is ready to strike if I don't do what she wants here and now. Losing face in front of all this media is not something she'll allow. I don't need to read her mind to know that much.

My legs feel like jelly. I stare out at the sea of reporters. "Um … Ms. Smith has just made me a very kind offer that will ensure the Youth Advisory Committee does not negatively impact my studies. As such, I am happy to join her in making Toronto a safe and environmentally sustainable city now and in the future."

A beaming Smith grabs my hand and raises it in the air with hers, putting just enough pressure on my skin that I feel a ring on her hand dig into my flesh. It's a subtle reminder of her power over me and her ability to inflict pain.

"We'll need to wrap up now," she says apologetically. "I need to get these two to my office."

Smith leans over to me. "Now get your ass into that car," she hisses. "And smile the whole time you're doing so."

Suddenly, I realize why she doesn't want Jade with me. She knows Seers are stronger together than apart.

# JADE

I watch Sandra Smith's car slide onto the road and pull away, taking Jasmine and Mr. Khan with it. I am paralyzed, trying to absorb what just happened. The reporters scatter like a swarm of mosquitoes bombed with insecticide. I guess they got their story and are now in a mad dash to be the first to get it edited and out there. Already loads of live feeds will be circulating throughout the city, and maybe even nationally.

"Well, this is thrilling," Mom says, her dark eyes glinting with excitement as we walk back into the building. A few residents are gathered on the sofas. I bite my lip to keep from saying something I shouldn't.

"Your daughter's quite the star," Mrs. Ford says, glancing up from her video watch. She's poured her large frame into a yellow sundress that's about three sizes too small, which makes her breasts pop out of the top like two bald men's heads. Patches of dark sweat stain her underarms, turning the fabric of the dress in that area from a sunny yellow into a colour closer to that of an alcoholic's urine. "The mayor's security person wouldn't let us out the door, but I watched the whole thing from in here and could catch what was being said on live feed." She taps her phone and grins. "Who knows? Maybe Jasmine will be mayor someday herself."

"We're very proud of her," Mom replies with a smile.

Mrs. Ford turns to me. "Sorry the mayor didn't pay you more attention. That couldn't have been easy."

"It was fine," I reply through gritted teeth.

"Did you know that Jasmine risked her life last year trying to save someone?" Mom says, talking loud enough that not only Mrs. Ford will be able to hear. "My best friend, Lola … you probably remember it being all over the media. She was killed in a fire at one of Mayor Smith's homes. Well, wasn't it Jasmine who ran into the house to try to save Lola, just when everyone else was running out? *Dios*, I don't know how my girl ended up being so brave."

"No one was in there when the fire started," I interject. "Remember? So no one was running out." *Except Mina*, I think. I'd never say that out loud, though. Sandra Smith made sure the entire incident was reported as an accident.

Mom shoots me a sideways glance. "I'm very proud of both my girls. Jade here is the smart one. Always the top in her class."

"That's nice," Mrs. Ford replies. "Well done, love." She might as well be describing a beige piece of furniture, her enthusiasm is that lacking.

I force a smile onto my face. Really, I shouldn't be wasting time standing around here talking to Mrs. Ford. Though I'm confused and more than a little hurt and annoyed that Jasmine, and especially Mr. Khan, didn't even say goodbye, let alone ask me to join them, I realize this media attention could be very bad for Beaconsfield and the Seers. They're going to want to uncover every juicy detail of Smith's new darling. I need to let the others know, especially Ms. Samson and the rest of the Protectors.

"I need to get to school," I say to Mom. "I've missed enough time already."

She turns away from Mrs. Ford. "Absolutely. Just give your hair a brush and be sure to take a full water bottle for the walk."

Not wanting to waste time going upstairs, I walk over to one of the cracked and mottled mirrors that line the rectangular pillars of the lobby. At one point in time this building must've looked pretty decent.

My dark hair is frizzy from the humidity. Perspiration moistens it along the nape of my neck. I quickly run a brush through it, pulling the hair off my face and into a high ponytail with an elastic I've got in my knapsack.

"I'm off," I say, giving Mom a quick hug and a kiss. "Bye, Mrs. Ford," I add, throwing her a quick wave.

Mrs. Ford waves back enthusiastically, putting her pit stains on full display. "You're camera-ready," she shouts as I head out the door.

*Aren't you the poster woman for feminism? Not!* I think as I start down the sidewalk, breaking into a light jog. Already, dark storm clouds are gathering over the lake, the deep, angry rumble of thunder rolling in the distance.

By the time I get to school, the entire sky is a deep grey, and sweat is pouring down my face in tiny rivulets.

Desiree looks up from her computer as I rush into the office and to the front desk. My mouth is so parched, it feels like my tongue is made of flypaper.

"Jade! Are you okay?" She stands up, pushes her red-framed reading glasses up onto her mane of bleached hair, and comes round to me. "Can I get you some water?"

I nod, wiping my hand across my forehead.

Desiree fills a cup with water from the cooler in the corner of the office and brings it over to me. "Lucky we're in an urban area and don't have to worry about dried-up wells or drinking water being rationed yet," she says with a smile. "Have a seat. It's good to have you back."

"Has Ms. Samson seen the news? About Jasmine?" I ask between gulps of water. The cool liquid feels like heaven as it hits my belly.

Desiree nods. "Mr. Khan hit 'record' on his video watch as he got into the mayor's car. Good thing he's wearing long sleeves today, though we suspect Mayor Smith doesn't care if he records the conversation taking place between the three of them. I suspect she's not too afraid of us, with the knowledge she has. You can go ahead into Ms. Samson's office. She's got Ms. Clarke in there listening to it with her." She smiles at me. "She'll be glad to see you as well. We all missed you very much."

"Thanks," I say, standing up and giving Desiree a quick hug. "It means a lot."

She places both her hands on my shoulders and looks me straight in the eye. "Don't let it get to you. You're just as special. The great thing about Seers is that we balance each other like yin and yang. Besides, being targeted for anything, positive or negative, by Smith is not something you should desire."

My heart skips a beat. I forget how good some Seers are at reading thoughts, unless you guard them, and even then we can still pick up fuzzy bits and pieces of what someone's thinking, or what their intentions are.

I refill my cup as I pass the cooler, thinking about how hard it must be for all the people in rural areas whose wells have dried up and who can't afford the tens of thousands of dollars to have new ones dug. Stories of families moving in with relatives and living in basement apartments or camper vans set up permanently in backyards are pretty common.

I knock at Ms. Samson's door. Ms. Clarke opens it for me, smiles, and puts a finger to her full lips. She's wearing an earpiece. I step inside, and she closes the door behind me.

Ms. Samson is sitting behind her large, wooden desk, leaning forward on her elbows with a look of complete concentration. A massive palm tree towers above her, its fronds reaching nearly to the ceiling.

"Jade's here," Ms. Clarke says, motioning for me to sit down on a leather chair across from her. A large monitor on the opposite wall shows the text of the conversation between Jasmine, Mr. Khan, and Mayor Smith. At the moment it looks like they're talking about the food on the table in front of them.

"Please carry on listening and let me know if anything critical occurs," Ms. Samson says, taking out her earpiece and tucking a renegade dreadlock behind her ear. She sits back and smiles at me.

"It's good to see you, Jade," she says, folding her hands on top of her desk. I stare at the multitude of silver and indigo rings on her fingers. "How are you feeling? A great deal has happened … and this latest turn of events is very worrying. We need to get you and Jasmine back into training as soon as possible. Two weeks off is a long time."

"I just want you to know that I tried to convince Cassandra and Jasmine not to go to the beach to train that night. All of this wouldn't be happening if they'd just listened to me. And he wasn't human. Jamie Linnekar, I mean. He was full demon when he attacked us." I pause. "How can that be?"

Ms. Samson nods, her dark eyes taking in every word. "We don't ever know what might or might not have happened on any given day. Cassandra's been spoken to about her choices that evening, and Jasmine will be as well. As for Mr. Linnekar, it's most unfortunate. Vulnerable souls are easily possessed."

"Sorry to interrupt, but I think you need to hear this," Ms. Clarke says. "Both of you."

# JASMINE

"Now," Mayor Smith says, taking a generous sip of her red wine. "Let's get down to business. I am well aware of your extraordinary courage and special talents as a Seer."

I raise my head from my plate of salad and chicken. It's so long since I've had meat, I don't care if I'm dining with someone who is very likely an enemy. I'm happy to bite the hand that feeds, and Mayor Smith will find that out really fast if she gets too close. Even though what Smith just said made my heart freeze, I plaster an expression of indifference on my face and shove another piece of chicken into my mouth.

"I don't know what you're talking about," I say between chews. "What's a Seer? I saved my sister and tried to save Mom's best friend. Anyone would do the same." I glance over at Mr. Khan, who hasn't touched his meal or water. His face is blank, purposely devoid of emotion. It also means I have no idea if I'm doing the right thing here.

Smith smiles, and I can't help but wonder how she keeps her teeth so shockingly white if she drinks red wine, even though it's a stupid thought to have in the middle of all of this.

She leans forward. The smile that seems to be permanently plastered on her face doesn't reach her eyes; instead, her gaze is full of frost and menace. "Jasmine, Lola was your Protector. I know *everything* ... and, just to let you know, she was sorry about Jade. It was the only way she could save Femi. It was a trade, you see. He was saved from his illness in return for your sister's soul being kept in the Ibeji doll. You're not the only ones with knowledge that our world contains the supernatural, the extraordinary ..."

I stare hard at the table, a lump of anger burning brightly in my chest.

"Jasmine," Mr. Khan says softly. "Emotions."

"What do you want from me?" I ask.

"I've chosen you because your story and your actions are inspiring. You have charisma and the type of fearlessness during these dark and frightening times that people decades older than you could only hope for. I want to be sure Toronto does not end up like LA or go the way Paris and New York seem to be ... they're ready to implode in civil war. All the mayors of the world's prominent metropolises, particularly the ones that stand poised to withstand the global economic and environmental changes that are happening, want to be more ... *proactive*. But we need the support of the people to do the things we feel are necessary. Part of getting that support is giving people hope in the form of someone or something they can believe in, that they can look up to." She sits back. "And for Toronto, that someone is you."

Her words tumble toward me like a landslide. I feel suffocated. One word in particular flashes in my mind like a red alarm. *Chosen.* Again, I'm reminded of the demon's raspy voice calling me *elegido*. The chosen …

"For years other countries, ones that have generally been frowned upon by Western nations, have broadcast the public executions of terrorists. It started in 2006 with the hanging of Saddam Hussein and became more commonplace in the early 2020s with the execution of members, particularly leaders, of other terrorist groups."

"Yeah, I wrote a persuasive essay on it last year," I interject, wrinkling my nose to show my distaste, "when certain broadcasters here and in the US wanted to publicly broadcast the executions. It's a disgusting thing for people to want to do to one another, let alone watch for thrills. I mean, we teach that it's wrong for a human being to murder another human, but then we murder the offender in return. It makes no sense." I look over at the bottle of red wine. Smith clearly has money. Wine and any meat besides squirrel and pigeon are now hot commodities. You can't even find them in grocery shops most of the time, and when they are there, they can cost hundreds of dollars for a bottle or for one roast chicken. Cattle production has been banned for years, so beef is like gold … rare and priceless.

"Is that what you're planning to do? Start broadcasting executions? Sell tickets so people can come and watch?" I ask sarcastically, spearing a piece of chicken with my fork.

"That's one part of it. Hopefully it will be a massive deterrent to terrorism and to terrorist-group recruitment for people to see the consequences awaiting. We also want to stop any new immigration into the city. Now that countries have closed their borders, we need to find a way to make sure all those refugees who have slipped into Canada over the last decade or so don't try to make Toronto their home. If people want to work here, particularly if they'd like to drive night taxis or subway trains, or work as identification and security officers in the evenings, we can provide them with housing on the outskirts of Oshawa and give them DNA-encoded passports to allow daily access in and out of the city. We have a need for workers in these sorts of employment and understand that these jobs are more challenging and dangerous. We wish to reward individuals who want to contribute to the smooth and safe running of the city. However, this means establishing a clear boundary between, essentially, 'old' Toronto, where no new population growth aside from live births will take place, and the outskirts, where new residents may be permitted to live."

"How very apartheid of you," Mr. Khan quips as he pushes his plate away. "This is insane. No one is going to support executing people, especially if you plan to turn it into public entertainment, like some sort of barbaric circus show. Besides, the death penalty doesn't even exist in Canada."

Smith directs her smile at Mr. Khan, regarding him silently for a few moments. "You'd be very surprised what people will support, and quite enthusiastically, I might add, when their own welfare is threatened, Jameela."

Mr. Khan's eyes widen with surprise. "How do you know my birth name?" His voice is unsteady with emotion.

"What Lola told me about all of you was so fascinating, I felt compelled to find out more about Beaconsfield, about the Protectors, and especially those Protectors and Seers whose twins are no longer with them. Mina ... what a tragic story. And Grace — I mean, your beloved Ms. Samson — her story is so very sad as well. But your story trumps both of theirs for tragedy and change, doesn't it? Gender reassignment for you, and, well, your sister's awful demise."

Mr. Khan doesn't say anything. Instead he just stares down at the table. He feels defeated and knows that Beaconsfield and everything we're doing there is at stake if he fights back. I can read that. He's also in immense pain. His heart feels as though it's been torn apart.

All of which makes me supremely pissed off. There's no way I want to be poster child for this demented bitch. But it looks like I might not have a choice ... for now.

"Stop it," I say. "Leave him alone." Meeting her gaze, I narrow my eyes. "What exactly do you want me to do? Because I'm not playing this game anymore." I follow Mr. Khan's lead and push my plate away, even though my stomach rumbles at the sight of the unfinished chicken breast perched on top of the last of the greens.

"I want you to stir up patriotic feelings in Toronto and the rest of Canada. Rabid patriotism. Make people feel that even the smallest contribution to the running of our city — for instance, bringing food to elderly residents trapped in their buildings due to power outages and elevator issues — makes a huge impact. I want the general public to understand that we're at war with *both* terrorism and the environmental changes happening around us. Make them understand that sacrifices will be required. Make them willing to turn on their own family members, if necessary."

I think back to my first journey to the Place-in-Between last year, when I found myself in the middle of the Blitz in London during the Second World War. The trapped souls there talked about the same kind of patriotic sacrifices. I'm guessing I'm going to be Smith's Churchill. Or that she wants to be Churchill and I'm some sort of personal assistant.

"Most importantly, I will need you to make people very afraid of the CCT and of the CCT's power to recruit the young people of Toronto. In fact, I want them to be terrified."

"And what do I get in return?" I ask, leaning forward onto my elbows and folding my hands on top of the table. "Because this all feels very one-sided right now."

Smith smiles again. "Oh, Jasmine, first off, you avoid being charged with the first-degree murder of Jamie Linnekar, because I can so easily have my technical department come up with a doctored video showing you attacking him first. It's so easy to change a narrative. And then, suddenly, it would be him acting in self-defence and not the other way around." She leans toward me. "The funny thing is, so many people in Toronto and beyond will believe anything I say." She sits back again and smiles widely. "So what you get is the assurance that all the Seers, as well as your precious little Beaconsfield, don't get exposed and dismantled for being a terrorist training ground. It would be very difficult to explain why such rigorous work on combative teachniques is being done on a daily basis, wouldn't it? Especially difficult to explain to a public that's scared to death of any more bombings and kidnappings. In fact, I question the curriculum there myself. Perhaps I need to make a visit one of these fine days."

"No thanks," I mutter.

She picks up her wine glass, regarding me as though I am some sort of fascinating bug. "We're at war, and we will not negotiate with terrorists," she says, taking a large sip and then holding her glass out in front of her. "Here's to alliances."

This is what it must feel like to be a fox caught in a snare. My choices are either to die or to chew my own leg off in order to survive. I stare at Smith, at the silver ring glinting on her finger as she holds her wine glass aloft in front of her.

She's very correct about one thing, though. We're definitely at war.

# JADE

Ms. Samson sent me to classes and training, despite my protests.

As my head hits the mat and Amara Jakande twists my arm behind me, placing her knee squarely in my back — a move that would effectively render me dead if she were a demon, but here in the gym, simply leaves me red-faced with embarrassment — I think about the danger we're all in. Not just from the demons, but from Mayor Smith as well.

"Jade, you're out!" Mrs. Jackson shouts from her chair on the sideline. She motions me off and over with a sharp wave.

I pick up my pole and jog over to her as Amara's sister, Vivienne, steps onto the mat.

"Where's your head at, girl?" Mrs. Jackson asks, getting up as I approach. She's at least forty and wiry, but strong. Her biceps pop out as she places her hands on her hips, regarding me carefully. "I know you've been through a bit over the last few weeks, but you need to get back on your game and get yourself together. We need to be ready for anything. You'd be dead in an instant with the kind of laziness I saw out there today. It was like watching a fish out of water, flopping around. Sloppy, to say the least."

I nod. She's absolutely right. I'm not even going to attempt an excuse. It would only make me look more pathetic.

"Now, take your seat over there by Cassandra." She points at the bleachers where Cassandra and Lily are sitting, poles in hand, waiting for their turn on the mat. It's the first time I've seen them since everything happened, and I'm still more than a bit annoyed at Cassandra for her part in dragging us to Cherry Beach to train.

Both Cassandra and Lily greet me with big hugs.

"So good to have you back," Lily whispers, leaning over to me, her dark eyes shining. "I was so worried. Did you know that Fiona and Jennifer were attacked the other night? They were in their yard. The demon tore apart their dog, Isabelle. That's how it lured them out."

My stomach plummets. Isabelle. Fiona and Jennifer had brought her to school a few times. (Ms. Samson doesn't like animals being inside, but understood that Isabelle was a retired guide dog and deserved not to be left on her own all day.) She was just this lovely, big-eyed chocolate Lab that had a kiss for every hand she could reach.

"Did they kill it?" I ask, hoping for Isabelle's sake that they smashed its head to bits like a ripe jack-o'-lantern.

"They tried. I think they were both so emotional because of Isabelle. She didn't die immediately … so the demon got away."

I look over at the mat. Amara and Vivienne are sparring with their poles, each careful not to hit the other with full force, since that could result in a fatal blow. Perspiration runs down their faces in rivers. I don't need to even watch them to know I messed up big time today. I'm lucky Ms. Samson didn't come in to watch like she often does. I'd be in detention training for a month if she had seen my pathetic display.

I lean back against the bleacher. I'm angry. Angry for Isabelle, who didn't deserve to die that way, especially after her years of service to others. It's stupid. There are people dying all over the world right now in catastrophic floods, hurricanes, and droughts. Countries that never used to eat dog and cat, like Australia, have been rounding up pets for consumption for the last few years. We haven't come to that here yet, but pigeon and squirrel are the only affordable meats at the moment.

"How's Jasmine? Is she coming back soon?" Cassandra asks. I can detect the hesitation in her voice. Try as I might to hide it, she knows how angry I still am.

"She's fine now. The doctors don't think there's going to be any lasting damage," I reply, trying to keep my voice as level as possible. "Which is lucky, considering she could be dead. Let's face it, I could be dead too. And you. Thanks to the stupid move we made going to the beach that day."

Cassandra sighs. "I get it, Jade. Believe me, everyone here has already taken a strip off me, so you doing the same isn't going to make a fraction of a difference."

Amara flips Vivienne onto her back, pins her to the mat, and then raises her fist in triumph, a wide smile spreading across her face.

"Beautiful!" Mrs. Jackson says, jumping out of her seat. She turns around. "Cassandra and Jade, you're up next."

I glare at Mrs. Jackson, hoping she'll somehow spontaneously combust as I slowly walk back onto the mat.

# JASMINE

"Our first news conference will be on Wednesday evening, as we want to ensure that we get across the message that the Toronto Youth Committee will not interfere with studies for those involved," Smith is saying to me as we approach the car. Her heels click along the sidewalk in front of City Hall. The sound is annoying. Everything about her is annoying. Everything is about appearance. This woman is the perfect example of smoke and mirrors. "The car will pick you up at six thirty p.m. sharp. It will pick up Jamil — Mr. Khan to you — just before that."

The driver opens the back door of the car for us. "There's water in the back if you want it, miss," he says. Though he shows little emotion, his brown eyes are kind, the skin around them deeply grooved, an indication that he's spent a good part of his life smiling deeply. I wonder how he ended up with the very shitty luck to be working as Mayor Smith's personal chauffeur.

"What about Jade?" I ask, turning back to Smith. "Why is she not a part of this?"

Smith, who is in the middle of slathering her lips with a shiny gloss, raises one well-manicured eyebrow at me. "Who said she isn't? You're going to recruit her for the committee, of course. However, we don't want to raise questions by including loads of identical female twins. With your other little Seer friends, you'll need to be selective in terms of who you invite. Like I said earlier, you're the one who has shown exceptional bravery over and over. Your sister has not risked her life to save another. Plus she becomes a gibbering idiot as soon as a camera is pointed in her direction."

"It's not like she wouldn't risk her life for someone," I say, crossing my arms in front of my chest. I hate not having my pole with me; it feels unnatural, like a chain smoker without a cigarette.

"Simply put, the reasons I mentioned earlier are why you were chosen. This first phase of the committee will focus on outreach work — things like taking food to the elderly, helping plant drought-resistant community gardens in inner-city neighbourhoods, talking up the infrastructure improvements the night workers are making. All good things."

I roll my eyes. "You're the boss," I say, getting into my side of the car. Mr. Khan's already in the other side, buckling his seatbelt and reaching for a bottle of water.

Smith grabs me by the arm; her fingers pinch into my flesh. I flex to show her it's a bad move. She squeezes harder in response and leans in close to me. Her breath is hot on my ear, and I can smell the minty scent of her newly applied gloss.

"Remember, you need to be one hundred percent when you're doing this. If you show the public that you don't believe in this, or if your flippant sarcasm slips through, I'll have you up for the manslaughter of Jamie Linnekar before you can blink an eye." She lets go of my arm and smiles. "See you on Wednesday."

I slide onto the seat as the driver closes the door behind me.

As soon as I'm buckled in, I turn to Mr. Khan. "Why didn't you say anything? You just sat there most of the time like some sort of slug. Like an elective mute." My face flares with anger. I'm not really that mad at him. It's the situation. But he did choose to just sit there after Smith brought up his sister, not saying a word. And that was cowardly.

"Not here, Jasmine," Mr. Khan says, nodding toward the driver. "I know you're upset, but …"

"Upset? Me? Not at all. I love being someone's puppet. Pull my strings and I'll dance. Just watch me go."

"Can you please take us to Beaconsfield Secondary?" Mr. Khan says, leaning forward in his seat toward the driver. Drops of condensation fall from the bottle onto his pants, leaving little dark teardrops along the tops of his legs. "At 898 Crossfield Boulevard."

"Absolutely, sir," the driver answers.

We sit in silence the rest of the ride. I stare out the

tinted windows, watching people shopping at small, makeshift stands set up in front of shops. Older people shuffle slowly along, most of them sporting oversized sun hats, their paper-thin skin being particularly vulnerable to the constant high heat and UV light that climate change has brought. The small selection of fruits and vegetables found in these shops is usually much less expensive than in the supermarkets, but more and more people are complaining that their gardens are being raided at night, the suspicion being that a lot of their produce is ending up in these stores. I guess that's something the Youth Committee could help with. Maybe some of Smith's new army of night workers could be put on shifts to patrol neighbourhoods where the raiding is a problem. There's also been a huge spike in lost and stolen pets, which makes me wonder if some of them are ending up on grocery shelves or restaurant menus, also advertised as chicken or rabbit instead of dog or cat.

As soon as we get through the doors of the school, Mr. Khan stops. "You really, really need to get your emotions under control," he says. "How could you think I'd talk to you about any of what's going on in Mayor Smith's car, in front of her personal driver, no less? Even if he doesn't tell her what was said, I'd bet she's got the car as well as her offices fully wired." He shakes his head. "I guess that's why first-borns are known for their bravery and not necessarily their grey matter."

"W–what?" I stammer. "This is really not what I need after everything that's happened today."

Mr. Khan leans in closer to me. "*You* don't need this? Do you realize just how much Lola told this woman about us? Lola betrayed all Seers and Protectors when she gave up Jade to the dark forces. And she didn't stop there. Mayor Smith knows so many things she shouldn't. Does she know about the Place-in-Between? About demons? About demons being here with us? God only knows how much Lola told her power-hungry little friend before leaving this Earth." He stops and stares at me, his brown cheeks flushed with emotion. "So, for just this once, can you stop thinking about yourself? Because if you are *elegido*, the Chosen One, we're in bloody big trouble."

"I need my pole," I say, turning on my heel and marching toward the office. I'm going straight to Ms. Samson. How can Mr. Khan speak to me this way? He's supposed to be my Protector. "FYI, you're not my father," I spit back over my shoulder. "Or my *mother*." It's a low blow, and I regret the words as soon as they escape my lips. Mr. Khan transitioned from being a female years before I even met him.

"Good thing, because no child of mine would be allowed to act like such a self-righteous brat," Mr. Khan says. I can hear the hurt in his voice. "And the police have your pole, not me."

I enter the office. Desiree looks up from her work. "Jasmine!" she stands up. "How are you?"

I rush around to her side of the desk to give her a hug and a kiss on the cheek. "I need to see Ms. Samson," I say. "Without *him*."

"You'll both see me right now, and Mr. Khan is very correct that you need to get a hold of yourself, young lady."

My heart jumps into my throat. I don't even want to turn around. Ms. Samson is slowly making her way down the short hall from her office, leaning heavily on her walking stick. She nods toward Mr. Khan, her large silver earrings glinting in the sunlight streaming into the room from the floor-to-ceiling windows on the far side of the main office area.

"You forgot to stop recording, Jamil," she says, pointing at her wrist. "A bit careless, but perhaps it's good, as I've been able to follow everything, including the conversation you two just had. And I'd expect your emotions got the better of you after Sandra Smith mentioned your sister. She hits low and hard, that one does." She motions us to follow her down the hall.

Once we're inside Ms. Samson's office, she closes the door and walks behind her desk. Dark, bruise-like circles frame her eyes. She looks beyond tired and seems uncomfortable lowering herself onto the leather chair.

"Other than two of our Seers being attacked the other night when their dog was let out to relieve itself, there has been virtually no demon activity noted. Nothing. No disappearances, no bodies found. Considering many of these entities would be vampiric, this is highly unusual."

"Whose dog?" I ask.

"Fiona and Jennifer's. Isabelle. Poor thing. I'd like to say she didn't know what hit her, but she did. Suffered quite some time after the initial attack while the girls tried to kill the demon. Fiona had to put her out of her misery." She shakes her head. "The agony of the world is increasing sharply. I can feel it in these old bones. They don't stop screaming in pain even when I sleep … if I sleep."

I feel sick. Isabelle was a beautiful, elderly chocolate Lab that wouldn't hurt a soul.

"What could be happening with the demons? Has the rift closed?" Mr. Khan asks.

"Why are there no demons during the day?" I ask. "When we were in the Place-in-Between, there were loads around all the time. Night and day."

"I wish I had all the answers. We just don't know. It's not like we've dealt with anything like this in modern times. In the last century there were some spots of demonic activity and horrific experiments done on twins, some of whom were Seers, by the Nazi regime during the Second World War, but nothing worth noting happened in Toronto. I'm not sure why the demonic activity is so prevalent here and now. Perhaps because we're relatively unscathed from climate change? Perhaps because your sister came back here from the Place-in-Between?" She sits back and curls her fingers around the top of her walking stick. The movement causes her swollen knuckles to bulge out like roasted chestnuts. "You're very lucky to have Jade back. My sister and I were so close. We were like panthers when confronting demons back home … black, fast, and deadly, we were." She laughs, but her laughter is tinged with a deep sadness.

I think about what Smith said today and want to ask Ms. Samson about her sister, but I don't dare. After all, I know how it feels to have a tragedy befall your twin, and how awful it is when people keep bringing it up.

"My sister, Grace, is in a home," Ms. Samson says, her chin quivering ever so slightly. "She was knocked down by a car filled with a group of very intoxicated sixteen-year-olds who were far too young and too stupid to be given a license to drive. She suffered immense brain damage and was left catatonic due to the injuries. That was over twenty years ago."

I stare down at my hands, at my chipped, violet-varnished nails. She just read my mind, but I didn't expect an answer, didn't want her to go back to that painful event, because I know when you've lost your twin, being reminded of that fact is like ripping a Band-Aid off a wound that isn't fully healed.

She clears her throat. "I do think we need to take Sandra Smith's threats very seriously. Jasmine, you have to play along with this, but keep trying to break into her thoughts and find out what you can when you're around her. Listen in on any conversations you can. Smith will be guarded. She knows what you can do. What's not clear is whether she knows about the demons or the Place-in-Between. Likely she just knows about Obeah from Lola. I have a feeling there's a lot more happening here than meets the eye."

"Obeah?" I ask.

"It's complex," Ms. Samson says. "Followers of Obeah

believe that spells for healing, wealth, and much more can be performed by certain people … shamans of a sort. Likely that is what Lola thought she was doing when she gave up Jade in return for Femi's healing. I can't imagine she'd have knowingly condemned her to live eternally without a soul in the Place-in-Between."

"There's nothing I wouldn't put past her," I say through gritted teeth.

Ms. Samson shakes her head. "Leave your anger, Jasmine. It will only eat you up from the inside out. We need you to be wise, to reflect. Everything said to you or that you see must be meditated on. Now, I need you to get to class. You and all the Seers have a great deal to learn."

"Before I go, can I ask you something?" I say, biting my lip nervously. I'm not sure I want the answer to this question but feel the need to ask. "The demon told me I was *elegido*. Chosen. Do you know what that might mean?"

Ms. Samson's eyes widen for a moment, and she quickly looks over at Mr. Khan, then down at her hands. She's clutching the top of her walking stick so tightly that her thin skin shines like plastic wrap.

"In time, you will find out. But you're not ready yet. However, it is the very reason we need you to be more careful and to begin to work on becoming wiser, less impetuous. You mustn't take the risks you have been taking. The one thing I can tell you is that it's absolutely essential you stay alive."

# JADE

It's been three weeks since the Youth Action Committee was created, and somehow Lily, Vivienne, and I all got roped — I mean recruited — by Jasmine. We joke that it's because we're all second-borns and therefore the brains of the committee, but it's likely because we're not stubborn and impulsive, like so many first-borns. We're not the only ones in the committee; in fact, there's a waiting list of over a hundred fifteen-to-eighteen-year-olds who've expressed interest in joining. At the moment Mayor Smith's capped us at thirty, which is good because it can be really hard coming to a consensus about things. Right now we're focused on helping those who can't help themselves and basically talking up the need for all Torontonians to cut back on water use by showering every second day and trying to eat foods that don't need to be boiled or mixed with water, which means a huge decrease in grains in people's diets, among other things. It seems to be going well, and Jasmine's also asked Mayor Smith if some of the night crew can be out on patrol to help protect people's private gardens from raids.

"I can't believe I'm up at this hour on a Saturday morning, let alone at a grocery store," Lily sighs, pushing her sunglasses up onto her head. "It's not even eight."

"It's that or delivering this stuff in over-forty-degree heat in a few hours. I'm more inclined to take a nap with my time later," I say, picking up some fruit bars.

Vivienne grabs a pack of the bars and turns it over to read the ingredients. "Seriously? Grasshopper protein powder?" She wrinkles her nose in disgust. "Desiccated apricots and powdered grasshopper? Ugh."

We're buying food to take to elderly residents living in the condos that line the waterfront. Many of the buildings stop running their elevators for hours a day, rendering Torontonians with any kind of mobility or health issues virtual prisoners in their homes. Even though keys were supposed to be given to any resident needing an elevator because of health or mobility issues, in practice it hasn't always happened, so the Youth Action Committee created a site where anyone needing grocery deliveries could sign up, and we'd deliver them. Hundreds of people signed up. It's not really surprising, considering nearly all of the buildings are over twenty storeys high. For us Seers on the committee, it's a great way to get in extra training, with all the stairs.

"It's not that bad. You can't really taste it," I say, shrugging. "Not everyone has generators when the power cuts happen. That means having meat or dairy in the fridge is too chancy. If you can even afford it in the first place."

Vivienne and Amara live with their parents in Rosedale, an expensive area of the city, and they have this massive generator that runs on propane and kicks in when the power cuts last for more than a couple of hours.

"Jade," Lily whispers, giving me a look that lets me know she thinks my comment was completely unnecessary.

"Believe me, I'd trade in our generator to have my grandparents alive and my friends not left behind. My country has been destroyed by climate change and war. We were once the Rainbow Nation. If my father wasn't a diplomat, we wouldn't have been on that plane. We'd be in South Africa and likely dead, or on a boat trying to find refuge with everyone else," Vivienne says. Her voice shakes. "You haven't got a clue what it's like to be a climate-change refugee, Jade."

My face burns. "Sorry, I wasn't thinking." I pop several bags of sweet potatoes and dandelion greens into my basket. My video watch buzzes. It's Jasmine.

"Hey, you," I say, bringing her up on the screen. Vivienne and Lily crowd around me to wave. "How's City Hall this morning?"

Jasmine grimaces. Her long, dark hair is curled to frame her face, and her eyes are darkly lined with makeup. "It's fine."

I laugh, knowing how much she hates being all done up. "Doesn't sound fine. Are you wearing a cocktail dress?"

"No," she says through gritted teeth, panning out to show us her outfit of a tight black tank top, skinny jeans, and black combat boots.

"I think you look great," Lily says from over my shoulder. "What are you doing?"

"A photo shoot for posters about the new train and vehicle stop-and-search bylaw and the importance of full compliance. Yet another way to try to keep immigrants out of Toronto. And then we're doing some sort of promotion for drought-resistant green garden roofs on residential buildings to increase the local food supply. Fun and games." She rolls her eyes.

No matter how tired we are being out at this time in the morning, at least we're involved in something good that directly helps people. Jasmine had to be at Mayor Smith's office at seven to start the photo shoot on the green roof at City Hall. The shoot is pure propaganda, according to Jazz, a first step to having every Torontonian question any and every unfamiliar face they see. Mayor Smith is starting checkpoints where any motor vehicle or train coming into the city limits will be stopped and thoroughly searched. And she's setting up an anonymous site where people can report suspicious activities or neighbours who seem to be acting strangely ... including anyone speaking out about the government.

"Listen, Sandra ... Mayor Smith ... she just told me to let you know that there's pretty significant delays expected on the subway today. Engineering work last night didn't get fully completed or something like that. She said you need to bus it to the condos."

"Great," I reply. "That should only add about half an hour and a ten-minute walk to our day."

"Don't shoot the messenger, kids. I wanted to let you know because she was pretty adamant that I tell all the committee members. Mom and Mr. Khan know that there is no other option." She glances over her shoulder at something behind her. "Gotta go. I wouldn't want to waste any of their precious time." She winks before ending the call.

I turn to Vivienne and Lily. "Ugh. I totally have to pee if we're going to be in transit that long. Can you cash out, and I'll meet you outside?"

"Sure," Vivienne says, taking my hemp bags from me. Her biceps bulge as she takes on the extra weight. All of us have become so lean and strong.

The washrooms are at the back of the store. My bladder is pressing uncomfortably, so I break into a light jog. It's like a ghost town in here at this hour anyhow, so there's no one around to give me stink eye for running to the bathroom.

I'm thinking about the stop-and-search laws, and the fact that anyone who doesn't comply, or worse, who is found to be harbouring or transporting climate-change refugees or immigrants of any kind, will face prison time … when this guy suddenly steps out in front of me, his arms piled high with bags of sweet potatoes and cornmeal.

My legs don't get the frantic message my brain sends them until it's two seconds too late.

I crash into him, and for a moment his grocery bags seem to hang in the air like hot-air balloons before crashing to the floor. One of the bags splits open, sending a tidal wave of tiny yellow fragments all over the floor.

"Well, I guess it's too late to tell you to watch where you're going," a soft voice says.

I look up, face burning. To my surprise, the guy is about my age. His hair is shocking orange, and his eyes are deep blue. He's got this strange, almost pinched look to his face. He flashes me a lopsided smile.

"Shit … I'm so sorry," I reply. I crouch down and attempt to scoop up some of the cornmeal, placing it back into the bag, which is split cleanly down the middle.

The boy crouches down beside me and starts laughing. It's a warm laugh that for some unknown reason seems familiar. He puts his hand over mine. Heat radiates from his flesh.

"Thank you for the effort, but I really don't think it's going to work." He pauses and shoots me a lopsided grin. "By the way, my name is Seth."

There's no way I'd usually be okay with some random guy touching me, let alone putting his hand on me, but I am actually liking this.

"I'm Jade." I stop my futile attempt to salvage the spilled cornmeal. "God, I really am sorry. I'll pay for it."

Seth shakes his head and runs a hand through his spiky

orange hair. "Don't be ridiculous," he says. He pauses and raises an eyebrow at me. "However, there is a way you could pay me back…." A pink bloom spreads across his alabaster cheeks.

I wait. I've got this strange, irresistible urge to touch him more, to reach out and kiss him. What the hell is going on? Have I been away so long that all of my puberty hormones have come rushing to the surface all at once?

"Would you meet up with me one late afternoon this week? Before curfew? Maybe for chicory or tea? We could maybe take our drinks and sit near the lake?"

My eyes widen with surprise. "Yeah," I say, without even taking a second to think about it. "Yeah, I'd love to."

We arrive at the condo buildings about forty minutes later than we expected to. Even with the windows open, the bus was suffocatingly hot and smelled strongly of unwashed feet and body odour, an unfortunate consequence of the humid weather and people taking Mayor Smith's calls for everyone to do their part cutting back on water consumption seriously. Definitely, fewer showers and baths seem to be happening in Toronto these days. Even though I'm doing my part and cutting back, I still make good use of a facecloth and soap on the days we're supposed to be skipping full-on cleaning. I'd like to know if our precious mayor ever sacrifices her daily cleanse. Somehow I doubt it.

"God, I feel sick," Vivienne says, holding her hand over her nose as we get off. She stops to readjust the knapsack full of food on her back. "That was vile."

"Look at this," Lily says, pointing at the cement light post we're standing in front of. It's covered with posters showing lost pets. "At least seven posters of missing dogs and cats have been posted in just the last week and a half. So sad."

I stare at the posters. Photos of happy, well-loved pets stare back out at me. Some of the images are in colour, some in black and white. Rewards are offered for most of them. For some reason they make me remember how desperately I wanted a kitten when I was young. The demon who abducted me from our front lawn had somehow known how badly I wanted a cat. That's how it tricked me into going with it. By the time I realized what was happening and began to scream, there was no one around to hear me. No one but the lost souls in the Place-in-Between.

"Probably some sick bastard who gets his jollies from torturing animals is responsible for the disappearances. Or maybe someone's eating them," Vivienne says as we cross the street and walk toward the condos where the deliveries are to be made. "I'm sure a few actual lost pets are in the mix as well."

We reach the condos and rest for a few moments

on a bench under the canvas awning at the front of the first building, listening to the grasshoppers sing as they jump up and down in the long, dry grass all around us. Like everything else, the grass is dehydrated and pokes uncomfortably into my legs and back each time I move even the slightest little bit. I find myself staring at the cloudless sky, thinking about Seth.

"What's with the Cheshire grin?" Lily asks.

"What?" I ask.

"You're sitting there smiling away like we're about to dive into an icy pool, rather than climb a zillion stairs in this heat." Lily gives me a playful punch on the arm.

For a half a second, I think about telling Vivienne and Lily about Seth. But for some reason, I kind of want to keep him a secret — for now, anyway. My life story was splashed all over the media last year, so it feels kind of good to have a secret all to myself.

"Naw, it's nothing. Want to split the buildings or just divide up the different floors in each?" I ask, getting up. I want to get this over with. Sweat is already staining the neckline of my cotton T-shirt and rolling down my back. With heat this insane, there's bound to be a severe storm and power cuts by midafternoon.

"Let's take a building each and meet back out here under this awning when we're done. Make it a bit of a race," Vivienne says, getting up and twisting a colourful cotton scarf around her dark, curly hair.

Lily frowns. "Sometimes they want to talk for a bit, the residents ... and I feel bad just dropping the food and running off. A lot of these people are really lonely. We're often their only visitors all week."

"Suit yourself," Vivienne says, shifting from side to side to stretch her long, lean legs. "I'll see you back here when you get done. Wake me up if I'm asleep." She grins widely and sprints across the empty parking lot between the building we're in front of and the one next to it.

"Do it whatever way you want," I say to Lily as soon as Vivienne's out of earshot. "And I agree with you about not just dropping stuff off and dashing. Sometimes I think our visiting the residents makes them happier than getting the food. Why don't you take this building? I'll take the far one."

"Thanks," she says, relief spreading across her face. She gives me a quick hug. "I just feel really bad for so many of them. See you soon."

I reach my building and discover that the elevators aren't running, which is no big surprise. I've got deliveries to do from the seventeenth floor down, so I decide to start at the top, since it will be easier.

Apartment 1705, where Mrs. Li lives, is my first delivery. She opens the door about half a second after I knock. It's clear she's been waiting for me.

"Jade!" she says, her wide smile creating ripples in her papery, sun-spotted cheeks. She's dressed in a faded floral sundress, her dark hair pulled back off her sagging face. Tufts of thin hair peek out from under the red fabric headband framing her face. "How are you, love?"

"Good," I say, letting the knapsack fall from my back to the well-loved, Moroccan-inspired carpet with a thud. It's such a relief to have it off, I feel like I could float away like a helium balloon. "I managed to get a bit of dry cat food for Pudding. It's made out of a variety of rodents and things, I think." Pudding is Mrs. Li's elderly grey tabby. Not only has it been hard for vulnerable people to get food and other necessities for themselves, it's been nearly impossible to keep their pets alive. And Pudding, last time I was here, was definitely walking a thin tightrope between life and death, her ribs jutting out of her body like skeletal fingers.

"Come in, come in," Mrs. Li says, putting her hand on my forearm. "Pudding will be glad to see you. I put out some traps the other night and managed to get three mice for her."

Staring at her painfully thin shoulders as she shows me into the kitchen, I wonder if she actually needed that mouse meat for herself.

"Do you want me to put the groceries away before I go?" I ask. "I can't stay long, unfortunately … subway delays and stuff … I had to take two buses to get here."

Mrs. Li's face falls with disappointment, and I think about how right Lily was about the importance of our visits for easing loneliness. I make a mental note to talk to Jasmine about the possibility of establishing a wing of the Youth Committee to do more outreach in terms of company for the vulnerable and ensuring their com-panion pets are as healthy as possible. Maybe we could even offer dog-walking or try to get vets to make the occasional visit with us.

"Any tasty spuds in there?" she asks, her eyes flashing with hunger.

I nod as I begin to unpack my knapsack. "I managed to get you a bag of sweet potatoes. And some really nice dandelion greens that will need to be eaten soon."

"You can leave a couple of the potatoes out with those greens, love. I'm going to have the last of my honey on them for lunch." She opens a cupboard and takes out a baking tray, her mottled hands shaking ever so slightly as she carries the tray to the counter. "Only a few years ago, I'd have thought nothing of boiling them up. But now ... I know it'll take triple the time, but at least baking won't waste water, and if I cut the veg up really small, it'll cook faster and I'll save more energy that way." Sadness fills her eyes. "My years on this Earth are numbered," she says, "but I worry about what the future holds for all of you young ones."

I smile at her. "Let me rinse and cut those before I go," I say. "And don't worry. Things will get better. I'm sure of it."

"Well, I don't know if it will get better, but at least we have a leader that's looking out for us. Didn't you hear that Mayor Smith is going to be giving all residents of Toronto drinking water? Delivered right to our front doors like this for people like me who can't get to the grocery shops any longer."

I shake my head. "I didn't know that, which is strange because usually my sister keeps me pretty updated on everything going down at City Hall. Do you have a peeler?" I ask, picking up one of the potatoes and absently scraping some dirt off of its orange skin with my index finger.

Mrs. Li nods, shuffles over, and opens one of the kitchen drawers. She retrieves a stainless steel potato peeler that looks like it's seen much better days.

"Did they say anything about the water supply for people outside Toronto? It seems like things are a lot more grim for people trying to live off well systems. Or in smaller communities. The groundwater's all dried up."

"Oh yes," Mrs. Li answers, her eyes lighting up from within the folds of crepey skin framing them. "I believe they're part of the water delivery scheme as well. And Smith is making sure they get tablets that will protect them from radioactive waste and also apparently help prevent dehydration. Maybe they've had some sort of intelligence about a threat. What do you think?"

It's hard for me to feel the same enthusiasm for Smith, though I wonder why Jasmine hasn't mentioned the drinking water stuff to me. The plan, at least from what Ms. Li is saying, sounds pretty good to me. Maybe Jasmine isn't being as open-minded as she could be. Wouldn't be the first time.

# JASMINE

The first bomb went off at 9:00 a.m. sharp. It detonated on a subway train that was snaking its way westward, leaving the platform of Bloor Station, bound for the underbelly of Bay Street. The subway wasn't packed because it was a Saturday morning, not the weekday rush hour. Still, there were at least a dozen passengers aboard that particular car, many coming back from night shifts as cleaners or security guards in office buildings. Others were just starting out on their journey to work long hours in retail shops and fast-food restaurants.

The second bomb exploded five minutes later, this time on a southbound train as it pulled alongside the platform at Queen Station. People waiting to disembark were blown out the sliding doors, resulting in bits of flesh and dismembered body parts being strewn all over the tiled floor of the station in a fifteen-foot radius.

One of Mayor Smith's assistants, a slim guy with ginger hair and a perpetually red face, came running across the roof in the middle of our shoot. I was standing in the centre of one of the vegetable gardens planted on the roof of City Hall, holding up a bunch of freshly picked chard and spinach with two little kids, the son and daughter of some city councillor, at my side. Neither of them could've been over the age of seven, and despite the giant straw sun hats perched on top of their heads, they were both sweating like lit candlesticks. The photographer kept snapping photos, but I stopped paying attention to the camera and instead focused my attention on Smith's face. It was pretty clear whatever was happening was serious. Mayor Smith's head was bowed over the assistant's tablet, her brow furrowed with concern.

"Jasmine!" Smith said, waving me over. I dropped the vegetables as her assistant approached.

"We're going to have to do this another time," he said. The tension in his voice was like a coiled spring.

"Okay," I replied with a shrug. If there is one thing I've learned since discovering that I'm a Seer, it's to try to keep my emotions as neutral as possible. So I wasn't going to worry or panic, no matter what was going on.

"The mayor needs you. Now," he snapped, his face turning nearly purple. "You two come with me," he said, holding his hands out to the two children.

It's hard to believe all of that happened just over twenty minutes ago. The shock of the news is wearing off, and now I'm sitting in a secure conference room in the depths of City Hall with a smattering of councillors, the police chief, Mr. Jawad, and Mayor Smith. It's the first time I've actually been in the same room as Mr. Jawad. He's wearing a navy linen suit, and his eye patch is silver today. When we were introduced, he wouldn't shake my hand.

"Superbugs. I don't take chances," he said with a smile, quickly moving his hand out of reach.

Weird, but I guess it takes all kinds. Besides, we've got a lot more important things to deal with, considering what's going on. I've managed to reach Mom and Jade, but Mr. Khan's phone is going straight to messaging. I hope he got my text earlier today about avoiding the subway.

"We've got our best people combing through all the video surveillance from last night as we speak," the chief says, folding his hands on the table. He shakes his head. "I was really hoping we'd be able to prevent something like this. It's hard to imagine how the bombs got under those cars."

"We're sure it wasn't suicide bombers? Absolutely, one hundred percent?" Mayor Smith asks, glancing at the wall monitors. There are at least five screens, all projecting different live feeds from newscasts and social media. "Because if those bombs were planted, this is something new for the CCT. They generally don't mind sacrificing themselves for their cause."

The chief's chocolate eyes darken with concern. "I don't think we can attribute this to any particular group at this point in the investigation. And no one has stepped forward to take responsibility."

"Who else would it or could it be?" Smith says, her voice tinged with frustration. "After all, they've been threatening to take action for the last while. We were short on subway engineering crews last night. It was also the first night starting garden patrols, so we were a bit understaffed in terms of the night workers who usually provide security on the transit system."

I glance at my video watch, willing it to come to life. With each passing minute, I'm getting more and more concerned about Mr. Khan. He would know to get ahold of me, would know I'd be sick with worry. Biting my lip, I force myself to pay attention to what's happening around the table.

There's a knock at the door. One of the uniformed security officers walks over and opens it. The same ginger-haired assistant who broke the news about the bombings comes striding into the room and up to our table.

"They've made an arrest," he says breathlessly.

We all stop and stare at him in unison like synchronized swimmers. The air in the room becomes thin and electric with anticipation.

"A person of interest was spotted on the security footage, and a short time later, a man fitting the description perfectly was found disoriented, wandering close to Queen Station." He looks over at the chief. "The deputy chief has requested you return to headquarters as soon as possible. There's a media frenzy both here and there. The suspect was taken to 52 Division."

Smith nods. "Thank you, Mitchell. We'll need the car in about five. Around back, please. And Jasmine and Mr. Jawad will be accompanying us."

"Yes, ma'am," Mitchell says, turning on his heel.

"Ma'am?" Smith asks, arching an eyebrow at him, her voice knife's-edge sharp.

"Sorry, I've just always wanted to say that … British crime shows…" His voice trails off as he leaves the room.

The chief's video watch buzzes. He looks at a message and frowns. "It seems they can't make a positive identification on the suspect. He was found wearing specialized contact lenses, and his fingerprints have been eradicated. Deep acid burns … about a month old. Which coincides with the exact time he claims to have become disoriented. He remembers nothing for the last four weeks and says his life before that is hazy. If this guy knows his own identity, he's not letting on."

# JADE

Mr. Butterman opens his door on my fourth knock. His face is flushed tomato red, and his bald scalp glistens with sweat. It's hard for him to move quickly due to bad knees, which are only getting worse with weight gain and age, and he's got the unfortunate luck of having an apartment located on the south-facing side of the building, which makes it feel like a sauna even this early in the morning.

"Have you heard?" he asks, somewhat breathless, moving to one side to let me in.

"Heard what?" I ask as I squeeze past his large frame and head toward the tiny galley kitchen. There's no way we'll both fit in here. Setting down my knapsack on the chipped countertop, I begin to unpack his groceries. Each week the amount seems to dwindle as things become more expensive. Soon Mr. Butterman won't need to worry about his weight, if shortages and food inflation keep happening at this rate.

"Oh, you obviously haven't," he says, following me a little more closely than I'd like. A wave of pungent body odour wafts over me, and I fight the urge to cover my nose. He's a nice man; I don't want to hurt his feelings.

"Bombs ... on the subway," he says, his eyes widening.

"Really? Where now?"

"Here in Toronto. At least two subway trains have been blown up. Downtown core." He leans against the doorjamb, breathing heavily. "They say the death toll is going to be well over two dozen for sure."

I feel like I've just been punched in the stomach. "I need to get in touch with my sister ... with Jasmine. Are you sure it's just on the subway? There haven't been any other attacks? On government buildings or anything?"

He shakes his head, causing drops of perspiration to fly from his hairline. "So far no, but who can say what these climate-change terrorists are plotting next. And communication lines are not dependable right now. The internet is overloaded."

I put a package of protein bars down on the counter and check my video watch. Nothing. No messages at all. Upon closer inspection, I see that Mr. Butterfield is right: I have no signal.

"Jasmine's with Mayor Smith. She's at City Hall. You're sure nothing's happened there?"

He nods and smiles kindly at me. "Jade, that's the most secure place in all of Toronto at the moment. Don't worry. She's probably trying to get through to you right now. If she knows that you were coming to the buildings at this time, *she'll* be more worried. After all, you could've been on that subway train at Queen coming down here. Why don't I make you a cup of dandelion tea?"

"No, thank you. I need to go deliver to the others.... We didn't take the subway, we took the bus today," I add, wiping away beads of sweat on my brow. I'm more thinking out loud than anything else now, trying to calm myself. "Jasmine told me not to take the subway. Said there would be major delays."

Mr. Butterman frowns. "Your sister warned all of you not to get on the subway system?"

I know what he's thinking. I don't even need to read his mind to know that he thinks Jasmine had something to do with the bombings. And I don't blame him. I'd think the same thing if someone told me their sister warned them not to take the subway on the day of a terrorist attack.

"It's not like that. Mayor Smith told her to tell us. The engineering work didn't get finished at track level last night, which meant delays today. Trains were going to need to slow down or something like that."

Mr. Butterman gives a low whistle. "The mayor told your sister to warn people close to her not to take the subway today? Jesus." He shakes his head. "There's something very rotten in the state of Denmark … or in this case, Toronto." He quietly watches me for a few moments, trying to decide if he can trust me with what he's just said.

My legs suddenly feel like wet strands of spaghetti, and I lean against the counter for support. "I think you might be right."

"Jade," Mr. Butterman says, "don't go telling anyone else that you were warned not to take the subway today."

"Too late. I'm with Lily and Vivienne, so they know about the warning as well."

"If you are sure you can trust them, trust them with your life, then tell them the same. Otherwise, don't mention it unless they do. And Jade?"

"Yes?"

He looks me in the eye. Deep fear radiates from him. "Do me a favour and don't tell anyone you talked to me about this, okay?"

Jasmine reaches me on video as I'm about to do two deliveries on the seventh floor. The reception on my watch is fuzzy, but I'm not sure if it's due to being in the stairwell or the ongoing communications disruptions.

As soon as I answer, relief spreads across her face. "You're okay," she says, smiling broadly. "Mom's at home, so she's safe as well. I told her I'd talked to you. Little lie, but I didn't want her to worry." She stops and bites her bottom lip. It's a nervous habit. "You haven't heard from Mr. Khan, have you?"

I shake my head. "Maybe he's just having trouble getting through. I haven't had a signal until now, and it's still weak. Where are you?"

"We're heading into a conference room to meet with the police chief and Mr. Jawad. Though I'm not really sure why I need to be there."

I pause. The stairwell is completely empty. "Are you with Smith right now?" I ask.

"No, I'm in the washroom just about to head back."

"Don't you think it's more than a little strange that she told you to warn us about the subway delays today? Smith? That she made sure we weren't on the subway?"

Jasmine frowns. "It didn't really cross my mind. Smith seemed totally shocked when the news broke. Believe me. I was right there when she was told."

I shrug. "Maybe she was surprised … or maybe she's just a really good actor. It seems a bit too coincidental to me. Were you able to get into her thoughts when it happened?"

There's a pause. "I didn't try. I guess I was so shocked about the bombing. The thing is, with Smith knowing what we can do, I think she guards her thoughts around me pretty closely."

"If she had been truly shocked about the bombing, you'd think she just might have forgotten to do that. Just promise to be super careful today, okay?"

Jasmine nods. I hope she knows I'm not just talking about the potential for further attacks. More and more, I get the feeling we're being drawn into a very dangerous game.

# JASMINE

"The suspect was identified within forty-eight hours of his arrest as Taylor Moore, a thirty-five-year-old man from North Bay who moved to Toronto several years ago after an acrimonious separation." Jade finishes reading and looks up from her tablet. "It says he'd had inconsistent contact with his family due to his ongoing battle with drug and alcohol addiction. Apparently, it was his mom who recognized him from the news and contacted the police." She holds her tablet up, screen forward, showing us a photo of a tanned, well-muscled Moore when he was a few years younger, in running clothes with a black Labrador beside him. The news site has juxtaposed that photo with one taken the day after his arrest. In the recent photo, he's gaunt, dead-fish pale, and his eyes are hollowed and haunted.

It's lunch, and we're sitting in the corner of the cafeteria with Lily and Cassandra. The place is heaving with bodies and loud conversation. Not an easy place to talk, but I don't want to take the chance of the others overhearing any of our conversation. Already I feel like a bit of specimen with everything going on. I stare down at my plate. Today's lunch is kale and sweet potato mash. The school is now strictly following the new government protocol for serving a plant-based diet of drought-resistant vegetables.

"It must've been really hard for her to contact them," Lily says, tucking her hair behind her ears and taking a bite of her mash. "It's a bit heartbreaking. I bet she didn't have a clue what Smith's new terrorism laws were really going to be like."

"Yeah, but the guy is clearly CCT and guilty. After all, it's not like we're all going around burning off our fingerprints and wearing contact lenses that prevent iris scans, are we?" Cassandra interjects. "Twenty-two people died, and others are in the hospital with limbs blown off. If that were my kid, I'd disown him too."

I shake my head. "I'm not sure it's that black and white. He looks like he's drugged or hypnotized or something. Have you seen the interviews with him? He's so confused. It's like his memory was wiped out or something."

"Maybe the CCT has some sort of mind serum to wipe out people's memories," Cassandra says. "Or he's lying. If they've already created specialized contact lenses, who's to say they don't have other crazy technology?"

Jade frowns. "Come on, this isn't science fiction. The guy clearly has amnesia. Maybe it's drug-induced or something, but that's as far as the science part of this goes. What worries me is the fact that I don't think he's going to get a fair trial." She looks over at me as she finishes speaking.

"Smith's going to make an example of him for sure," I say, pushing my plate away. My appetite's been pretty much nonexistent lately. "She's planning to follow through with the death penalty on this, and I think she's going to want a public execution … or at least have it available to be live-streamed."

Lily makes a face. "That's barbaric. People aren't going to allow that, for sure."

"Actually, you'd be surprised. Most of the surveys Smith's government has done in the last few days show the majority of Torontonians are in support of executing anyone who commits an act of terrorism. And Moore is on camera planting those bombs, whether he remembers doing it or not," I say. "I'm not saying I agree with Smith wanting to execute him, but a lot of people in the city and the country want exactly that to happen. In fact, tonight I'm being filmed beside her night-work crew with one of the little kids who was injured in the blast. That will create even more support for getting his balls to fry."

"That's a lovely way to put it," Jade says with a grimace.

"Well, I agree with the majority," Cassandra says. "This isn't the time to be a bleeding heart. There's enough hardship with climate change, and don't forget our demon friends who are likely around the corner.… So if someone wants to commit a crime as disgusting as blowing up innocent people on subways and buses, then I say, no matter what the reason, they deserve the same happening to them. It's time to take back this city."

"Excuse me," Jade says, standing up. I notice she hasn't finished even half of her lunch either. "I need to go finish some reading for one of my classes this afternoon."

That's a lie. Jade always finishes her homework well before any deadline.

"I'll join you," Lily says, getting up and gathering both their trays.

As soon as they're out of earshot, Cassandra leans toward me, elbows on the table. "Second-borns," she says, rolling her eyes. "They don't get it. I don't care if the terrorists have family out there on ships or whatever. Closing our borders is a good thing."

I shrug, not wanting to get into a conversation that feels like sister-bashing. "I know Moore is guilty, because I've seen the security videos; they show him entering the station late at night and putting the bombs under the trains. But what I don't understand is how he got in after hours in the first place. Unless he hid somewhere until the station closed, it makes no sense. That also means he'd have had to hide there until morning. And it doesn't explain how two bombs went off in different stations. He couldn't have been in both stations overnight."

"Which station did you see the footage from?" Cassandra asks.

"That's just it … I saw footage of him in both stations the night before the bombings." I shake my head. "He'd need help to have pulled it off. Someone on the inside, a night cleaner or security guard, someone helping him get in and out undetected."

"I don't believe in conspiracy theories, Jazz," Cassandra says. "And you'd know if they were looking for other suspects before any of us anyhow. Not only that, but it would be all over the news. But if you're right, and the CCT have got people on the inside … you've told Smith about your suspicions, right?"

I shake my head. "I guess I can mention it tonight if I get the chance."

Cassandra arches an eyebrow at me. "It's your duty to do that, when you think about it. We need to be reporting anything we're suspicious about in order to keep the city safe."

Mayor Smith's driver picks me up at 8:00 p.m. sharp. Mr. Khan's already in the back seat when I get in.

"Frederick got me first for once," he says with a wry smile. "Our destination tonight is somewhere closer to here, apparently." I know he feels as uneasy as I do about these publicity stunts we're doing for Mayor Smith.

I glance at his bandaged hand. "Is it feeling any better?"

He nods. "It's getting there. I'm using silicone sheeting

on it at night. Supposed to help the burn heal." Glancing at the back of Frederick's head, he leans closer to me. "This is crazy, you know. I wasn't even the one who helped the little girl. After the bomb went off, I stayed with an elderly woman whose right leg was blown off. It's propaganda, what we're doing tonight. A complete and utter lie."

"Well, you were helping people after the bombing. You didn't have to do that. You could've just run to safety like nearly everyone else did."

"You know what I'm getting at. It's wrong. Full stop. We're colluding with a government that's asking a four-year-old child to lie to the public in order to gain support for its crazy policies. I don't know who helped that little girl the morning of the bombing, but it certainly wasn't me." He sits back heavily in the seat and sighs.

It's pitch black as we pull up to the train station, and the streets are so empty you could bowl down them. A camera crew guides us to a room where our makeup and hair will be done. The little girl is in there already.

I smile at her as I'm led to one of the chairs. It's like a chair at a hair salon, with a foot pump to change its height and a large, fully lit mirror directly in front of it. I sit down heavily, and makeup and hair people immediately swoop down on me.

The little girl smiles back at me. Her dark hair is pulled into two pigtails and tied with red ribbons. The skin on one half of her face is bandaged, and her left arm is in a cast.

"My name is Aaliyah," she says brightly. "What's yours?" She points at the bandages on her face. "They sprayed new skin on my ouchie."

I plaster a smile onto my face. God, what do you say to that?

"I'm Jasmine," I reply. "Sorry about your face … your facial ouchie. I'm sure it will be better soon." It's kind of nice to talk to someone who doesn't recognize me right away, even if she is only four.

"And this is Mr. Khan," Aaliyah's makeup person says in a singsong voice. She points at him as he takes a seat on the other side of me. "He's the man who helped you when the train crashed and you hurt yourself."

Aaliyah looks over at Mr. Khan for a few moments, her face scrunched in thought. He smiles back at her, though it seems like more of a grimace to me. I know he's hating this more than words can express. Aaliyah shakes her head. "No … that's wrong. That's not the man who helped me. The man who helped me was fatter and whiter. And he had no hair. His head was shiny."

The makeup person frowns, speaks into her video watch, and within a few seconds, Smith's assistant, Mitchell, appears. He smiles at Aaliyah. It's a smile that doesn't reach his eyes.

"Hello, Aaliyah, darling," he says, teeth gleaming. "You bumped your head when the train crashed. Your memory of it all would've gotten a bit mixed up because of that … like a dream. Believe me, this *is* the man that helped you."

Aaliyah shakes her head, her dark curls bouncing up and down in their respective ponytails. "No, no, no! That's not the man," she says emphatically.

Mr. Khan looks at me. I know he wants to say something to reassure her, to confirm that she's right, that he's not the one who helped her.

Mitchell leans forward and whispers in Aaliyah's ear. I can't catch what he says but get the general message as her face crumples like a week-old birthday balloon. Tears fill her eyes, and her bottom lip trembles.

"What did you just say to her?" Mr. Khan asks, his face reddening as he gets up out of his seat. His makeup person stands over him, brush hovering in the air, unsure of what to do next.

"Everything's fine," Mitchell says, his face slowly turning red like a ripening tomato. "Isn't it, Aaliyah, darling? Everything's just fine, isn't it?" He clamps a pale hand on her shoulder.

She stiffens at his touch but nods, the first tear trickling down her cheeks, leaving a salty trail on her brown skin.

"Thank you," she says to Mr. Khan, her voice barely a whisper. "Thank you for helping me with my ouchies on the train."

Mr. Khan opens his mouth, then shuts it again as Mayor Smith strides into the room.

"Is there a problem?' she asks, looking first at Mitchell and then at Mr. Khan. Her hair has been dyed a deep burgundy since the last time I saw her, and she's wearing a fitted black dress that looks like it would be better suited at a cocktail party than here.

Mitchell rushes up to her, smiling brightly. "Everything is absolutely, one hundred percent under control now. We're a few minutes behind on makeup and hair. Just wanting everything to be perfect." Beads of perspiration dot his forehead, and he gestures wildly as he speaks. Clearly Mayor Smith makes him very nervous.

"Perfection means getting this wrapped on schedule. And I'm sure no one here's causing trouble and causing delays, because time is money," she says, her gaze coming to rest on Mr. Khan.

Our makeup and hair is finished within the next five minutes. I'm put in a crisp black dress and silver ballet flats, with my hair left in loose curls down the middle of my back. The flats make me feel shorter than I already am (if that's even possible) and vulnerable. Obviously I couldn't bring my pole with me to this (and I'm still getting used to my new one anyhow, since the pole used on Jamie Linnekar became police property the night of the attack), and I feel susceptible without a weapon, especially when my location is being broadcast live across the city and beyond this evening. Even though there hasn't been much demon activity in the last while, I can't shake the words the demon said to me about me being the chosen one, the *one* they were searching for. I also can't forget the look on Raphael's face when I told him the demon had said that.

I need to find out what it means to be chosen, and what exactly I've been chosen for. I also need to get out from under Smith's thumb. I'm angry with myself for not speaking out more, but torn because I want to be sure the Seers and Beaconsfield aren't put in danger; I know Smith is deadly serious about framing me for Linnekar's death. Any careless action could put a lot of people I care about in danger.

"Come with me," Mitchell says, motioning us out the door and down a dimly lit hall. "Aaliyah, hold onto Jasmine and Mr. Khan's hands as we walk out, please. And don't answer any questions until I say something first."

Two security guards lead us into a large, industrial-sized elevator. Mitchell leans against the railing and gazes at me, his eyes moving slowly from my legs to my face. It takes everything in me not to hit him. I feel uncomfortable enough in this outfit without his visual molestation.

We step out of the elevator and are immediately greeted by four more meaty bodyguards. Their faces are serious, devoid of any emotion, even when Aaliyah waves and smiles at them. As they fall into step with us, Mitchell links his fingers together as a reminder for Aaliyah to grab hold of our hands.

Mr. Khan wipes his palm along the leg of the black dress pants they've dressed him in before taking Aaliyah's hand in his own. He's nervous, which makes me nervous. It takes a lot to ruffle him.

Two massive, reinforced steel doors swing open, and suddenly we're outside, the humid night air wrapping itself around us like a moist blanket. Floodlights shine down onto the platform. Mayor Smith and Mr. Jawad are already here. Directly in front and below us are train and tram tracks. It seems we're at the back of Toronto's largest train station. The zigzag of tracks is also brightly lit, and at least fifty members of Smith's night crew are hard at work down there. They don't even pause to look up as we walk out. I watch their methodical work. They seem to be synchronized in their task. It's like they're working to some musical rhythm we can't hear. And then I notice something even more bizarre.

*Every single one of them is wearing sunglasses.*

The floodlights make it bright, but not that bright.

I look over at Mr. Khan and see him staring down at the workers as well. I catch his gaze and raise an eyebrow.

The broadcast starts a few moments later, and Mr. Jawad says nothing the entire time. Instead, he simply nods while Smith talks about how Aaliyah could easily not be with us right now if it weren't for Mr. Khan's heroics in staying and helping her rather than leaving the station like the majority of passengers. Most of all, she emphasizes that it was a stroke of luck Aaliyah was in the carriage directly behind the one under which Taylor Moore actually planted the bomb.

"This type of terrorism cannot — and must not — be tolerated in our city. That is why I am implementing the War Measures Act and calling for the execution of Taylor Moore. We have video evidence of Moore planting the explosive devices under the carriages. By his own admission, he says he does not recall what he did or where he was the night before the bombings. He has no alibi, nor has he put forth an alibi. He also admits recognizing himself on the security footage in question."

At that moment she motions for a pause in the filming. "When I announce the date of the execution, I want you to turn to Mr. Khan and hug him," she says to Aaliyah. "And all of you," she says, bringing the mike closer to her mouth and walking to the front of the stage to peer down at the workers, "need to cheer at the same time. I will signal you like this." She raises both hands into the air, palms facing upward.

Filming begins again, as though there's never been a pause. I continue smiling; my face feels like cardboard from the effort.

"As I've said, this kind of barbaric act simply will not — and, most of all, cannot — be tolerated." Smith punctuates each word with her index finger. "In order to send a very clear message to the CCT and anyone else thinking of taking the lives of innocent Torontonians, Taylor Jeremiah Moore will be put to death by lethal injection on October thirteenth, on this site, at nineteen hundred hours. This is not something I wish to do, but the CCT must be stopped."

On cue, Mr. Khan bends down, and Aaliyah puts her arms around his shoulders to hug him, though her eyes are wide with confusion. At the same time Mayor Smith throws her hands in the air like an overexcited orchestra conductor. The workers immediately stop what they're doing, look up at the stage, and roar with approval.

Someone shouts "cut," and Aaliyah comes running over to me. "Does putting him to death mean they're going to kill the man they arrested? The man on the videos?" she asks breathlessly.

I nod. "Yes," I say, keeping my voice low. "But it's not something we should talk about here." Smith is only about four feet away, already watching the playback of the video, no doubt ensuring it meets her standards.

A look of slow understanding mingled with horror fills Aaliyah's eyes. "But how do we know he really did it? Because they said Mr. Khan helped me, but he didn't. The man who really helped me had eyes that changed colour. And he wasn't as old." She pulls her bottom lip into her mouth and bites on it nervously. "Why are they lying? I thought only the bad guys lie."

I stare at Aaliyah in stunned silence for the next few seconds. "You said the man who helped you was bald. And larger than Mr. Khan," I say, my voice barely a whisper.

"I kind of forgot about the other man until now. He was the one who touched me where the bomb ripped open my tummy." She stops speaking, and tears fill her eyes again. "He had black hair that was really shiny and made the really bad ouchie go away. The one that was killing me."

I don't know what to say, because I agree with Aaliyah that it's becoming very hard to tell the good guys from the bad guys. And I can't tell her that I know exactly who saved her. It rips me apart inside wondering why, if Raphael is around, we're not in contact.

# JADE

"I looked like an idiot, like a complete hypocrite," Jasmine says, throwing herself belly down onto our bed. Her face is still caked with the thick makeup they put on actors for high-definition broadcasts. I want to tell her to be careful not smear it all over our comforter but restrain myself. Sometimes, as a second-born, I'm too uptight for my own good.

"It was fine," I say. I'm lying, though. The broadcast tonight was the most contrived, uncomfortable thing I've watched in a long time, and that's saying something, considering the propaganda that Smith and other city and government leaders have been broadcasting lately. Maybe to a non-Seer it wouldn't have been as obvious, but I could tell the little girl was very scared and uncomfortable when she was thanking Mr. Khan for saving her life on the subway.

Jasmine flips over on her back and rolls her eyes at me. "The whole thing was crazy … dressing me up like some kind of doll, making Aaliyah and Mr. Khan lie about him helping her during the bombing …" She pauses and links her hands behind her head, deep in thought. "Even this night crew stuff is weird … I mean, something's really not right. All these people, working without a sound, all in sync like zombies. And get this, they're wearing sunglasses. Every single of them. It's pitch black outside, and every one of the workers has on shades."

"Well, Smith and her government did make it pretty clear they want to respect the workers' anonymity," I say. "Maybe that's part of it?"

She stares at the ceiling for a moment, then shakes her head. "I really think something more is up with it. I don't believe they volunteered for this project. And, get this — I wasn't allowed to be anywhere near them. Why don't they want me talking to the night crew? Mr. Jawad's orders, apparently. The guy wouldn't even shake my hand when I met him. He's more than a bit of a freak himself."

"You think they're drugged?" I ask, knowing full well this is what she's thinking.

"It has to be something like that. Why else couldn't I meet any of them? I said I just wanted to thank them for everything they're doing for the city and was told absolutely not, even though I've been doing all this stuff promoting the program. And it would've been a super photo op for Smith's government, so you know there's something really fishy when she isn't taking advantage of that."

"Well, with the kidnappings and disappearances having pretty much stopped, no one's going to want Smith to step down. And if any disappearances do happen, she'll likely say it's just a case of recruitment by the CCT." I open my tablet and search for comments and polls about Moore's execution. The vast majority are not only positive, but also strongly in favour of having his death broadcast publicly. Many of them praise Smith's "no-nonsense" attiude toward the terrorists. Some are perversely excited about the entertainment they expect to see, as though they're travelling back in time to see a gladiator being ripped to shreds by a lion. Executions used to happen only in countries with governments that were considered primitive and backward, or ones that had been taken over by the military. "I mean, even some of our friends, even ones who are Seers, are beginning to sound really closed-minded about it. Look at Cassandra the other day, for example. Pretty soon people won't be able to speak out against Smith and her government without fear of reprisal."

Jasmine nods. "The thing I don't get is if vampiric demons need to kill to survive, how are they surviving here? If the disappearances have stopped, who are they feeding on?"

I shrug. "Maybe there aren't as many of them as we think? I don't know. Could they have gone back to the Place-in-Between?"

"I don't think so. Raphael said something really strange to me in the hospital ..."

"Come on, Jazz," I say. "How can you really be sure you saw him that night? I mean, you were pretty out of it on painkillers and stuff."

Jasmine narrows her eyes at me and sits up. She hugs a pillow to her chest. "I wasn't out of it. Raphael was there. It wasn't a hallucination or my imagination, or whatever you think. And he told me that something or someone is controlling the dark forces from this side, which makes sense when you think about it. Things have been much too quiet … I don't think demons have a huge amount of self-control. It's not like they'd all get together and decide to fast or take a break from drinking blood."

I have to agree with her. But there haven't been any new disappearances, which makes me think Mayor Smith was right and most of the missing persons reports have been down to people being recruited to the CCT, and that her campaign against them is now working. The bodies that were found, she claims, were those recruits who didn't make the cut, but knew too much about the CCT to be let go.

"We need to find out exactly what is going on. I want to get together a bunch of Seers and get closer to the night crews, check out where the demons could've disappeared to. And I want to shake Mr. Jawad's hand … or at least touch him. He's so careful not to have any physical contact, and though it might mean nothing, I need to find out. I'll make it look accidental. Like tripping into him or something. And I don't think it will be hard to find demons...." Jasmine pauses and picks at an invisible flaw on the pillow with one darkly varnished nail. "I didn't tell you this yet, because I didn't want you to worry, but the night Jamie Linnekar — I mean the demon — attacked me, he said something to me. Something I think I'm not supposed to know, but I don't think it believed that I was going to survive. It was while the demon was strangling me."

"What? What did he — I mean, it — say?"

Jasmine's face grows dark. "He said they'd been looking for me. Hunting me. The demons. He said I was *elegido*."

Words escape me. I stare at my sister. Before I have a chance to stop myself, I think, why would she be chosen by the demons? Does she seriously expect me to believe that the entire demonic race somehow has anointed her as special, just like Mayor Smith did? Either her new-found fame has completely gone to her head, or she knocked it harder than previously thought against that sidewalk the night of the attack.

"It's not like that," she says, her voice full of hurt. "And whatever it means to be chosen, it isn't the least bit positive. I'd gladly give away the honour. In fact, I think it scared Mr. Khan and Ms. Samson when I told them."

I realize she's just read my mind. And I feel like a traitor.

# JASMINE

Risks. I know they're something I'm supposed to be avoiding like the plague, which is a bit funny when I think about how I actually survived a plague-filled London in the Place-in-Between last year, but I feel it's important to discover what's happened to the demons, as well as to find out who or what might be controlling the dark forces. No demonic activity has been sighted during the day, so it seems only natural to start investigating what's happening in the city at night. I also want to go undercover to find the reason why Smith's night crew is kept sunglassed and secret.

"Mr. Khan would kill us if he knew what we were planning. All the Protectors would," Jade says, her face twisting into a frown as she laces up her black Doc boots. She's dressed in a black T-shirt and black jeans. We're all wearing black. This way we'll blend in with the night and hopefully be safer.

"Well, he'll thank us afterward if we can figure out what's happening with the demons," says Cassandra as she tucks her ponytail into a black ball cap. "It's been way too quiet. And besides, I've been dying for a little action. I mean, what's the use in doing all this training if we're just going to be like caged birds and get locked away every night?"

"No one's arguing that we need to discover the reason the demonic activity stopped," Jade says. "It's just last time we were out late, I nearly lost my sister, so forgive me for feeling a bit hesitant doing this."

The air in the room thickens with tension. There are eight of us crammed into Vivienne's bedroom, some of us sitting on the bed, some on the floor, backs leaning against the wall. We all had to come in through the window, since otherwise her parents would wonder why we were all here, and we'd also be made to leave long before curfew. This way we can all leave the way we came in, and hopefully the parents won't be any wiser.

Vivienne and Amara are the only Seers we know living in a home big enough to risk meeting together like this. It's their mother's book club night, and their father is tucked away in his study doing work, desperately trying to appeal to the Canadian and American governments to accept a boat full of South African and Swazi refugees that's been drifting off the Atlantic coast for a few weeks, its resources and passengers quickly dwindling. It's a terrible situation that I'd never even have known about if Amara and Vivienne hadn't told me. The media is careful to avoid covering stories that might cause people to empathize with the plight of climate-change refugees and the goals of the CCT, since Los Angeles and other west coast cities were basically destroyed. Images broadcast around the world at the time by the CCT showed scores of ulcerated sores covering the faces and bodies of the unfortunate Californians who hadn't left before the riots. The CCT attributed the sores to radiation poisoning from both the Pacific Ocean and abandoned nuclear power stations along the coast that had ruptured during some of the quakes right before the riots. People took to the streets, asking for freedom of movement and demanding to know why they hadn't been better informed by the ruling parties of North America about the seriousness of the situation. It was after that that the crackdown on the CCT really began.

I look around ... I've only asked the Seers I trust with my life to come tonight, those who won't run to Ms. Samson and sacrifice me like a spring lamb if things go wrong. A small worm of doubt twists uneasily in my stomach. Maybe we shouldn't be doing this, but it's not like I'm the ringleader. Well, not really. I mean, no one's said that, but it's weird how they're all waiting for me to decide exactly how this evening is going to play out.

Fiona nods, her blond curls bobbing up and down with the movement. My stomach knots with worry when I think about how easy it will be to spot her and Jennifer if they don't have something covering their heads.

"I agree that we need to be careful," she says. "But the thing is, after what happened to Isabelle, I want to hunt down every one of those walking dead bastards, slice their heads clean off, and then kick them around like soccer balls. One thing I know for sure — I'm not going to wait around for them to come to me again. Not after they tortured Isabelle and tried to drink her blood." Her bottom lip starts to tremble, and she stops talking to wipe at her eyes.

"Yeah, it's not like there's been *no* demonic activity. There's just been nothing happening recently that directly impacts human beings. I'm sure Isabelle isn't the only animal they've killed in the last couple of weeks. After all, there aren't going to be news alerts about loads of missing stray cats, are there?" Jennifer says, taking over for her sister, who is clearly too upset to continue.

Jade snaps her fingers. "Actually, I've noticed a massive amount of notices up about missing pets. If that many pets are missing, I'm sure there's double or triple that amount of stray animals being eaten. I mean taken." She pauses, an apologetic look spreading across her face. "But … you're right that it's not something that's going to get any major attention."

I sit back against the wall under the window. "Where are the bodies, then? I agree, there are lots of missing pet posters and online postings lately, but if these pets are being taken by demons, where are the bodies? The demons drain them of blood, so you'd think the leftovers …" I pause, trying to avoid Jennifer and Fiona's gaze "… would be discarded. After all, I don't think that demons are into composting or making sure the animals they kill are neatly buried."

"Well, there's only one way to find out," Cassandra says, getting up and grabbing her pole. "It's nearly dark, so time to head out there."

She's right. The inky blackness of the night is slowly creeping forward, devouring the dusky shadows in its path. I swallow hard. There's no telling what we'll find out there. Maybe nothing. But if we get caught doing this, it'll be a massive fine for our parents, which Mom can't afford. I'm pretty sure it would be a hardship for all the girls' families, except Amara and Vivienne's.

It's weird. I wouldn't usually stop to think about things like this. Maybe the attack really did change me, somehow shaking me up inside. Whatever's happened, I admit I feel responsible for what might or might not happen tonight.

"Okay," I say, standing up, trying to ignore the feeling that Jade might be thinking my ego is taking over again. "Let's divide into parties. We shouldn't go too far away from each other tonight. If we don't find anything at all, we can always expand our search next time. I want safety to be the top priority. No matter what, we don't want two sisters to be at risk of being harmed at the same time … especially by the same demon."

Everyone nods, their eyes solemn. We've been taught about the fact that as Seers we are faster and stronger than most human beings and that we have the ability to sometimes read thoughts and feel what others are feeling. But we have one huge weakness: we only have half a soul. The other half resides in our twin. I guess you could say we're the real deal when it comes to soulmates. This means we're stronger physically and mentally with our twin, but if we're killed together by a demon, it can then possess an entire Seer soul, which means the demon becomes extraordinarily strong, kind of like the Superman of demons. Even if a demon killed one Seer, it would be a lot stronger than your everyday demon, from what I can gather. But a demon with an entire Seer soul? I imagine that would be a very difficult, if not impossible, demon to defeat.

I once asked Mr. Khan if that had ever happened.

"It's not something often spoken of," he said, staring down into his cup of chicory like he wished he could crawl inside it to avoid the conversation. We were at a cafe after one of Mayor Smith's boring city council meetings, the ones for things like water reservoir levels and pharmaceutical shortages at some of Toronto's hospitals and pharmacies.

"So it has happened?" I asked, leaning forward on my elbows, eyes wide with curiosity ... and fear.

Mr. Khan scanned the room before answering. "Not yet," he replied, his voice low.

"What? What do you mean, not yet?"

His eyes darkened. "I don't know if I am supposed to be telling you this ..."

"Come on. I'm somehow special, *elegido*, remember? Shouldn't I know these kinds of things? In case it comes after me?" Completely inappropriate, maybe, but sometimes I can't help it. Actually, joking about the whole chosen thing sometimes helps to take the edge off a bit. It's better than lying awake, staring at the ceiling, worrying that something might pop out from under my bed and take me to the Place-in-Between (or worse), which I've done plenty of times.

Mr. Khan looked up at me, alarmed. "Don't say that, Jasmine. Don't ever say that. You don't want that to happen. I can't see how you'll survive it."

A wave of terror swept over my body. I felt like someone just dumped a bucket of ice water over my head. Why was Mr. Khan suddenly talking in the future tense?

"It will go by several names. The Darkness being most common," he said quietly. "According to the scrolls, it will be present at the Final Battle."

"What do you mean it will be present? How do you know? Crystal-balling it much?"

Mr. Khan shook head. "The scrolls and other ancient literature describe many elements of the Final Battle. *It*, this Darkness, will somehow originate during the Final Battle or shortly before. During a time when the survival of the human race and of the divisions between here, the Place-in-Between, and the other plane of existence, are torn apart. Or maybe it would be more appropriate to say they will collide to create a new existence."

You sometimes hear people use this expression to describe feeling a deathly chill: someone is walking over their grave. Well, that's the exact feeling I had at that moment.

"Is there a way we can stop this from happening?" I asked.

"We're done talking about this," Mr. Khan replied, placing the lid on his chicory and standing up. "You mustn't ever tell anyone about this conversation. Because it shouldn't have been spoken of in the first place."

I glance around the room again, thinking about just how much I don't want anything to happen to the girls who are here with me. Then I look at my video watch and swallow hard. It's ten to eight. Nearly curfew.

"Okay," I say, "we need to have a good mix of first- and second-borns out together. That way we're balancing and making the most of our strengths. *Everyone* gets listened to. We're trying to find out anything we can about the demons and about Smith's crew of freaks."

"How do we make sure everyone gets back safely? And home safely?" Amara asks, leaning against her pole.

"Don't worry about that. I've taken care of it. We just need to make sure we're all in the lobby of One Oak Street at ten p.m. sharp."

All eight of us touch the tips of our poles together before sliding silently out the window and into the humid night.

# JADE

I'm with Amara, Fiona, and Lily. Two first-borns and two seconds. And no twins together. I've got mixed feelings about Cassandra being with Jasmine after what happened on the night we encountered the demonic Jamie Linnekar, but I know that Jennifer and Vivienne will keep things in check as much as they can. However, I have to admit I'm really glad that Cassandra wasn't put with me. More and more, I'm finding her personality as annoying as nails on a chalkboard.

"It's strange being out this late," Fiona whispers as we walk along the inner edge of the sidewalk. "I really hate the curfew, but it's also uber creepy being out here." She looks around us. "There are more people on the street than I expected there would be, but — and maybe this sounds totally paranoid — I can't shake this feeling that we're being watched. It's intense."

She's right on both counts. A couple of weeks after the disappearances stopped, people tentatively began to return to the streets at night. This was depicted by Smith as Torontonians taking back their streets from the terrorists. Of course, things aren't back to being completely normal, but it's a huge change from the empty streets and sidewalks you could bowl down. I look around. The shadows of the trees seem to stretch out like fingers. It's like they're alive, pulsating.

More people on the streets when darkness falls also means we're that much more likely to be caught being out after curfew.

"Here, tie this around your head, Blondie," Amara says with a wink as she hands Fiona the black bandana tied around her own wrist. "Your hair is like a screaming alarm bell, girl."

"So our job is supposed to be to just hang out, looking for demons? Should we be putting out an advertisement or something? Like demons wanted for observation?" Fiona asks, her voice thick with sarcasm as she stops to tie her hair up and back with the bandana.

Amara frowns. "Agreed. Why didn't we get to go and check out Mayor Smith's night crew?" she asks. "There wasn't even a discussion of what each group was going to do. We got the boring task for sure."

"It doesn't have to be. Boring, I mean," I say. "Listen, if there are still demons around, many of them will need to feed. We need to be somewhere where there might good supply of small animals for them to take."

"That's awful," Lily says. "I hate thinking of all those innocent animals not knowing what they're in for."

Amara looks doubtful. "The drought's killed off a lot of strays … but I suppose we could check out Kensington Market and Chinatown. If any feral cats are still surviving, they'll be around there."

"Are you serious?" Fiona asks. "We can't possibly go on the streetcar after curfew. The driver will call us in for sure. And it's at least a twenty-five-minute walk."

"Come on, you're a Seer," I say. "We'll run it. Back streets, mainly. That way we can hopefully stay unreported. And I doubt the demons are going to be strolling Yonge Street anyway."

Amara rolls her eyes. "Fiona, how come Jade's talking more like a first-born than you? You need to step it up."

"Well, for starters, maybe because my dog, who we had since she was a puppy and Jen and I were six years old, was torn apart last week. Her stomach was ripped open, and she still tried to crawl to defend us, whimpering with pain the entire time. So going out looking for demons that are feeding off animals is pretty far down my list of things to do tonight. Kind of equal to poking out my eyeballs with hot sticks."

An uncomfortable silence descends on us.

Lily clears her throat. "I think," she begins, "that the best revenge for Isabelle would be to find and destroy each and every one of the demons that might be feeding off innocent animals. And to remember that at any time, they could turn to humans for nourishment. So … it's kind of urgent that we do this."

With that, we begin to jog in and out of the shadows along the side streets that run parallel to Carlton Street, heading west. The houses are large and old in this area. Once-grand brick exteriors loom out at us, their dark windows like empty eyes. A few are still well kept and fully lit, but most have been abandoned for small apartments; the cost of maintaining them became too much a decade or so ago, when the cost of electricity and fuel skyrocketed. Some of the abandoned gardens seem to have taken on a life of their own, with long tendrils of green ivy. For a moment it feels like, if we became tangled in their reach, we'd be pulled into the dark abyss of the homes behind them. I shudder, knowing I'm letting my imagination run wild. Thing is, these houses clearly show that the world would go on perfectly fine without humans. Better, in fact.

We're just passing somewhere near the University of Toronto when we hear a high-pitched scream from one of the houses directly behind us. And it's not a human scream. It's the kind of squeal you might hear when a cat's tail is stepped on. Hard.

We stop cold on the sidewalk and crouch behind an abandoned car that's been barbequed. A lot of gasoline-fuelled cars have been abandoned over the last few years. They quickly became too expensive to fill, on top of having to pay the carbon/climate-change taxes to drive, and thus they became virtually worthless. Many people tried to at least save on the cost of towing their vehicles away to become part of a scrap heap. Those who could afford it converted their luxury model cars into fully electric vehicles.

"That sounded like a cat," Lily says, the whites of her eyes growing large. "Like a cat getting its tail stomped on."

"More like getting it chopped off," Fiona says, her voice quiet.

I realize I've been holding my breath, waiting for the next squeal of pain, but nothing comes. Instead the sound of crickets fills the night again.

"We need to check it out," Amara says, standing and raising her pole to her waist. "Because if those were demons grabbing that animal, they're going to be gone as soon as they can be."

"Wait," I say, as the rest of us get to our feet. I want to tell everyone to take it slow, to discuss keeping safe, to have a plan in case someone gets hurt. As usual, the urge to be cautious is overwhelming.

Amara is already sprinting across the street with Fiona beside her, the two of them pausing for just a second to wave Lily and me over.

"The scream came from behind one of these two houses," Fiona says. "We need to split up and check both."

"Is that really a good idea?" I ask. "Shouldn't we stay together? In case there are more of them than we think?"

"We'll only be a few hundred feet away from each other. Whistle loudly if you need the help of other Seers," Amara says, raising an eyebrow at me. I may be imagining it, but her voice seems to be tinged with mockery.

Lily and I jog off toward the house to the right. It was clearly abandoned a few years ago. In the front, a large wraparound porch sags like a new mother's belly, and the first-floor windows are all either loosely boarded, or else the glass is shattered, making it a good shelter for displaced people and animals alike. Being so close to campus, it was likely occupied by students at one time. Of course, there's virtually no need for student housing now that there are only a handful of foreign and out-of-town students, and those who are here usually live in residence to avoid the massive cost of a rental property, especially old houses like these, which were built before climate change was even an issue.

We move together in silence to the left side of the building, which is adjacent to the right side of the house Amara and Fiona are exploring, making sure to press as thin as paper against the exterior wall as we move. Lily's directly behind me, close enough that I can hear her breathing. We reach the corner of the house and stop to peer into the overgrown backyard.

It takes a moment for my eyes to adjust to the tangle of bushes and grass nearly as tall as a young child. Then I spot them. A pair of demons, one holding the front end of a fox and the other the hind end, their razor-like teeth sunk deep into the still-twitching carcass. My stomach does a somersault as I watch streams of hot blood leak out of their mouths and down their chins before spilling onto the ground.

A low, loud whistle from behind me sings out into the night air. Lily's given the signal.

Amara and Fiona spring over the fence. The black bandana falls from Fiona's hair, exposing her white-blond curls. Both of them hold their poles defensively in front of them the way we've been taught at Beaconsfield.

The demons drop the fox, which continues to twitch in the long grass, and that's when I realize it's still alive. And with this realization, a tidal wave of anger is released in me as Lily and I charge the demons that are advancing on Fiona and Amara from behind.

With a shout, I bring my pole up and across one of the demon's necks as it swivels in surprise away from Fiona and toward me. There's the satisfying squelch of the pole moving into the demon's flesh and then the resistance of bone against bamboo. The familiar smell of rust wafts over me.

I hear Lily shout in panic as the other demon turns and lunges at her. Amara leaps after it, swinging her pole forcefully. It grazes the back of demon's neck, leaving a superficial scratch that's not enough to even distract it.

Within seconds the demon is on Lily, knocking her to the ground. Amara throws herself at it, screaming, but the demon is strong and doesn't budge. Its hands are firmly around Lily's neck, causing her eyes to bulge like a goldfish that's been tossed from its bowl. A purple tinge is slowly blossoming across her lips.

The demon I attacked is not dead yet, because my pole didn't fully sever its spinal cord. Instead it shuffles toward me, head hanging awkwardly at an angle that shouldn't be physically possible, its tongue lolling out the side of its mouth.

As soon as it's within arm's reach, I swing at it, using my pole like a baseball bat. My pole is on target and the demon's head drops to the ground, followed by its body. A few seconds later, tendrils of grey smoke slowly unfurl from the corpse.

I turn toward Lily and Amara just in time to see Fiona swing her pole and smash the other demon's skull in. Bits of bone, brain, and blood fly everywhere. She retracts her pole less than a second later and swings again, this time slicing clean through its neck.

Amara and the demon roll off Lily like a pair of Siamese twins. Fiona turns toward the fox, which is still softly whimpering and twitching where the demons dropped it. She brings her pole down, silencing it.

"Rest in peace, little one," she says, walking toward us. Chunks of grey, spongy brain matter and bits of bone are stuck in her curls and on the bandana, and her face is splattered with blood.

"Looking good, Goldilocks," Amara says, her voice full of admiration. She puts her arm around Lily's back, helping her to sit up. "Great job. Though you're going to need a shower for sure."

Lily coughs and shakes her head. "It bit me," she says, pulling the sleeve of her T-shirt up to her shoulder. Rivulets of blood that look almost black in the dusky light of our video phones slide along her skin.

Fiona unties her bandana, gives it a shake, and hands it to Amara. "Tie this around the wound," she says. She looks toward the back fence and into the darkened yards around us. "Well, now we know there are still demons out here. And because of that, I think we should get outta here and back into the street as soon as possible."

"We need to get your arm cleaned," I say to Lily, who is slowly getting to her feet with Amara's support.

"And where exactly can we do that?" Amara says. "Any hospital we go to will report us for being out after curfew, and I don't think arriving with our poles is a good idea anyway, especially with blood and guts all over ourselves."

"I'm going to message Mr. Khan," I say. "We're going to get it in the neck for being out here, but none of us knows what a demon bite might do, and any bite needs to be cleaned. After all, the demon was using a human's mouth to do the deed, and our mouths are notorious bacterial breeding grounds."

"Okay, Dr. Guzman," Amara says sarcastically. "Just tell him not to let Mrs. Jackson in on this. She'll chew me up and spit me out."

"All of the Protectors, not to mention Ms. Samson, are going to kill us," Lily says hoarsely. "But at least we can say we know that there are demons still here and how they're feeding and surviving. Right?"

I nod. There's no way more than a handful of demons could survive on the blood of stray animals. Which means maybe Ms. Samson was wrong when she told

Jasmine that there was a legion of demons here. Maybe only a few were actually able to get through the rift that opened between here and the Place-in-Between.

"I really think we should head back toward your place," Fiona says to me as I bring up Mr. Khan's contact details on my video watch. "In case there are more demonic bastards lurking out here."

"Actually, all of you need to stay just where you are," an unfamiliar voice says from behind us.

# JASMINE

"We need to go to the hotel where the night crew is housed. They're never out during the day. Smith claims it's because they're working all night and need to go to rehab and other training programs during the day, but if we can catch them before they're sent out to their different projects, maybe we'll get a better idea of why they act so robotic. I bet Smith and Jawad are drugging their food or something equally sinister," I say as we make our way along Front Street toward Union Station.

"You're sure this is the right hotel? It seems pretty central, considering Smith wants to keep these people's identities secret," Jennifer says.

"Who's in charge of these people, anyway? Is it Mayor Smith?" Cassandra asks, tossing her dark hair behind one shoulder. She looks around us, her eyes widening with concern. "I think we should be moving a little more into the shadows," she says as two orange school buses pass us. "It's busier here than I feel comfortable with."

I look around. The buses — no longer used for school
excursions, as the cost of the electricity to run them is
too great — are used to ferry the night crew around.
That means they're going to be leaving soon.

"We need to hurry," I say, walking faster. Cassandra's
right. We really should be taking the back streets, but add-
ing time getting to the hotel would mean possibly missing
the night crew. "Just keep close to the buildings. As far as I
know, Mr. Jawad's in charge of the night crew. Smith only
comes around if there's a chance to impress the media."

We're half a block from the hotel. The buses are out
front. Mr. Jawad is standing on the sidewalk, his bul-
bous stomach silhouetted by the lights at the entrance
of the hotel. Mitchell, the ginger-haired assistant, is
buzzing around Jawad like a hungry mosquito. I hadn't
thought about the actual logistics of how we'd get close
enough to actually see what's going on. Now that we're
here, I realize just how difficult getting closer is going to
be. We slow and duck into a doorway, flattening against
the stone.

"What now?" Cassandra asks, wiping at the sweat
on her forehead. "We can't get closer without them
noticing us."

Six eyes turn to stare at me. I pause. Again, it's
unspoken, but I'm being looked to for leadership.

"I know. That's why I'm going to go over there," I say.
"Alone. Everyone else should stay put. I'll make up some
excuse for being here. And I'm going to make Mr. Jawad
touch me."

"Ewwwww," Jennifer says, wrinkling her nose as though she's just gotten a whiff of a pile of soiled diapers. "Why would you want that old fat man to touch you?"

My face burns. "Not like that. I didn't mean it like that. Pervert."

Cassandra laughs. "How was it meant then? You did just sound uber creepy a second ago."

I narrow my eyes at her, remembering how she'd seemed to compete with me for Raphael's attention when I first met her. "He wouldn't shake my hand when we met. In fact, he's made sure that we've never had any physical contact, and I find that strange. He blamed it on fear of superbugs, but I've seen him shake other people's hands. Just not mine."

Vivienne shrugs. "C'mon, Jasmine. You're probably reading into it. Maybe he's a selective hypochondriac. I really don't think there's some sort of conspiracy theory to be had." Her condescending tone only adds to my irritation. "Did you try to find out what he was thinking when he refused to shake your hand?"

I nod. "That's precisely it. I couldn't read his mind. It was impossible. And I don't mean just fuzzy, like it is sometimes with people; it was a complete blank. Like running up against a brick wall."

"You said Smith knows a lot about us, right? Which means she's blocking her thoughts from you a lot of the time, or at least she's trying to, so maybe it's the same thing with him. After all, if she knows a lot about Seers, you can guarantee he does," Cassandra says as she peers around the corner of the stone archway. "They've got the workers lining up in groups on the sidewalk, so you'd better hurry if you want the chance to see them up close and personal."

"Watch my back just in case anything goes wrong," I say, slipping out of the doorway and onto the sidewalk. My heart is pounding against my ribcage with the ferocity of a tiger. Mr. Jawad's back is to me as I approach. He's speaking to one of the groups of workers. Though they're all facing him, their orange jumpsuits clean and unwrinkled, I can't get any sense of what they're thinking or feeling, mainly because they're all sporting their sunglasses. Also, when I try to tap into any of their thoughts, a tsunami of voices, a thousand of them all jumbled together and screaming like trapped animals, comes at me. Maybe it has to do with their addictions, but not all the night crew workers are addicts, according to Smith. I can't distinguish any of the voices, and they feel distant, as though they're coming at me from somewhere deep underwater. The only other time I've experienced anything like it was when I was able to faintly pick up on Jamie Linnekar's memories of his mother. His thoughts were so distant, they were almost imperceptible.

"Mr. Jawad," I say when I'm close enough to touch him.

He spins around, his sausage-like lips forming a capital O of surprise. Tonight's eye patch is a matte black. Slightly boring but tasteful.

"What are you doing here?" he asks. There's no denying the tone. I'm definitely not welcome. "It's after your curfew, Jasmine."

For a moment my mouth feels like it's been stuffed full of peanut butter, and I'm unable to speak. The way Mr. Jawad is looking at me is different than before. The fatherly friendliness he's always shown me in front of Smith has evaporated, to be replaced by a much darker, threatening tone.

"I thought Mayor Smith might be here ..." I say, noticing him glaring at my pole. "And ... I was heading home after my martial arts class and realized I hadn't seen my identity banking card since we filmed last night, so I came down here, hoping you or Smith or Mitchell —"

"Hoping what? Why would you come down here, at this time of the night, when you know Mayor Smith is staying in this evening?" he asks, leaning toward me. Foamy spittle flies from his lips as he speaks, and I swallow back the impulse to vomit. "You knew she had a dinner party this evening. I was there when she told you." As he's speaking, I focus hard, trying to crack my way into his thoughts, but once again there's nothing. Common sense tells me he's thinking he'd like to squash me like a bug, though....

"I — I forgot," I stammer, glancing over his shoulder at the rows of orange-suited zombies that are standing, every single one of them with his head cocked slightly to the right, as if listening to something or someone only they can hear. The light from the hotel windows glints

off their sunglasses. It's as though they're zombie sol-
diers waiting for their next command. And that's when
it hits me. My eyes widen as I realize just why the sunglasses are necessary, and why no one is allowed to see
the workers. To *really* see them.

"Why don't you just take a seat inside the hotel lobby,
and as soon as I see the workers off, we can go and look
for your card?" Mr. Jawad says, suddenly smiling. "I'll
contact Mayor Smith and tell her you're here. She might
know where your card is. And I know she'd want to be
sure you got home safely. After all, you never know if
the CCT are out there waiting, like boogeymen, to grab
people, do you?"

Mitchell is suddenly beside us, laughing at Mr.
Jawad's comment. His laugh is like a donkey's bray —
shrill and irritating.

In an instant I realize I've screwed up. This was too
large a risk. Mr. Jawad's just read my mind, rather than
the other way around, which means I'm in danger.
Then I see something that makes me suck in my
breath: Smith's ring, the one she always wears, with
the Star of David thing on it. It's hanging from a thick
silver chain around Mitchell's scrawny neck. The light
from the hotel catches it, and it glitters at me like a
chip of ice.

Mr. Jawad's eyes narrow as soon he sees I've noticed
the ring, but before he has a chance to react, I reach
out and rip the chain from Mitchell's neck, pushing
my other hand against Mr. Jawad's upper chest as I do

so. And although our physical contact only lasts for a fraction of a second, it's enough.

My knees buckle, and urine, warm and wet, leaks from my bladder as tortured screams fill my head. The shrieks are loud, louder than a jet plane taking off, and filled with immense pain. Images of faces, half-eaten, wild-eyed, and infested with maggots that dance like whirling dervishes come tumbling at me. I wish I could block them out, but can't. I tumble to the sidewalk, scraping the skin off my knuckles as I fight to keep a hold of both the ring and my pole.

"Jasmine!" Cassandra shouts. The girls spill out of the doorway and move toward me.

"No!" I yell, picking myself up and stumbling forward. My legs feel like jelly. "Run!"

The work crew *is* coming after us. They're the wolves, and we're the prey.

I'm racing as fast as I can behind everyone. Jennifer looks back and nearly trips. I don't want to turn and attack, because there's a part of me that questions my theory about the night crew. What if they *are* human? Smith would have me up on murder or terrorism charges in the blink of an eye if I were to defend myself. On the other hand, why would they chase us if they weren't demonic?

*Maybe because you just mugged the mayor's assistant and then assaulted her right-hand man?*

My hand throbs as I run. The sensation is partially from the nerve endings in my skin reacting to the scrape, but the ring itself, secure within my clenched hand, also feels like it's beating. I know that seems crazy, but there's definitely a vibration coming from it … it's like it has some kind of a life force of its own. I try not to think about it. I need to stay focused on not losing sight of Cassandra, Jennifer, and Vivienne.

Lungs burning, I increase my speed as I approach Yonge Street. I'm keeping my gaze on Vivienne's long brown legs as she runs onto the road when something suddenly grabs me around the shoulders and pulls me sharply to the right. I'm spun around like a crazed ballerina and have just enough time to see the blur of a few faces and the bright graffiti collage on the alley walls before my head is draped, effectively blinding me. My pole is ripped from my left hand, but I somehow manage to keep the ring enclosed in my right palm. There's not even time to scream as a hand is clamped over my mouth. More than one person is grabbing me, and I try desperately to fight, flailing my arms and legs at my unseen assailants, but it's no use. I slip the ring into the front pocket of my jeans moments before multiple arms wrap around me and I am hoisted vertically, somewhere into the sky, away from Smith's night crew and away from the rest of the Seers.

# JADE

I jump and nearly shout out. Heart racing, I turn and see Amara throwing her arms around the man who's somehow managed to sneak up on us. I smile at Lily, but it's a shaky smile because all I can think is one or more of us could be dead right now if this man had been a demon.

"This is my dad," Amara says, grinning widely, her white teeth gleaming like Chiclets. She turns back to her father. "Dad, this is Jade, Lily, and Fiona. How did you find us?" Her admiration for her father shines in her eyes.

Mr. Jakande shakes his head. "No need to worry about that right now." His voice is deep and strangely reassuring. "None of you should be out after curfew, and you certainly should not be out here." He glances down at the decapitated bodies lying near our feet but doesn't look shocked. In fact, not even a glimmer of surprise registers on his face. "As such, I need to get all of you home and safe as soon as possible."

"We can't go with you," I say. "We're supposed to meet my sister and Vivienne and the others in the lobby of the apartment building where I live. They'll be waiting for us."

Mr. Jakande nods. "Yes, we knew that was happening, and it's been taken care of. A ride home has been arranged for them already. No worries."

I raise an eyebrow at Lily. Who is this *we* he keeps referring to? Considering he's Amara and Vivienne's father, I don't see what choice we have but to trust him.

Fiona and Lily are dropped off first. Then Mr. Jakande drops Amara off. A worm of worry unfurls in my stomach. Why is he dropping off his daughter? I can see the question forming behind Amara's eyes as well, though her father seems to inspire such reverence, she doesn't even ask.

"See you soon, my Bokkie," Mr. Jakande says as he opens the car door for Amara. "I'll watch until you get inside. If your mother notices, which I don't think she will, judging from the amount of wine her book club has consumed this evening, tell her I'll explain everything when I get home." He leans over and gives Amara a kiss on the forehead.

"See you tomorrow," Amara says, leaning back down to peer into the car and wave at me. She smiles widely.

*I'll see you tomorrow as long as your father isn't a serial killer or rapist*, I want to answer. I remember a sex education class from grade seven or eight in which our phys. ed. teacher, Mrs. Pringle, who looked like she'd be more at home on a Paris runway than standing in work-out clothes in front of thirty teenagers, told us over and over again that four out of five times, victims of rape know their attacker.

I glance sideways at Mr. Jakande. He's actually quite good-looking for being somebody's father. He's got a really strong jaw and chin, and his deep-brown skin is smooth and shiny.

"I'm sure you're wondering why I'm taking you home last," he begins, not taking his eyes off the road.

"Yeah, kind of," I say, twisting the corner of my black T-shirt round and round nervously.

"You could've tried to read my mind, though, right?" he says, his voice gentle.

My blood turns to ice. "What? That's crazy," I say with what I hope is a convincing laugh, though I have a feeling it's anything but. How does he know I can read his thoughts? Does that mean he also understands what his daughters are?

"Everything I'm about to tell you stays between us. Not even my girls know. If they did, it would put them in danger." He pauses, pressing his full lips together. "Jasmine's not coming home tonight. I'll let your mother know. I'm going to say she's staying with us … with my family to work on a school project with Amara. But that's not the truth."

"What? What have you done with her?" I ask, my voice rising. I glance out the window, wondering if he's secured the locks so that I can't jump out and escape.

"It's not like that, Jade. She's safe." This time I do reach out to try to read his mind. He's unguarded, trusting me with his thoughts, and I need to know whether he's telling me the truth about Jasmine. He is. She's safe.

"You're working with the CCT?" I ask. "You're a terrorist?"

He shakes his head. "I certainly don't consider myself as such. But I guess it depends on whom you ask. Mayor Smith would say we are, but going by the amount of daily suffering she causes, both her action and her inaction look like terrorism as well. In fact, I would consider Smith, if not a complete sociopath, then definitely a terrorist. She fits the definition quite nicely." His voice is filled with deep sadness. Memories of his parents dominate his thoughts, of their kindness and pride in him. "Many years ago, when my parents were children, my country, South Africa, was in turmoil. A very few people held all the wealth and freedom. Others were virtual slaves, made to work in the mines and in the houses of the wealthy. One man, whom we called Madiba, along with others, formed the African National Congress. They sought to bring the country together and to allow everyone to live in harmony as equals. The corrupt government at that time declared Madiba to be an extremely dangerous terrorist and imprisoned him for decades. However, the world soon saw the truth of what the South African government was doing and declared Madiba to be a freedom fighter and a symbol of the global fight against injustice."

"But what about the subway bombings? The kidnappings? What the CCT does hardly seems like freedom fighting to me. I mean, who or what are all of you fighting for anyway?"

We're close to my apartment building. I have serious doubts that Mom's going to be all right with some strange man dropping me off, let alone informing her that Jasmine is staying at his house, especially in light of my abduction when I was younger. Mr. Jakande obviously hasn't experienced my mother's protectiveness, if he thinks she's going to be the least bit okay with what he's proposing.

"We haven't harmed a single person, Jade. The CCT hasn't abducted anyone or bombed anything. We don't even know Mr. Moore. None of us had ever set eyes on him until his arrest for the latest subway bombing. Smith saying he is a member of the CCT is a complete and utter fabrication. In fact, nearly one hundred percent of what Smith puts out there about the CCT is nothing but lies and propaganda. We're actually Climate-Change *Transitioners*. We want to advocate for a socially just transition into this phase of human existence. But our manifesto never made it into the media. And that's directly due to Smith. What she's doing stirs up support for her policies and draws attention away from the very disturbing things her government is doing behind the scenes. Not us."

"What about the terrorism in London? New York? Are you telling me there are no climate-change terrorists?

That the bombings, the fires, all of that isn't real?"

Mr. Jakande stares at the road ahead for a few moments. "Many years ago, the truth began to be elaborately dismantled by certain governments. There was some resistance amongst a number of global leaders and the general populace...." He trails off. "However, as climate change worsened and resources became more and more precious, those leaders resisting were either deposed or they succumbed to the corrupt. Knowledge is power, Jasmine. Tell the people a lie for long enough, and it becomes truth. That's the ultimate power: the ability to manufacture truth. The bombings and destruction may be real. The perpetrators are fabricated."

We pull up and park on the street just in front of my apartment building. Instinctively, I scan the bushes out front.

"How do I know I can trust you?" I say, leaning back to grab my pole from the back seat.

"My parents died a slow and terrible death this year," Mr. Jakande says quietly. "They were deprived of water for days and died of dehydration. Perhaps it's a godsend that delirium would've set in toward the end." Tears shine in his eyes.

"I'm so sorry," I say. "Is there really that little water left in South Africa?"

He nods. "The Orange River is barely a trickle, and what is left of it is so polluted, the water would kill. However ..." He pauses and looks at me, his face grave.

"My parents did not die in South Africa."

"But Vivienne and Amara said ..."

"I know. That's what I told them happened. It's also what I told my wife. Still devastating news, but not as gruesome as the truth. My parents died here only a few short months ago. They were on one of the refugee boats that came down the St. Lawrence. I made sure they had passage to leave South Africa before we left for Toronto by plane. They were following us and nearly made it here. Smaller ships came and got the refugees from the larger ships that were turned away off the Atlantic coast. These smaller boats brought people inland. Near Kingston. However, once they landed, some of the boats were detected, and the army and police were dispatched and ordered to round up all the refugees they could find. Then they took them to the camps."

A feeling of dread invades me. "Camps? What camps?"

"Prisoner camps filled with climate-change refugees. Smith set some of them up. The federal government established others. She's not only been given the authority to run Toronto as a city state, but also the control over much of the wider area in this part of Ontario. There are dozens of internment camps around the province, including two north of Toronto. We're taking Jasmine to see one near Muskoka tonight. This government is savvy. The smaller the camp, the less likely it is to be noticed. So they keep the prisoner numbers around a hundred. That's not to say the conditions are humane. They're anything but. However, Smith's doing a great job making the public believe there's a terrorist around every corner and that any immigration will just add to the threat. Pretty soon she won't have to worry if the camps are discovered, because people will support any violation of human rights if they're fearful enough. Even torture … or murder."

I take a deep breath. I'm overwhelmed by this information. "So why Jasmine? Why not take Amara or Vivienne? Since they're Seers as well, why not take them to the camps?" I don't ask why not me, even though that's what I really want to know. Jasmine and I share the same DNA, and yet something obviously makes her stand out as being so much more special than me. Something that makes her *elegido*.

"Jasmine is being used by the mayor to bolster her little propaganda machine. And the safety of Beaconsfield and all the Seers is being actively threatened to make her go along with the mayor's every demand. Smith could do serious damage just by revealing the truth about the school to the public. My greatest fear is that she'd turn all of you in modern-day science experiments. The thing is, Jasmine's in a position to destroy Smith, if she can get her hands on the right information. I don't think our mayor is fully aware of that. In fact, I don't think Smith is aware of everything that's going on in terms of her night crew."

"How do you know so much about us?" I ask. "About the Seers? My mom has no idea what Jasmine and I are. And the thing is, tonight when you found us there were two bodies lying on the ground. Bodies without heads. But you didn't even blink an eye. You just gave baby wipes to Fiona to clean herself up in the car like she had nothing more than a runny nose. She had brains, blood, and bone in her hair."

It's Mr. Jakande's turn to glance uneasily out the window. "We can't stay out here too long. There's no guarantee that we aren't being tracked or followed by either Smith's cronies or our demonic friends. I know about the Seers because in my former life, before my political position in the South African government, I was a professor at Durban's KwaZulu-Natal University and one of the world's top Aramaic experts. As such, I was given the task of trying to piece together more fragments of the Dead Sea Scrolls from what archaeologists called Cave Four. I discovered the scroll that speaks clearly about the Daughters of Light, the identical twin descendants of Lilith. It says they will be instrumental in the Final Battle of the Apocalypse."

"The Seers," I say.

"Yes. You and Jasmine. My daughters. And about two dozen other women, young and old, scattered around our crumbling world. It's my understanding that as many as possible were brought both here and to London as soon as it became clear the countries least impacted by climate change were going to close their borders to those displaced by environmental destruction."

"So you know about the demons too? And the Place-in-Between?"

He nods. "The scrolls mention both quite extensively. I believe it is where the idea of limbo originated many centuries ago. But what is most worrying …" He trails off, looks out the windshield window into the darkness, and clears his throat uneasily. "We really need to get inside," he says, grabbing hold of the door handle.

"Wait," I say. "You can't leave me hanging like that. "What is it? What's worrying?"

Mr. Jakande turns to me. "According to the signs mentioned in the scrolls, it would seem that the Apocalypse may be near."

"What exactly is this Apocalypse?"

"It's the end of time and this world as we know it. The Final Battle." A heavy quiet spreads through the car like a blanket. "We need to go and speak to your mother," Mr. Jakande says, opening his door. I watch, speechless, trying to digest what he's just told me, as he slides out of the car, his long legs stretching into the night.

# JASMINE

The hood is removed from my head, and my eyelids automatically slam shut to shield my eyes from the light. Yet as soon as the arms holding me loosen, I instinctively begin to swing. I don't have my pole, and a moment too late, I remember my legs are tied together. Arms pinwheeling, I open my eyes just in time to see a cracked and worn cement floor hurtling toward my face.

At the last second — and I mean literally the last second, when my nose is millimetres away from brushing the grime off the concrete and smashing open like a vandalized jack-o'-lantern — I'm caught around the waist and hoisted back to my feet.

"We're not going to hurt you," the man who just saved my face says as he bends down to untie my legs. "You need to trust us." His voice is gentle and kind, and as I stare down at his shiny scalp, I reach into his thoughts and realize he's sincere. He's also one of the people who just abducted me from downtown Toronto, which means he's not really in any position to tell me what I need to do, in my opinion.

"Screw you," I spit back at him.

I stretch my legs and look around. The place is dimly lit by a few overhead lights and candles. About a dozen people are seated, most of them in a loose circle on stools and chairs, watching me. A few are at tables that have been turned into workstations. The crowd is diverse in terms of age and race. One boy looks like he might be only a year or two older than me, no more than eighteen at the most, and then there's an elderly woman I'd guess is nearly seventy. We seem to be in some sort of abandoned industrial building, maybe an old warehouse, judging by the high ceilings and sparse interior. There are a couple of futons in a far corner of the cavernous room. Clearly a few people are calling this dusty place home.

"I swear we're not here to hurt you," he says.

"Trust you?" I laugh sarcastically. "You grab me, blindfold me, and then throw me, like I'm nothing more than a sack of potatoes, in some kind of vehicle for more than an hour, and I'm supposed to *trust* you?"

A door opens at the opposite side of the room, and three people walk in toward us. As soon as he steps from the shadows to where I can focus on his face, my heart jumps.

One of them is Raphael.

*What's he doing here?*

He runs a hand through his black hair and catches my eye before quickly looking away.

"What's going on?" I ask, my voice shaking.

The bald man finishes freeing my legs, stands up, and begins to wrap the rope used to restrain me neatly around his left wrist. He's wearing a tight black tank top, his biceps bulging like overblown birthday balloons every time he moves. Tattoos snake their way up and down both his arms. Even if this guy who looks like the poster boy for anabolic steroids were holding me, I still should've been able to break free easily. It makes no sense.

"What happened to everyone else? To Cassandra, Jennifer, and Vivienne? And my mother and sister are going to totally freak out. I really don't think my mom should have to deal with the abduction of another one of her children." An uncomfortable lump forms in my throat at the thought of Mom and how worried she'll be. I should never have tried to pull off this stupid plan tonight.

"We're sorry for the way this had to be done, Jasmine," the woman with Raphael says, stepping forward. She's tall and lean, with cheekbones that reach for the sky and chocolate skin that glows in the soft light. Her voice is like a purr. "The other Seers are fine. We arranged for Frederick to pick them up on Yonge Street and drive them home. You did a good job gaining his trust, as he did yours. Your sister is home and safe, and your mother thinks you're safe."

I look over at the other guy who's with this woman and Raphael. He's taller than Raphael and slightly thinner, with a lighter complexion and honey-coloured hair that hangs over one eye. He smiles at me. God knows that's a lot more than Raphael's doing. I get the sense that Raphael is purposely trying to avoid looking at me, which makes me feel like my heart is being crushed between two very strong hands. It's like I'm invisible.

"What are you talking about? You're saying Smith's driver was in on this? That he helped you abduct me?" I ask. I'm starting to feel a bit like a zoo animal on display with everyone staring at me. "Can I at least sit down?"

The bald man pulls a wooden chair over to me. "Sorry," he says with an apologetic smile. "My name is Harry, by the way."

I make a point of moving the chair about half a foot from where he placed it. At this point I have no desire to play nice. "Thanks," I mutter, sitting down. The ring in my pocket digs uncomfortably into my upper hip, and for a moment it almost seems to heat up and pulsate, like a tiny creature. Either I'm really losing it or this is no ordinary ring. Which might explain Mr. Jawad's reluctance to let it go.

Thing is, I don't think Mr. Jawad is an ordinary human being either. When I touched him, it reminded me of kissing Raphael. As soon as my lips touched Raphael's, I felt like my life was ending. Visions of incredible suffering, of war and hell, invaded every cell, every atom of my being. The difference is that with Raphael, it felt like I was seeing things he'd actually witnessed. With Mr. Jawad, the screaming people, the animals being torn limb from limb and boiled alive, seemed to be inside him. Like they were a part of him.

The woman places a chair across from me and sits down. She crosses one long leg over the other, raises a finger to her full lips, and regards me closely.

"I'm Noni," she finally says. "And I apologize for the way you were brought here, but many of our members are uncomfortable with you knowing how to get here, knowing our location ... despite Raphael's constant and very passionate protests that you are absolutely trustworthy. He's quite a fan. Perhaps in time you'll gain the rabid admiration of the rest of us." She pauses, a smile dancing across her lips.

"Am I here for your amusement?" I snap. My face burns. If Raphael is such a huge fan of mine, why does he seem to be pretending not to know me? "So what makes you so special that you needed to keep me blind-folded on the way here? From what I can see, all of you are just squatting in an abandoned warehouse. I couldn't care less where this dump is."

A few of the people on the computers leave whatever they were intently working on and turn in their chairs to watch.

Noni tilts her head and silently studies me in a way that makes me feel almost naked, like a bug under a microscope. She's not sure if she can trust me.

"I'm sorry. For saying what I just did. You can trust me."

Noni nods, though I know she's not entirely con-vinced. "The reason we're so secretive is that this is the CCT headquarters ... or the closest thing we've got to headquarters." She waves a hand toward everyone sitting on the chairs. "You've met Harry, and these are our other members, whom you'll meet in due time. And, of course, you know Raphael...."

"I'm Gabriel, Raphael's brother." The boy with the floppy hair steps forward and holds out his hand. He smiles widely at me.

I raise an eyebrow and shake his hand. Is Gabriel an angel as well? I'm guessing he must be some sort of supernatural being. I look over at Raphael. He's taken a seat on one of the stools with the others, where he's staring intently at the floor as though something fascinating is stuck there.

"We've brought you here tonight because Smith's recent decision to execute Moore and to falsely identify him as a member of our organization means we need to move faster. As such, we felt that it would be very beneficial for you to be aware not only of our plans, but also of some of the things Smith's got going on behind the scenes. The position you're in is unique. You could help us greatly in our quest."

I'm confused. Why is Raphael here, amongst terrorists who bomb and kill innocent people? What kind of an angel supports murder? I look over at his brother. I assume Gabriel, with his floppy hair and puppy dog smile, is also an angel. Regardless, Noni has piqued my interest.

"Okay," I say. "But for the record, I am disgusted by terrorism, and you're terrorists. You've bombed and killed people in this city and in other cities around the world.

People just going about their business, even children. In fact, I just met a little girl who is permanently scarred from the bombing at Queen Station, so I have no idea what makes you think I'm going to want to help you. And if Moore wasn't a member of the CCT, then who exactly was he working for?" I sit back and cross my arms over my chest.

Noni nods. "You should be skeptical, Jasmine," she says. "This is a world where questioning everything and everyone is necessary for survival. You're right. Moore was working for someone. Well, working might not be the operative word. Perhaps associated with … but it wasn't us. It was Sandra Smith."

We're nowhere near Toronto, or any urban area as far as I can tell. I'm guessing we're somewhere very north of the city. The stars glitter like chips of ice, and the trees are tall, towering over us like giants. The ones that have managed to remain somewhat healthy despite the drought provide us with a leafy canopy, while others sway unsteadily in the night breeze, their barren branches creaking arthritically. It's weird that this abandoned industrial building is even here in this forest clearing, but maybe it was used for some kind of agricultural or lumber production at one time. Whatever its original use, it's pretty evident, as we move away from the massive concrete walls and twisted metal that it's been abandoned for decades, if not longer.

We move silently through the forest with Harry at the front. We're using only the faint glow from our video watches to illuminate our path. There's six of us altogether: Harry, me, Raphael, Noni, Gabriel, and another woman named Sarah who is heavier-set but moves with the grace and fluidity of a panther. The path is fairly well worn, which helps because I can only see about two millimetres in front of my face. All I can make out are Noni's shoulders and the back of her head, her tightly curled hair fanning out like an enormous halo. Before leaving, we were given metal bars and an axe. Harry's holding the axe at the front, and both Gabriel and Raphael declined weapons, but the rest of us armed ourselves. I made sure to take the longest, slimmest metal pole of the bunch. It's about three hand-lengths shorter than my pole and a lot heavier, but at least it gives me some sense of comfort. I grip it tightly and scan the forest on either side, though it would be impossible to detect a demon approaching until it was almost on top of us.

Raphael's directly behind Harry. I can't see him at all. It's not clear where we're going, and it's also not clear to me whether anyone other than Raphael (and likely Gabriel) knows about the demons.

A sharp whistle sounds, and Harry drops into a crouch. Everyone else does the same and dims their video watches. I follow their lead, balancing on the balls of my feet, my calf muscles quickly protesting this new position by tightening up and cramping painfully.

Noni turns to me and leans in close. "We're nearly there. Harry's whistle is the signal for our approach. If it's safe for us to proceed, one of our people will let us know." Her breath is hot on my ear, making me shiver. She smells of vanilla and freshly washed clothes.

I place my right hand on the ground in front of me to help steady me, the dry grass stabbing into the fleshy pads of my fingers.

After a few minutes, a low whistle that sounds like a bird call echoes, and we begin to inch forward, hunched and lower to the ground than before.

The trees ahead thin, and light shines into the sky in the near distance beyond them. It's now easy to follow Harry's lead, as he's fully silhouetted by the light. He dives onto his belly and begins to crawl, using his elbows to propel him, toward the border between the last of the trees and the light.

We all do the same, and I gasp as I move up beside Raphael to stare out from the trees and down a steep embankment toward the source of the light.

There's a clearing below us, an almost perfect circle completely empty of trees. It's occupied by what looks like a summer camp, the type kids used to get sent to. I count at least eight to ten small cabins and one large one. Thing is, I don't think kids' camps were surrounded by tall barbed-wire fences or lit up like a full moon at night. I'm also pretty sure they didn't have guards, especially sunglass-wearing, semi-automatic-weapon-toting ones.

The camp is being guarded by members of Sandra Smith's night crew.

I automatically reach out and touch Raphael's arm, wanting to tell him about Smith's crew, about the fact that I'm nearly one hundred percent sure they're demonic, that they might be doing her bidding somehow.

But Raphael jerks his arm away as though he's just been jolted by about a million volts of electricity and then continues to stare, his eyes cold and emotionless, silently down at the camp. It's like he's trying to pretend I don't exist, and maybe, if he tries hard enough, he can wish me away.

Once more my face burns with embarrassment, and I'm grateful for the cover of darkness. Thankfully, everyone else's attention is also firmly fixed on the camp below.

Something rustles in the long, dry grass and bushes just below us, and I freeze, holding my breath and gripping the metal pole even tighter.

A slender, hooded figure emerges. Judging by the silhouette of her chest, it's a woman. She stays low to the ground, letting the overgrown weeds and bushes camouflage her until she's nearly on top of us.

"It's safe," she whispers. "We can go down into the detention centre via the east side and then to Cabin Five. That cabin did work duty today, so they've been given the night off. None of the guards will bother going inside there for at least a few hours. And we're short on guards tonight, anyhow. Apparently something happened to the work crew that was supposed to join us. Usually they switch them up every couple of evenings, so these guys are beyond fatigued and pretty jittery. I guess they need their fix."

Or they need a feeding, I think. If I'm right and the night-crew members are actually demons, a few of them might be getting more than just a little hungry. The ring begins to pulsate again from deep within my pocket. I reach down and place my hand over it. The movement is definitely not my imagination, because the rhythmic beating coming from the little band of metal reverberates into my palm. What is this thing?

I'd like to ask Raphael but am not feeling like being publicly rejected and humiliated again. I wish Mr. Khan were here. Even if he'd never heard of a ring that can do this, I know he'd be able to do the research to find out exactly what's going on with it and where it's come from.

# JADE

"Where exactly is your sister, and who is this man?" Mom asks me, cocking her head toward Mr. Jakande. She stands in the doorway, hands on her hips, her dark eyes narrowing. Mr. Jakande just tried to explain that Jasmine is going to be staying at his house overnight to work on a project with his daughter, Vivienne, who is her assignment partner. He didn't get very far.

"He's Vivienne and Amara's dad. They're friends of ours. From Beaconsfield," I say, shrugging to try to make the situation seem as normal and casual as possible. It doesn't work.

"So why is he driving you home alone? Where are these *friends* of yours? His daughters?" Mom asks.

I open my mouth but can't think of an answer. This is going exactly the way I knew it would — very badly.

She turns to Mr. Jakande. "And what were you thinking driving only one of my daughters home in the dark? Why didn't you call me to ask if it was okay for

Jasmine, my daughter, to stay at your house? I have a good idea to call the police right now. You've got about thirty seconds to convince me why I shouldn't."

I've got to admit, Mom's right. If I were in her shoes, I'd be pretty suspicious of some grown man — a complete stranger at that — driving my teenaged daughter home at night. Mr. Jakande clearly didn't prepare himself very well for this conversation.

"Mom, you know how Jasmine is helping the mayor?" I begin. I'm not sure if what I'm about to do is the right thing, but I can't see any other way to keep her from calling the police at this point. And really, having Mom know about Jasmine and I being Seers would make things so much easier. The one thing I'll never tell her about is Lola's part in my disappearance. That would break her heart and likely kill her. Literally.

I look over at Mr. Jakande. He shoots me a warning look. He obviously doesn't think this is a good idea, and I need to know why. I usually feel a bit like a perverted Peeping Tom when I read people's minds, but knowing he's letting me makes me feel better. And because he's open to it, his thoughts are crystal clear: it's as though he's speaking directly to me. He feels that the more Mom knows, the more at risk she'll be. He fears it may even put her life in danger. Most of all, he doesn't want her to know about his involvement with the CCT.

I bite at my lower lip, unsure of what to do.

"What does your sister helping the mayor have to do with this situation?" Mom asks impatiently.

"Well, the thing is …" My mind races. Improvisation has never been one of my strengths. "She's actually there tonight. At City Hall. There's an emergency meeting about a refugee boat from Turkey or Greece or somewhere like that … and it's full of women and children and lots of teens our age that's made it down the St. Lawrence to Lake Ontario. There are not enough resources on the ship, especially water, and, of course, Mayor Smith made that pledge about no more immigration into the Toronto area. So now they're trying to decide what to do. Like if they should make the ship turn back. Jasmine suspects the meeting will go for hours and hours. All night."

Mom raises an eyebrow. She's still dubious, but her face falls with sadness. "Those poor people," she says. "I know my daughter will do the right thing and advocate for them to be let in. We can't leave them just to die."

I feel terrible for lying. It's an awful story to make up. I'd prefer to tell Mom everything about Beaconsfield, about being Seers, about Raphael and Michael, and the Place-in-Between, but I don't want to put her in danger.

Mom's silence only lasts a few moments. "So why did you lie to me?' she asks, turning her attention firmly back on Mr. Jakande. Her dark eyes snap with anger, though her voice is remarkably steady. "I get one story from you and another from my daughter. What is the real deal? Tell me before I call the police to come."

"Mr. —" I begin, but Mom cuts me off.

"No, Jade. I want to hear from *him*."

The blood drains from my face. I can only hope that
Mr. Jakande can think fast on his feet. Hopefully all that
university training prepared him for situations like this.

"No one, in terms of the public, is supposed to know
about this meeting," he begins. "However, I'm involved
with a group that Mayor Smith is well aware of, and
because we're also working on some high-level, secret
projects that will greatly impact local government policy,
Jasmine felt it was okay to let me know. My daughters
aren't aware of Jasmine's actual whereabouts tonight.
They thought she was just going home earlier than Jade
when she was actually being picked up by the mayor's
chauffeur to go to City Hall." He pauses, letting Mom
digest all of this for a moment. I have full respect for
how he's trying to avoid lying to her as much as possible,
but am not sure Mom's going to let Jasmine out of her
sight overnight without more evidence. Not after losing
me for years.

"Okay," Mom says. Her voice is slow and deliberate.
"I know Jasmine sometimes works on things that need
to be kept quiet from the public. I'll just video message
her to make sure she made it there safely. Don't worry.
I won't let on that I know about the actual reason for
the meeting."

Before either of us has the chance to protest,
Mom speaks into her video watch. Mr. Jakande and
I exchange worried glances as it lights up and begins
calling through to Jasmine.

# JASMINE

Only Noni and I are going down to the camp. The others are staying up at the top of the hill. We advance, keeping low to the ground and as quiet as we can behind the hooded woman. She moves carefully through the areas where the grass and brush are longest, slowly descending down the hill toward the high fencing that borders the camp.

As we get closer to the periphery of the fence, I see a section of it has been cut and then carefully put back together so that the wire is flush. We drop onto our bellies again, even though the area is in the shadows behind one of the larger cabins and away from the glare of the lights.

The hooded woman comes closer to me. I can smell her body odour. It's a strong, cloying smell reminiscent of apple cider vinegar.

"I'm Eva," she says, her voice barely a whisper. She's got an accent. "You're Jasmine, right? We've been hoping to get you here ... to show you what's going on." She pauses. "*¿Habla usted español?*"

I shake my head. When we were much younger, both Mom and Dad spoke equal parts Spanish and English to Jade and me. After Dad's death and then Jade's disappearance, it stopped, though, and now I can barely speak the language at the level of a three-year-old.

"Well, I've dreamed about you, about what needs to be done ... about what's going to happen in the near future. You have so much responsibility on your shoulders."

My heart freezes. Who the hell is this freaky chick?

"I'm a Seer as well. I arrived here about four months ago. Left Cuba and then made my way up the eastern coast of the United States as a stowaway on various boats. Not something I'd recommend." She lowers her hood, revealing a head that is partially bald. The skin of her scalp on one side is raised in ropey scars that remind me of the mountainous regions left behind after centuries of earthquakes. There's also a raised, linear scar along her cheekbone on the same side of her face. It looks awful. She reads my mind. "Courtesy of a couple of assholes who thought I owed them a little something for hitching a ride and didn't expect that I would fight like a super-strong Muhammad Ali."

I'm grateful that the darkness at least partially hides my shock at seeing her severe scarring. "What is this place?" I ask, keeping my voice low.

"A detention camp for climate-change refugees. It's been set up for those of us who risked our lives to make it to the shores of Canada, only to be captured, taken into custody, and immediately shipped here. And make no mistake, it is hell. However, I try to remind myself that there are hundreds of thousands of others that didn't even make it this far. Some are still stuck on ships that no longer have enough food and water for everyone … and then there were those who didn't make it at all." She pauses. "Survivors from some of the ships have told stories about passengers who became sick or lost their minds due to fear, as well as the elderly and disabled … all being thrown overboard in the dead of night by crew members worried about disease and discord. They'd strip them naked and then gag them with their own clothes in order to muffle the screams."

I stare at the razor wire running along the top of the high fence, then back at Eva. Just the thought of people being tossed overboard into the dark waters as if they were nothing more than excess baggage makes my stomach turn. "How can people just be put in here? In this camp? I mean, what have they done?" I ask, keeping my voice low.

"That's just it. We didn't do anything except have the misfortune of being born in countries that were amongst the first to be completely decimated by climate change. I would never have left Cuba, but my beautiful island home is sinking and sinking fast due to the rising sea levels. Not only that, but the ferocious hurricanes never stop now. One hits right after another. The country couldn't even catch its breath. There was no choice for many of us but to flee and try to make it somewhere that hadn't hit the tipping point. The alternative was simply to stay and die."

Noni slides over to us. "A few night ago we gave video watches to several of the prisoners in Cabin Five. They've been documenting their experiences as much as they can since that time. We're going to retrieve the footage and make sure it gets out to the general public." She nods toward the fence. "We need to get in there. It's not safe to be out here longer than we need to be."

"Just one thing before we go in," I say. "Why hasn't everyone just escaped through this cut in the fence?"

"It took me over three weeks to do that," Eva says. There's more than a hint of pride in her voice. "The guards are pretty vigilant, so I could only get tiny bits done at a time. They're also armed with semi-automatic weapons. Now that it's complete, we need to find a way to safely get as many people as possible through it. Thing is, no one knows what might happen to those who don't make it through. That's the predicament we're in. If we just take a few people out at a time, the guards will notice when they do their count the next morning. There might be severe repercussions for the prisoners who remain. And we can't chance that." She pauses. "Alternatively, if we try to make a massive break for it, there's no way everyone will get out, the guards will discover the cuts in the fence immediately, and who knows what that will mean for those who don't make it through to the other side."

Noni moves up to the fence, pushes the wire apart, and slips through, pausing for a moment as the rough edge of the cut metal catches on her shirt.

Eva pulls her hood back up. "You need to prepare yourself for this," she says. "It's not pretty."

I move with her to the fence. Noni holds it open for both of us. We run forward and press as flat as possible against the back of the cabin, which I assume is Cabin Five, then move in unison from there to the side of the building. Here the light reaches us more. We'll be completely exposed if anyone looks this way. My heart thumps heavily in my chest. This is dangerous. There's nowhere to run and nowhere to hide.

Eva moves in front of Noni and peeks around the front of the cabin. She motions us to follow with a wave of her hand as she disappears around the corner.

Bright light shines on us as we race toward the front door. Eva throws it open, and we run inside.

The stench hits me before my eyes have the chance to adjust to the murky darkness, causing me to tear up. Smells of shit, bad breath, and general body odour mingle together in the air like a toxic stew. I look around. Columns of bunks beds from floor to ceiling occupy the length of two of the walls. These beds are filled with children and women. Two worn sofas line a third wall, and an open doorway on the fourth leads to what seems to be multiple toilet stalls and showers, judging by the fact that the horrific smell is originating from that end of the cabin.

Several of the women get off the bunk beds and cross the room to embrace Noni and Eva. They're handing the video watches they were given to Noni, who then puts them into a nylon bag that she secures tightly with a drawstring. I can't stop staring at the children. They're bone-thin, and nearly all of them have a haunted look in their eyes that makes me shiver. The women whisper with Noni and Eva, keeping their voices low and heads bowed so I can't make out what's being said.

There's a tap on my right elbow, and I jump, my heart pounding as I swivel around. A little girl who can't be more than seven or eight years old, her eyes hollow and darkly framed in the ghostly skin of her face, steps away from me and holds up her hands in self-defence.

The metal pole. I've got it raised in front of me, ready to strike. It's an automatic reaction. I slowly lower it.

"It's okay," I whisper, crouching down and placing the pole at my feet. "You just scared me. That's all. I wouldn't hurt you."

She tilts her head, one tangled blond pigtail coming to rest on her shoulder, and regards me closely. Cautiously. I've made her unsure and afraid of me, and I feel sick to my stomach about that. No kid should have to live in here, behind barbed fences like a criminal.

"I'm Jasmine," I say, keeping my voice low. I reach out my hand, but she doesn't take it. "What's your name?"

"Penelope." A tentative smile tugs at the corners of her lips. "I'm from Australia. We came here on a ship from England because Canada is where my nanny lives, but the policemen who met us on shore put us here instead of letting us go to my nanny's house. They weren't very nice." She pauses, her eyes dark with the memory, and bites at her lower lip. "Have you come to rescue us?"

I'm silent for a moment, not knowing how to reply. Penelope's sunken eyes fill with hope as she waits for my response. I want to answer her with a huge yes, but I can't. Are we here on a rescue mission? I don't know much other than the fact that Noni and the others want to help everyone imprisoned here, and now that I'm in this cabin, I understand why.

She holds up one of her arms. There's a bandage on the nearly translucent skin at the crook of her elbow.

"Did you hurt yourself?" I ask. I have to admit I'm pretty surprised they're even given Band-Aids here.

She shakes her head. "They bled me today. Our cabin was on work duty. Some of us were sent to do chores like cleaning the toilets." She wrinkles her nose in disgust. "That job is really smelly and gross. I had to do that last time we were on work duty, but today some of us were sent to be bled. It was my first time for that." Her voice trails off. There's a haunted quality to her last few words.

"What do you mean you were *bled*?" I ask, though I'm pretty certain the answer isn't going to be something I want to hear.

Penelope's eyes shine with tears. She nods her head. "We were taken to their cabin; the one the guards stay in. They stuck a needle in our arms and took blood out. A lot." Her bottom lip quivers like an arrow about to be released from its bow. "I fainted after a while. When I woke up, I was back here in the cabin. But they give us more water when we're bled. Sometimes people drink their pee here, because there's not enough water to go around."

The force of her words hits me like a slap. These people risked their lives to try to get here, and now they're barely surviving and being kept like cattle. I look around the room again. One woman is keeping guard at the window, peeking out from the side of a worn sheet that's badly in need of washing. I assume it's been hung to block the light from outside and to give the women and children some semblance of privacy. She is painfully thin, like everyone else in here. It's clear these people are not getting enough food, on top of the disgusting living conditions and lack of drinking water. And if they're being used as involuntary blood donors on top of that, the situation is ripe for diseases stemming from malnourishment. A part of me is grateful that the only light in the room is provided by a smattering of candles encased in glass lanterns. I don't want to see how much of this place needs cleaning ... or how many creepy-crawly creatures are sharing the space with us right now.

"Guards!" the woman at the window says. Her voice is sharp, rife with panic. Noni grabs my arm and pulls me under the closest bed. Something furry scurries past me as we slide underneath the low frame, and I close my eyes as a rat's long, worm-like tail comes within millimetres of my face. A ragged blanket falls from the bed, acting like a curtain to conceal us, just as the door swings open. The bright light from the communal yard in front of the cabin spills into the room, making the blanket translucent. I hold my breath, terrified.

If these guards are demons, they'll be ecstatic at finding me here. Imagine the Chosen One being stupid enough to walk right into their prison camp. A sudden thought pops into my mind. *What if this is a trap?* After all, I was abducted tonight trying to escape from Smith's demonic workforce, and now here I am, surrounded by them once more in the middle of nowhere. How could I have been so stupid to mindlessly follow Noni and the others into the forest in the dead of night?

Except I know exactly what caused me to do it. Or more to the point, who caused me to act so recklessly. *Raphael.* I wanted to leave the warehouse and join Noni and the others because he was going with us. And it is really only when I'm around him that I feel whole. I'm like a moth being drawn to a flame; that's how crazy I feel in his presence. And though he hasn't exactly been warm and fuzzy toward me lately, I'm still certain he wouldn't betray me. It wouldn't make sense after all the times he's given me advice that's helped me avoid danger, not to mention actually saving my life when I was trapped in the fire at Susan Smith's house.

I peer through the blanket. My breath is machine-gun rapid and shallow, making me feel like I'm teetering on the edge of a panic attack. We're screwed if the guards decide to look down here. I don't really like the idea of becoming as full of holes as Swiss cheese from the bullets in those massive rifles slung around their shoulders.

The guards aren't saying anything, but they are definitely part of Smith's workforce. For one thing, they're wearing the trademark sunglasses. And they haven't said a word the entire time I've been here. They've basically just gestured.

Everyone in the cabin is now standing at attention, arms stiffly at their sides, including Eva. This is good for us because the legs of the women and girls who were sitting on the lowest bunk are providing some coverage. As the guards walk around the room, they click a small metal thing in their hands. I realize they're doing a count.

Seemingly satisfied, they nod at one another and turn to leave. The door was left open the entire time they inspected the cabin. I guess with sunglasses on it would be impossible to see anything by just candlelight. Relief washes over me as they depart.

And that's when my video watch lights up and begins beeping.

The sound shatters the tense silence of the cabin. Immediately the guards stop, swivel around, and march back into the cabin. Their guns are now at chest-height and ready to be used. By the time they reach the middle of the room, I've turned off my phone, but it's far too late.

Everyone's back on their feet, and now some of the youngest children are whimpering, burying their heads in the sides of their mothers' bodies. The older ones cover their mouths in an attempt to muffle the sound.

But the guards aren't paying attention to them. After all, they did their count and everything was fine. Fine until my watch went off. One of them marches over to the bunk Noni and I are under, violently forcing the women standing in front of it aside with the butt of his gun. The other guard leads the rest of the children and women out of the cabin in two straight lines.

I reach out, concentrating hard on the one closest to us, and try to get into his thoughts. There's only an insect-like buzzing. White noise. Nothing. He's one of them. A demon.

And that's when the ring in my pocket starts to pulsate again. Not only does it feel like it's breathing now, it's also growing warmer. If I didn't know better, I'd swear it was alive.

Noni grabs my upper arm just above the elbow, her fingers digging into my flesh like pincers. "We need to just go out. We're putting all the others — the entire camp — at risk by staying under here."

I nod and begin to move forward on my elbows. It was so stupid of me not to turn off my video watch before the Seers set out tonight. Not that that matters now.

The guard catches me by the back of my shirt as I'm emerging from the bunk. Hauling me to my feet, he begins to shove me toward the door. Noni screams from behind me.

Turning, I see that the other guard has come back into the cabin and is pulling her out from under the bed by her right ear. The silver hoop earring that had just a few seconds before been dangling from her earlobe clatters to the ground. Drops of blood rain on top of it from the tear in the flesh of her earlobe.

"Leave her alone!" I shout, breaking free from the guard's grasp. My pole. It's under the bunk. I move toward the bed again.

Out of the corner of my eye, as I drop to my knees and reach for my pole, I notice something strange.

The demon that was holding Noni has let her go. It's moving away from her and toward the door. In fact, it's about to walk right out of the cabin, leaving Noni completely alone.

Just like I told it to.

The ring is now burning like a flame inside my jeans pocket. It feels almost hot enough to brand itself into my flesh.

I grab my pole just as the demon that's after me lunges once more. The sudden motion causes the sunglasses its wearing to slip. Exposed, the demon's flat black eyes meet mine. I seize the moment and firmly plant a kick to its chin.

It reels backward, howling.

And that's when the chaos really begins. From outside in the yard there are screams and shouts of fear and pain. The voices are both female and male, adult and child.

Noni's already halfway out the door. The sound of gunfire punctures the air like July fireworks. I sprint after her, but the demon grabs my right ankle. My feet slide out from under me and for a brief second I'm suspended in the air.

I shout in pain as the side of my body slams to the floor. At least I've managed to use my right arm to stop my head from connecting with the rough wooden planks. I roll over just in time to see the demon getting ready to pounce on me, teeth bared.

"Back off," I shout, thrusting my pole in front of me like I'm about to do a chest press.

The demon immediately stops, cocks its head sideways, and regards me carefully.

I scuttle away, crab-like, toward the opposite end of the room without taking my eyes off it. My ribs and left hip hurt, but it's more a throbbing burn than sharp pain, so I'm pretty sure nothing's fractured. The ring is no longer as hot as it was, but it's still beating like a Kenyan runner's heart in my pocket. I reach into my jeans, fish it out, and slip it onto my ring finger. Though it looked like a large-sized man's ring when I first got it, somehow it now fits me perfectly. Just one more strange thing to add to the list.

Breathing hard, I lean back against one of the sofas. I need to get out of here. Though it's gotten quieter, the air is still pierced every few moments by shouts of pain and cries that serve as a reminder that I screwed up, and people are suffering now because I wasn't smart enough to turn off my video watch.

The demon hasn't moved. It's still watching me, teeth bared, but it's not attacking. If I didn't know better, I'd almost think it was some kind of wax museum dummy.

I look down at the ring again. It's no longer pulsating, and the metal is room temperature. Though I have no idea what the deal is with this crazy piece of jewellery, something tells me I need to keep a hold of it, even though it's creeping me out. Without taking my eyes off the demon, I rise to a standing position and move sideways toward the door. That way I can keep an eye on both it and the doorway to be sure nothing comes at me from either direction.

But the demon doesn't move a muscle as I leave. Instead it just sits there, watching me, head in the same cocked position the entire time, as I slip out the cabin door.

Nothing could've prepared me for the scene unfolding outside the cabin.

About a hundred women, children, and men are lined up, row upon row, facing each other in a square formation. Their faces are solemn. A few of the guards stand around them, guns drawn, but the majority of them — about a dozen in total — are standing firmly within the centre of the square.

And they're not alone.

A handful of children are also standing in the middle of the square in a straight line, their faces frozen with terror. Large spotlights illuminate the area where they are positioned. A row of guards stands directly behind them, each with gun a pointed against the back of a child's head. In front of the line, lying face down, arms spread like a snow angel, is a tiny, crumpled body. A pool of red-black blood fans out like a halo around its head.

One of the demonic guards has grabbed Noni. Its arm is hooked around her neck like a noose. Every time she struggles, the guard tightens his grip.

I've got to do something. Where are the others? They must've heard the gunshots and realized we were in trouble down here. Maybe they've decided it's too dangerous to come in through the fence. Besides, what can they do against at least twenty machine-gun-wielding demons?

The ring is pulsating again. It pushes against my finger every few seconds like a beating heart. Every cell in my body wants to take it off and throw it as far into the bushes beyond the fence as possible. There's something sinister about it. Something dark. Maybe it's just my imagination running wild, but something tells me I need to be careful while it's in my possession.

It only takes about two seconds for me to realize I'm completely exposed, standing here in the doorway of the cabin. Two of the guards have turned and are intently watching, like cats getting ready to pounce. In contrast, the one inside hasn't moved and doesn't seem like it's planning to anytime soon. If I didn't know better, the way it's looking at me, head still cocked in that weird, dog-like way, I'd swear it needs permission to.

*It is waiting for permission … permission from me.*
This realization hits me like a punch to the stomach. The
guard hasn't moved even a fraction since I commanded
it to stop attacking me. And the other one has left Noni
completely alone since I told it to.

But what if I'm wrong? What if it's just some fluke
that the two guards stopped attacking us? As a Seer, my
gut instinct is usually right, so I'm hoping not only that
the plan I've just thought up will work, but also that it
will guarantee the child lying in a pool of blood is the
last fatality tonight.

As I make my way down the cabin steps, I scan the
crowd again, holding the pole firmly. And that's when
I spot her. It's hard to believe I didn't notice Penelope
standing there before. She's fifth in the row, a guard's
gun resting against the golden curls at the back of her
head. Tears glisten on her cheeks.

"Penelope!" I yell, leaping from the bottom step.
She doesn't even flinch.

The two guards that've been watching me spring into
action. One launches itself at me, hands outstretched,
teeth bared. It stinks of fresh blood.

I bring my pole up and swing, putting all my weight
into the movement. The demon guard is decapitated
smoothly. Its head lands about five feet to the left of me
with a loud thud that is barely audible above the screams
of a few of the prisoners. After all, they don't know that
these guards aren't human. I must look as dangerous, if
not more dangerous, than those who have marched them

out here. In their eyes, I've just murdered someone in a really gruesome way.

Gunshots shatter my thoughts. My gaze pivots away from the dead demon and back to the line of children just in time to see Penelope fall to her knees. She looks almost like she's praying until her mouth opens in a silent scream, a river of dark blood gushing out from between her lips. Her tiny body crumples onto the parched grass.

"No!" I shout. And before my brain can signal my heart and emotions to think, I'm leaping forward, stabbing my pole into the midsection of a demon that's rushing toward me. Of course that hardly even slows it. They need to be decapitated, otherwise they don't die. Like cockroaches, they can withstand even the most catastrophic injuries. We've been taught this over and over at Beaconsfield.

The demon continues to run at me, my pole sliding deeper into its midsection, steaming intestines leaking out the sides of the wound like hot vomit. I've screwed up. My pole is useless. I kick out as the demon closes in. It grabs my leg and twists it violently. Something pops and I scream as pain radiates from my knee in both directions up and down the length of my leg.

The pole is being torn from my grasp. I'm so weak with pain that I'm barely clinging to consciousness, so there's no way I've got the strength to hold on to it. It's pulled through the demon's abdomen and out the other side, leaving a gaping wound that's framed with an ever-increasing circle of dark blood.

More gunshots. Tears spill out of my eyes. My stupidity cost not only Penelope's life, but also the lives of multiple climate-change refugees tonight.

The demon pulls a gun from a leather holster at its hip, its cracked lips drawing upward into a smirk.

A crack like thunder shatters the air and warm liquid splashes across my face. I smell blood but am in no pain other than a loud ringing and sharp ache in both ears, worse than any infection I've ever had. Everything else is strangely silent. Am I dead? Was the liquid hitting my face my own blood and brains? Is that sensation going to be my last living memory?

Shaking. Someone's shaking me. I open one eye, then the other. Eva's face floats above mine, filled with concern, eyebrows drawn together in a deep frown. Her mouth moves, but no sound comes out. Reading her lips, I realize she's saying my name over and over, but can't hear her over the buzzing in my ears. It's as if a thousand bees are partying in my skull.

She hoists me up, throwing my left arm around her shoulders. That's when I see it — she's got my pole in her other hand. Eva just saved my life.

Out of the corner of my eye, I see two more demons rushing toward us.

And that's when I remember the ring … and what I think it can do.

"Stop!" I shout in the demons' direction. I'm not even sure if my words are audible or understandable. It seems the gunshot has made me totally deaf.

The ring is heating up again. I raise my hand.

"You need to stop attacking us. Drop your guns," I say, leaning heavily on Eva. Each word echoes uncomfortably in my head, causing the world to spin and tilt like a giant kaleidoscope. Vomit rises in my chest.

My hunch appears to have been right, because the commands are working. The guards lower their guns, then straighten to a motionless standing position, passively watching the camp's inhabitants. From inside my fishbowl of white noise, I watch Noni begin to cautiously direct the surviving prisoners over the dead bodies and puddles of blood toward the fence behind Cabin Five. They're making a break for it.

Eva and I stay at the back of the crowd, continuing to pay close attention to the guards. Though I can't hear anything, it's clear from the grief-stricken faces of the prisoners, some of whom are weeping, open-mouthed, that their cries of sorrow and relief must be filling the air. Yet the guards remain static.

I glance down at the ring glittering briefly like a chip of ice as it catches a ray of light from one of the spotlights. It sounds totally insane, but I feel like it just winked at me. Like it's alive.

My stomach churns uneasily. Every cell is screaming for me to remove the ring, to destroy it. Whatever this thing on my finger is, and despite the fact that it just saved my life, I'm becoming more and more certain it's inherently dark and dangerous.

# JADE

Mom frowns down at her video watch. The screen's gone completely dark. She glances up at Mr. Jakande and me, her lips pressed so firmly together, they're almost bloodless.

"What's going on?" Her voice barely reaches the level of a whisper, but the tone is deadly serious. "Jasmine — or someone who has control of Jasmine's video watch — just hung up on me. And my daughter wouldn't do that unless something was very, very wrong."

Mr. Jakande opens his mouth to speak, but I lift my right hand, palm facing forward, to stop him. Mom won't accept any more of his half-truths. And quite frankly, she shouldn't have to.

"I need to tell you something," I say. "Actually, I need to tell you a lot of things … and I'm not really sure where to begin." I look over at Mr. Jakande. "Could Jasmine be in trouble?"

He nods. "Theoretically, yes. Smith is always on the

hunt for us, and if something went wrong with the plan
to take her to see the camp ..."

My heart freezes. "Or if something went wrong when
she was already inside the camp ..."

Mom's gaze follows our conversation. "What camps?
What are you two talking about?"

I open my video watch. "I need to contact Jamil Khan
and ask him to come over," I tell Mr. Jakande. "He's our
Protector. Obviously it's not safe to tell him anything
until he's here with us." I grab Mom's hand and squeeze
it tight. "Come and have a seat on the couch."

By the time Mr. Khan arrives, I've managed to tell
Mom nearly everything — from my abduction to
the Place-in-Between at the hands of a spotty teenaged demon to Jasmine being taken to see Smith's
climate-change refugee camps. I don't mention Lola's
involvement at all. There's no need for Mom to know
about her best friend's betrayal. At least not when
that best friend is dead. It's not like she can hurt Mom
anymore. I also don't mention anything about Raphael.
Learning that both angels and demons are roaming
around our dying planet might be a bit much for even
the sanest person to digest in one sitting. Not to mention the fact that one of her daughters is clearly in love
with said extraterrestrial being.

"And you've known about all of this ... this *locura*?"
Mom says, staring at Mr. Khan in disbelief. "Am I
dreaming? This talk of my daughters being descendants
of Lilith, the first wife of Adam? Adam from the Bible!"

She laughs, but it's a tense laugh that teeters on the edge of hysteria like a circus tightrope walker. "Does that mean I'm a Daughter of Light as well? Can I fly out the window and into the night like an owl?"

Mr. Khan grimaces, his eyes dark with concern. "I know it's a lot to take in. It sounds like utter madness, but it's not. And Seers can't fly. They have strength and speed that is much greater than that of a normal human female, as well as some psychic abilities, but no superhero-type powers. No invisibility cloak or power of flight, I'm afraid…. As for lineage, it seems to come from a combination of DNA and being an identical twin."

"Let me get this straight. On top of all of this about my daughters being Seers, I'm supposed to believe the mayor is holding people hostage in concentration camps around the province?" Mom smacks her forehead with the palm of her hand. "And — I forgot — a climate-change terrorist is here in my house, politely sipping dandelion tea?"

Mr. Jakande's eyes widen as he places his mug down on a nearby side table. Mom is all about proper manners. Despite all the madness of tonight, she still made sure her guest was treated properly.

"We prefer the word allies rather than terrorists," he says, clearing his throat uneasily. "Remember, we're not behind the violence and abductions that've been plaguing the city. We're trying to make sure humanity stays humane during this transitional period brought on by global climate change."

Mr. Khan nods and turns his gaze firmly back to Mom. "We haven't been sure that the CCT wasn't behind the bombings and some of the abductions, but we strongly suspected, especially once Jasmine and I became more privy to the inner workings of City Hall, that things weren't as clearly defined as Smith would have the people believe. However, I didn't — we at Beaconsfield didn't know that Craig here was a part of the CCT, nor that they were planning on abducting Jasmine this evening."

"Abduction seems a bit harsh," Mr. Jakande says, his voice soft.

Mr. Khan raises an eyebrow at Mr. Jakande. "I certainly call taking someone forcibly outside of the city limits to an undisclosed location abduction." He turns his attention back to Mom. "Regardless, we only knew Craig as a parent of two of our Beaconsfield girls. Two of our Seers. Alejandra, knowing this information puts you at risk. It mustn't be spoken of outside these walls. Ever." He looks down at his video watch. "Has anyone tried to contact Jasmine since the first call ended?"

"No," Mr. Jakande and I reply at the same time.

"And how long ago was that?"

"At least twenty-five minutes," Mom says quietly.

He frowns. "I would hope she'd contact me immediately if she were in trouble. If she *could* reach out, that is. What I don't understand is why all of you were out after curfew in the first place."

"Smith's work crew. We were trying to find out if —"

"Find out what?" Mr. Khan interrupts, his voice terse. "What could possibly be so important as to risk your lives, to risk one of you — worse yet, two of you — to the demons?"

I look down at my hands, my face reddening. He's never spoken to me like this. I feel like a six-year-old being admonished. His thoughts are raw.

*So much can happen in twenty-five minutes. Jasmine would've seen that it was her mother who tried to get ahold of her. Jasmine would've contacted her mother straight away because of how she worries about her daughters after Jade's abduction. She would've contacted me….*

"You're Seers, not a bunch of wannabe Nancy Drews," Mr. Khan interrupts.

"Nancy *who*?" I ask.

He glares at me. "After what happened to Jasmine only a few months ago, I would've expected all of you to be more cautious, not less. The forces of darkness are strengthening. More importantly, the different planes of existence are closing in on each other, colliding. This isn't some little adventure game, Jade. We're heading toward what could be the end of time and human history as we know it. You should realize that from what we've taught you at Beaconsfield. I'd expect so much more of —"

"Of *me*? Because I'm a second-born? Well, you know what? I'm tired of having to be the sensible one. I'm not Jasmine's keeper!" I snap, leaping up from my chair.

Even this feels uncomfortable to me. Impulsive displays of emotion are definitely more my sister's thing.

Mr. Khan raises an eyebrow. "Actually, as a second-born, you kind of *are* her keeper."

I clench my fists until my nails are digging into the fleshy part of my palm. I'm shaking.

"Well, I don't want to be. And why should I be, anyhow? I look after her, I'm sensible and make all the right decisions, and *she* thinks she's somehow special. Wait, what is it she says? Oh yeah, chosen. That she's been chosen but can't seem to figure out for what." I say it with a laugh that is so tinged with bitterness, it surprises me.

"What is this Chosen One stuff about? What exactly is it Jasmine's been chosen for?" Mom asks. "Another one of Mayor Smith's initiatives?"

Mr. Jakande clears his throat and frowns at me. "We should try Jasmine again. If we still can't contact her, I'll get ahold some of the others who are supposed to be with her."

"Absolutely," Mr. Khan says. "You're absolutely right. We need to at least try her before jumping to conclusions." He presses his video watch and glances up at me as it rings through, his gaze steady and serious. "Imagine if something has happened to your sister. A little over a year ago, she went back down to the Place-in-Between to bring you back here, even though she knew virtually nothing about it, about the dangers she was facing down there. I have to wonder if you'd be willing to do the same for her tonight."

# JASMINE

"Want to tell me what that was all about? How come I don't have your special Seer power?" Eva's suddenly beside me. "I've got to admit, it was pretty cool how you commanded that crowd back there." Her comments have a playful tone, but her eyes are deadly serious.

I pause. My hearing is still not fully back to normal, and I'm having to strain to hear what Eva's saying over both the din of the room as well as the residual buzzing in my ears. I rest a hand on my right hip. The ring is back in the front pocket of my jeans, where it currently feels like nothing more than a tiny circle of metal.

"Yeah," I say with a shrug. "They can't hurt us if we're not afraid, right?"

She raises an eyebrow at me and smiles. "If you say so, but I certainly think those demonic *tipos* in that camp back there could have hurt me whether I was afraid or not. That's not what I'm talking about, and you know it. I can do things like slay demons and run fast. I'm pretty strong. Sometimes I can even read minds if I work hard enough at it. In fact, I dreamed about that shitty refugee camp before even getting on the ship to come here." Her eyes darken. "But I couldn't even get a guy to video message me back before I left Cuba. My powers certainly didn't translate into mind control. Because if they had, I would've made damn sure I wasn't dancing reggaeton by myself at the clubs before becoming a climate-change refugee."

I pause and look around. We're back at the warehouse. The cavernous room echoes with the sounds of the survivors' grief. Some of them are openly weeping, others are leaning on one another's shoulders, bodies heaving with emotion. Some of the cries are nearly silent, while others whimper loudly like wounded puppies. One woman sitting near me is rocking back and forth catatonically, her arms wrapped around her shins, fingers clasped tightly together. The entire place is beginning to smell of body odour, bad breath, and farts. It's enough to make someone's sanity walk a circus tightrope.

I swallow hard and try not to stare at them. I can't allow my feelings to get the better of me. It's important to try to stay as hardened as possible. After all, there's no guarantee that the power of the ring will continue to work on the demons once it is a certain distance away from them or after a certain amount of time has passed. And if that's the case and we've been followed, then the negative emotions here will draw demons to our location like moths to a flame.

"Well?" Eva asks, breaking into my thoughts. "Are you gonna tell me how you stopped those demonic psychopaths or not?"

I turn to her. "How do you know about demons? I only found out because of getting sucked into the Place-in-Between and from ..." My stomach does an uneasy somersault. I press my lips together, unable to say his name "... from being at school at Beaconsfield."

"My sister and I were taught about it all — about what it means to be a Seer, about the demons, about the predictions," Eva says, reading my mind. "We learned everything from a local *santera* who took us under her wing, so to speak."

"Santera?" I ask.

Eva nods. "A Yoruba priestess. They were the first to really understand our powers as Seers ... to know that we are descendants of Lilith and that we exist in order to keep balance in the world ... and to keep balance and harmony between the Archangels and the Archons. That's why Ibeji dolls were created. To house the other half of a Seer's spirit. To keep the living twin strong. Unfortunately, many men didn't like the power given to us. That's why so many religions and governments around the world have actively enslaved and disempowered women since ancient times. And when our powers were diminished, the Archons used their gift of sorcery to create demons, which threw the balance off even more. The rest is ... well, you know. History. Get it? His story."

The Ibeji doll. That was what Lola used to keep Jade's spirit here after the demon had abducted her, allowing her to remain, imprisoned for years in the Place-in-Between. I've got no idea if Jade was actually dead during the time her spirit was in the doll, or if she was still a living being. When we touched down there, she certainly felt alive, and her body had aged normally, as far as the naked eye could see, which means she had the molecular consistency of someone here on Earth even then. I guess maybe her body was still alive but kind of empty inside. Sometimes I catch her staring off into space in this eerie kind of way, with a blank look. She always laughs when I call her on it and says she just spaced out for a moment. But I sometimes wonder if there's more to it than that.

"Where's your sister?" I ask. I've been holding back on this question and, considering the craziness of this night, there really hasn't been a good time to ask anyway. "Is she here?"

In response Eva clenches her teeth so tightly together that her jaw muscles pop out from the corners of her face, making it look like she's storing walnuts back there. "No," she finally replies, "Princess didn't make it here. Those same men who attempted to have their way with me tried to do the same with her." She stops, her eyes hardening with a cold anger. "No, that's not true. They did rape my sister. Four men were needed to hold her down. I didn't know it was happening, because Princess ventured up on the deck one evening in the middle of the night while I was sleeping. She suffered from bouts of anxiety, and I guess being down in the hold twenty-four hours a day, staying as silent as a mouse, and having to shit and piss in the dark corners amongst the piles of supplies got to her. I guess she figured she'd be safe … but she wasn't. Her pain and fear woke me up. I could feel it. She bled to death because of what those animals did to her."

I stare at Eva as she tells me the story. It's beyond nightmarish and makes me realize things could've turned out so much worse for Jade and I. At least I got my sister back. Eva's story is exactly what everyone feared had happened to Jade after her abduction.

"They tried to do the same to me but stopped trying after I killed two of them."

"You had your pole on the ship?" I ask. As soon as the words tumble from my lips, I regret speaking them. What a stupid response to such a horrific tale.

She shakes her head. "No … with my hands. Snapped their necks like they were nothing more than a chicken's wishbone," Eva says, her voice void of emotion. She might as well be reading from a menu. "The others didn't bother me at all after that. Was able to sleep in my own cabin, eat, and go to the bathroom in complete comfort and privacy. Not that I could sleep or wanted to eat. What I wanted was to kill myself. Sometimes I still find it nearly impossible to get up in the morning and go on without Princess."

We sit in silence for a moment. I have no words to offer, but I'm hoping she's feeling my empathy. Tears fill my eyes at the thought of anything like that happening to Jade or any of my loved ones.

I dig my fingers into my front pocket, fish out the ring, and place it on my open palm. "It sounds crazy, but I think this ring is what stopped the demons. Sometimes it doesn't seem to be just a ring. It almost feels like it has some kind of a lifeforce of its own. Not all the time; just some of the time." Biting my lower lip, I gauge Eva's reaction. The last thing I want is a fellow Seer to think I'm a complete lunatic.

She leans forward and squints at the ring. "Can I touch it?"

I nod. "It feels normal right now. I mean, how it *should* feel. Like just a bit of metal."

Eva picks the ring up and holds it carefully between her thumb and index finger. Her eyes widen ever so slightly as she examines the design on the front of it, the star created from two overlapping triangles, before handing it back to me.

"You just felt it, didn't you?" I say.

"Yeah, I felt it," she answers, nodding. "I don't know what it is, but it's got power. I need to get Noni over here," she says, getting up and heading across the room to where Noni's comforting an older woman.

I put the ring back into my pocket and fish out my phone instead. Holding my breath, I press it on. After a few seconds the screen lights up. I sigh with relief.

Knowing I still have a way of communicating with everyone in Toronto makes me feel much better. For some reason, I'm still not one hundred percent sure I can trust everyone here yet. Even if …

My eyes scan the room again, this time with purpose. However, despite the number of bodies and the shadowy light, I already know.

*He's gone. Again.*

Though I'm used to Raphael disappearing on me, this time feels different. There's something about this place or the people in it that isn't sitting right with me. Maybe I've become a victim of Smith's propaganda machine, and despite knowing that she and Mr. Jawad are up to some pretty shady stuff, I find it difficult to believe that the CCT aren't terrorists — even though everything I've seen this evening should confirm that they're not.

I check my phone. It was Mom who called earlier when we were in the cabin. My heart sinks. She's going to be so worried. And angry. If I get out of here alive, there's a good chance I'll be dead anyway, because she's going to kill me. I've also missed two calls from Mr. Khan. Jade must be getting so much heat right now from all sides because of my decision to go out last night after curfew. My heart sinks.

"Jasmine?"

I look up from my phone. Noni's standing over me.

"Yeah?" I answer, casually turning off my phone. For some reason I don't want her to see who has been trying to contact me in the last few hours.

"Eva said you have some sort of ring that you took off of Mr. Jawad earlier this evening?" She squats down beside me. "Can I please see it?"

For some reason the question strikes me as more of a command than a request.

After a moment of hesitation I fish the ring back out of my pocket and hand it to Noni.

She looks at it briefly, her eyes widening with surprise. "Put it away. Now," she says, glancing around the room as though trying to be sure no one else saw it.

"What? Why?" I ask, stuffing the ring back into my pocket.

"It's Solomon's Ring. It controls demons. Not only that, but its reappearance is part of the prophecy in the lost scrolls about the Final Battle. If it is here in this time and place, it could change everything. We need to get it back to where it belongs."

"How do you know all of this?' I ask. "And I don't have a clue where it belongs. Sandra Smith's been wearing it for as long as I've known her, but Mitchell, he's Smith's assistant, had it on earlier tonight. That's how I got it. I grabbed it off a chain around his neck. But it belongs to Smith."

Noni shakes her head. "No, it doesn't belong to her, and it shouldn't ever have been in her hands. That's for certain. The fact she's had it explains some of what's been going on, though."

"How do you know all of this?" I ask again.

For a moment she doesn't answer. Instead she looks

around the room, her eyes wary, then back to me. She presses her lips tightly together.

"My colleague and I have been studying the fragments of certain Dead Sea scrolls for years. These are scrolls that were never made public, nor was the information contained therein. And they contain a great deal of information about the Daughters of Light, amongst other things. Because of that, we've been waiting in particular to have a chance to meet and hopefully collaborate with you, Jasmine." For a brief moment she smiles. "Craig Jakande and I know what the other members of the CCT don't: that global climate change is only part of the transformation happening to our world. You see, we know all about the Seers." She pauses and regards me solemnly. "We know about you."

# JADE

Mr. Khan powers off his video watch and sighs heavily.

"Why isn't she answering?" Mom asks. Worry and panic rise in her voice like hot lava. I walk over, sit down beside her on the couch, and put my arms around her shoulders in a loose hug. My own worry is beginning to intensify, but I also feel that Jasmine is okay. At least right now. Somehow I know that if something really bad were happening to her, if she were in pain, I'd feel it to a degree.

"Where did you take her? Where is she?" Mr. Khan asks, swinging around to confront Mr. Jakande.

Though his voice is steady, there's an undercurrent of detectable anger. And worry. "I'm sorry, but I can't tell you that," he replies, folding his hands on his lap. His calmness is shocking. "One of the reasons the CCT has been able to continue our planning and work is due to the fact that we've largely avoided surveillance and detection. Even Jasmine doesn't know where we've taken her. "

"I'm Jasmine's Protector. Do you have any idea the danger you've put her in? That you've put all of us in? You mean to tell me that Jasmine can't find her way back here if she needs to? The arrogance of your organization is incredible." Mr. Khan stops speaking for a moment, his cheeks flushed with emotion. "If anything happens to her, you won't have to worry about climate change. The consequences of us losing Jasmine will have far-reaching implications for the future of the human race — implications you can't even begin to fathom."

"She's the Chosen One, isn't she?" Mr. Jakande asks. "We suspected as much, but couldn't be one hundred percent certain. From what you've just said, it's evident."

These words seem to hit Mr. Khan like a tsunami. Visibly shaken, he sits down heavily on a chair. "I'm not telling you anything," he answers, his voice quiet. "You're not the only ones trying to keep quiet. We've also only been able to survive until now by keeping under the radar of society … and under the radar of those in power. And we were fairly successful at doing so, aside from a relatively brief period known as the witch trials. Unfortunately, that's changed."

"Smith is one of the greatest threats our global community faces," Mr. Jakande says. "We need to warn Canadians, and the world, about the truth. The CCT requires just a bit more time. Our people are working on a way to disrupt her plans as we speak."

"If you can't tell us where Jasmine is, then take us to her," I say. "She's my twin, and Mr. Khan is our Protector.

You are part of a plot that saw my sister abducted tonight. If you think I won't contact the police right now and have you arrested, you're very, very wrong. And FYI, the Toronto police are pretty hyped up about abductions right now."

"Jade's right," Mr. Khan says. "You can take me to Jasmine without giving away the location. Blindfold me. Throw me in the trunk of a car." He turns to me. "Jade, I know you want to come, but we just can't risk it. Not knowing where we are means having to rely completely on Craig here and the rest of the CCT members that are with Jasmine right now. It's just too dangerous —"

"To lose two Seers together," I finish. Despite my best efforts, my words are tinged with sarcasm. I get it. Well, I guess I do. Somehow it just makes me feel, once again, like Jasmine is the focus and I'm the afterthought. I know that's not really the situation, but my Cinderella complex is taking over: I feel like everyone else gets to experience the excitement and glamour of the ball while I'm stuck at home.

"There's no way both of my girls are going to be taken to some unknown place by someone I am not even sure isn't a terrorist," Mom says, getting up off the couch. "Jade, you'll stay here with me." She walks over to Mr. Khan and grabs his hand. "Thank you for this. For everything you're trying to do for my girls to keep them safe, even if I wish you'd left them alone — Seers or not." Then she turns her gaze to Mr. Jakande, her dark eyes snapping with emotion. "As for you, should anything happen to Jasmine, I will hunt you down and personally tear your heart out with my own hands. And you can tell the police that, if you so desire."

Mr. Jakande is silent for a few moments, then he nods. "I understand. These are difficult times, and to make sense of things in the midst of chaos is hard. I'll take you to Jasmine. But only under my conditions."

# JASMINE

I'm given one of the mattresses in a far corner of the warehouse, which seems highly unfair considering the number of children and elderly from the camp here with us. Noni insists, though. The mattress is damp with humidity and smells like unwashed socks. I fold my arms under my head, unwilling to let my face touch the fabric. My body is beyond exhausted.

But sleep doesn't come. Every time I close my eyes, the image of Penelope crumpling to the ground floats up to haunt me. I caused her death. There are no two ways about it. If my phone hadn't been on, she'd be alive. Instead, my stupidity and recklessness caused the death of more than a few people tonight, including children. Rolling over onto my back, I link my hands behind my head and stare at the ceiling. How can I possibly be chosen for anything when I can't even trust myself to make smart decisions?

Noni knows so much about the Seers, the Place-in-Between, and the demons. It's more than just a bit uncomfortable realizing that she possibly knows more than even Ms. Samson and Mr. Khan. Does this mean that someone, like maybe Smith, knows a lot more about me, about my weaknesses, than I'd ever imagined?

I play my conversation with Noni just after I showed her the ring over and over again in my mind.

"If the ring doesn't belong to Smith, then whose is it?" I'd asked after putting it back into my jean pocket.

"The ring belongs to no one. Many centuries ago it was given to King Solomon, apparently in the hope of eliminating the demons. Solomon was supposed to use the ring and the power inherent in it to control the demons, to make sure they could never roam the Earth again. Except that's not what happened."

"So it *was* the ring that controlled the demons tonight? Not some kind of special, previously undiscovered Seer power of mine?" I said. Really, I was only half joking. The idea that I was able to completely stop the demons from killing all of us with just a little circle of metal was still pretty mind-blowing and hard to believe.

"It was. Whoever has possession of the ring is able to control the demons."

"Do demons have their own thoughts?" I asked.

Noni nodded. "You mean like free will? I suppose, but as far as we know, their main drive is one of feeding on blood in this plane — the Earthly plane — and feeding off the negative energy of the Place-in-Between. They are consumers, carnivores, driven by an insatiable hunger. And they are programmed to partake in and celebrate human-made chaos. Oh … and to destroy Seers."

"Lovely," I replied. "Seems to me that this Solomon dude could've done us all a huge favour if he'd followed through."

"The history of the ring is no joke." Noni regarded me solemnly as she spoke, her dark eyes revealing her worry about me.

I wanted to tell her it's a two-way street: I wasn't exactly feeling totally warm and fuzzy in terms of trusting her yet either.

"However, once the ring was in his possession," she continued, "Solomon decided to wait before keeping his promise. Instead he used it to build a temple, with the demons utilized as slave labour, and then he went on to use the power of the ring to compel a woman to marry him. You see, even though Solomon was a very good man, power corrupts. It's a nearly universal human weakness. Just one of our many Achilles heels."

"Yeah, humans can really suck," I said. "So what happened? I mean, it's pretty obvious the guy didn't follow through with his promise — ever. 'Cause tonight, as you know, a bunch of those bastard demons murdered people, including kids." I paused, my bottom lip trembling, as Penelope's face floated into my mind's eye again. Taking a deep breath, I pushed it away. Guilt wasn't going to help the rest of us in the here and now. "Where did the ring come from then? I mean, who gave it to Solomon in the first place? Why didn't that person take care of the demons himself?"

"As far as we know, the Archangel Michael devised the ring and infused it with the power to control demonic entities. The Archangels and the Archons are two great forces balancing each other. They are supposed to be the bookends, so to speak, for our world. The Archangels balance the light and the Archons, the dark of humankind. However, both needed to do so without interfering in the structure of this realm — especially without interacting *intimately* with humans. Very early on, the Archons broke that rule."

I raised an eyebrow at her. "This realm? What do you mean? Earth? The Milky Way?"

Noni shook her head. "This realm encompasses both the Earth and the Place-in-Between. There may be other components to it that we don't yet know about … there is some evidence of a lower level, a deeper level below, but we've only come across fragments of the scrolls alluding to that. Of course, the scrolls mention a heavenly plane from where both the Angels and the Archons come. What we do know is that the demons are a creation of the Archons. Both the ring and the demons are abuses of the gifts given to the Archons and the Archangels. Just as the Archangels cannot undo something the Archons create, so the Archons cannot directly use the ring, nor destroy it. The thing is, the Archangels may not use or destroy it either. Same with demons."

I tried to take in all of this information. But it was a lot, and I was beyond exhausted. I wondered if Noni knew that Raphael was an angel. Probably, because she seemed to know everything, but I couldn't be entirely sure. And she refered to his brother, Michael, as an angel.

"What do you mean they weren't supposed to interact *intimately* with humans? What did the Archons do exactly?"

"The Archons involved themselves emotionally, physically ... and sexually with humans. The result was the exchange of Archon powers with a group of humans who were filled with much more darkness than the average person. Emotions like greed, anger, hate, and jealousy attract the Archons. They then gave this group of humans the ability and strength in the afterlife to move their souls into the bodies of vulnerable humans in order to make them do their bidding. They were also given the ability to move between the Place-in-Between and Earth when conditions allowed it. In essence, they taught them the art of the darkest magic. Whereas these souls should've spent eternity on the lowest plane or in the Place-in-Between, instead they were able to become predators. As in life, so in death. And that is how demonic beings came into existence."

My stomach felt like it was being pulled inside out. So that's why Ms. Samson was so concerned about Raphael and me. My mind drifted back to our kiss under the tree last year. Did that mean Raphael had broken the same rule? And if so, what did that mean? Had we somehow changed the way our world and the Place-in-Between are supposed to function? I desperately wanted to ask Noni if she knew, but didn't want to reveal what had happened between Raphael and I. It felt like too much of a risk.

"So how did the ring get here, to Smith, after all this time? Did Solomon pass it along to his children or something like that?"

Noni nodded. I noticed deep purple circles under her eyes and wondered how much sleep she actually gets at night. It seemed to me like she was kind of in charge of things with the CCT.

"Solomon realized the power of the ring was corrupting him, so he passed it along to his two daughters. Twin daughters. On the advice of Michael. It was hoped that, with Seers having the ability to control the demons and keep them in the Place-in-Between or in the Darker Place, some balance would be restored here on Earth. And as far as we know, it worked for a while, though the opening between the two worlds was still there. The next time the ring was used here, that we know of, was around 60 CE. The Iceni ruler, Boudicca, used it to brutally defeat the Romans and destroy London after she was tortured and her twin daughters were raped by the Roman army. Boudicca led a violent army to avenge her family — an army that not only killed, but also devoured some of their enemies. She realized the incredible power of the ring to corrupt and decided it shouldn't be in any mortal's hands — ever. Just before her suicide, she placed it between some of the rocks that would, a century later, form part of the foundation of the Roman wall built around Londinium."

"Londinium?" I asked.

"The Roman name for the city of London. They ruled the city until the early fifth century," Noni answered. "Someone must've discovered the ring, perhaps on an archaeological or building-site dig, and removed it. There was no record of it until the mid-twentieth century in Germany and India. A few decades later it reappeared in Saudi Arabia. After that, we lost track of it. We didn't know what had happened to it … until now."

"So where exactly does the ring belong, if it doesn't belong to anyone?" I asked. "If it's being used to help Smith with her twisted plans to make Torontonians turn on each other out of paranoid fear, I'd say it belongs at the bottom of the ocean. Or at least at the bottom of Lake Ontario."

"There's so much more to the mayor's plans than you could ever imagine, Jasmine. Her reach and plans are international in scope." Noni paused and clenched her teeth together, causing her jaw muscles to pulsate. Her hatred of Smith came to me, loud and clear, at that moment. "The ring needs to be placed back at the Roman Wall in London. Into it, actually."

I laughed. "Well, good luck with that. England's borders are closed, like everybody else's."

Noni ignored my comment. "According to the fragments of the scrolls Craig and I have managed to piece together thus far, the global events happening right now may signal the coming of the Final Battle. At that time, the Daughters of Light — the Seers — will be pivotal in deciding the fate of humankind. If the ring is not in its rightful place when that happens, and someone has control of the demons during that time …" She trailed off and gazed at me, her eyes darkening with concern.

"Let me guess. It would be a very bad thing. I still don't see how anyone can get the ring back to London, though."

"You're right. Virtually no one can do it with the borders closed the way they are. The thing is, the ring needn't be returned, as far as we can tell, to the wall at this precise moment in time. And that's where you come in, Jasmine."

# JADE

To say I barely slept after Mr. Khan and Mr. Jakande left would be a massive understatement. By the time the sun begins streaming into my window, triggering the birds to act as my alarm clock, I realize sleeping isn't going to happen for me.

Rubbing the grit from my eyes, I swing my legs to the side of the bed and grab my video watch off the side table. It's only a few minutes past six. Nothing from Jasmine, and nothing from Mr. Khan. Not that I really expected to hear from them yet. And Mom will be asleep for another couple of hours, if not longer. I heard her quietly sobbing in the living room for at least an hour last night after she thought I was asleep.

I'm going to lose it if I just wait around to hear from Mr. Khan. And god only knows how long that will be.

Slipping into a light dress and ballet flats, I decide to walk. I won't go far, and I'll take my pole for good measure. But if I don't move and get out into the fresh air (or at least into the humid morning air of drought-ridden Toronto), my sanity is going to disappear like a magician's bunny.

My pole is stuffed under my bed. I grab it and a water bottle out of the fridge and tiptoe my way out of the apartment. Once outside, I pause for a moment, holding my hand over the top of my eyebrows to shield my eyes from the bright morning sun and take in my surroundings.

It's quiet. Maybe a little too quiet. After the events of last night, I realize this walk is probably a totally stupid move, but there's this annoyed feeling building up in me like a sneeze, and I need to try to walk it off. It's seems to be constant now, simmering just below the surface. I guess it's mainly directed toward Jasmine and Mr. Khan. Walking might allow me to work it out, sort of like a knotted and sore muscle.

I begin walking without any real destination in mind. The streets are virtually empty, with only a few people out walking their dogs and some either leaving for work or coming home. No one can travel during curfew unless they have a special pass, so a lot of employers schedule their workers' shifts around it. Of course a few drones buzz overhead, competing with the cicadas. They're used by the police and Smith's government to try to thwart future CCT terrorist attacks. Basically, they're insect-like, robotic spies. And they're everywhere.

As I walk, I think about how easily I become annoyed with Jasmine. It makes no sense. I mean, it's not like she's really doing anything on purpose to me. If I'm dead honest, she's not doing anything at all. She can't help that she was chosen by Smith to be the youth representative. And really, would I want to be running around being the mayor's little puppet?

"Penny for your thoughts?"

I jump at the sound of the voice directly to the right of my shoulder, swivel around with the speed of a ninja, and raise my pole to strike. My heart's pounding, jackhammer speed, in my ears.

It's Seth, the cute boy from the grocery store.

"How did you sneak up on me like that?" I ask, slowly lowering my pole.

He holds his hands over his head in a gesture of mock surrender. "Don't kill me. I honestly just wanted to see when we might be able to go on that date," he says, shooting me a lopsided smile.

My heart is still doing nervous flip-flops in my chest. "Do you live around here?"

Seth shrugs. "I guess you could say not far from here." His eyes travel to my pole. "You're pretty fast with that. A very famous man once said it was a good idea to walk softly and carry a big stick. He'd likely be impressed with you. What's it for?"

I can't tell if he's making fun of me. The pole, and my reaction with it when he scared me, must've seemed more than just a little over the top, even with curfew and the kidnappings and murders happening in the city.

"Um, I … I'm learning kendo," I reply. "And I figure it's better safe than sorry to carry it at this time of day when I'm on my own. Especially with everything that's going on. It's hard to believe how our world changed into being crazy violent and everything so fast."

Seth's smile fades a bit, but his eyes stay fixed on me. His gaze is full of understanding. "It's pretty crazy for sure. Makes everything seem so unfamiliar, doesn't it? That must be hard."

I pause. The loneliness … that sense of being empty that I'd felt the entire time I was captive in the Place-in-Between comes flooding back. It's like he's just read my mind. I reach out and try to listen to his thoughts. Nothing. It's like hitting a blank wall.

"I …" Words escape me. Why am I drawn to him so strongly? Every molecule in my body wants to reach out and touch him.

He slips his hand into mine. His freckled skin is warm and sends little sparks of electric energy into the core of my body.

"Let's go for a walk," he says. "I'd like to show you some of my favourite spots, if you'll let me."

I nod. Mr. Khan and Jasmine can wait. God knows they don't respect what I have to say most of the time. But I should get home to Mom. She'll worry so much if she wakes up and I'm not there.

"I just need to contact my mom and let her know I'm going to be out for a while," I say, slipping my hand out of his. Despite the sun already heating the air like an oven, my hand suddenly feels cold, and I want to message Mom as fast as possible so that I can be touching him again.

As though sensing this, he puts his arm around me as I text her.

"You're very special to me, Jade," he whispers.

# JASMINE

It's hard to tell whether it's day or night in the warehouse. Most of the sobbing seems to have stopped, and I guess that's because a lot of the survivors have fallen asleep. I wonder if they're dreaming of a happier time, of a time before they had to flee their homeland, before climate change made them refugees, and then prisoners.

It makes me think about Jade. Did she dream about Mom and I, about Toronto, about her life here after she was abducted and taken to the Place-in-Between? She says she doesn't remember a lot but recalls that her memories of life before slowly faded away during her time there. Kind of like the way a mug of hot water can dissolve sugar cubes. They were there, but she just couldn't detect them any longer. I don't really get it, and that must be hard for Jade. Sometimes I think the loneliness she feels now must be even worse in some ways. At least when she was trapped in the Place-in-Between, she didn't fully realize what she was missing. Now everything she missed during those years she was gone is painfully clear.

The heat in here is getting unbearable, and the darkness from the covered windows makes it impossible to tell the time. I roll over on the mattress and check my video watch. It's nearly 6:00 a.m.

A faint shadow falls over me. I look up.

It's Raphael.

"What the ..." I begin, but he crouches down and places two fingers over my lips. The touch is gentle, but it's effective. I fall silent.

"Shhhh ... the others can't know I'm here with you. No one can. But I wanted to tell you I'm sorry. You don't know how sorry I am." He stops speaking and looks at me. The pain is evident in his eyes. "I know you were hurt tonight."

"Really, Sherlock?" I whisper. "Do you think so? Or maybe I love being treated like the Invisible Man." Despite trying my best to push his affection away, I'm unable to.

"I can't be around you. I've been told that."

"Told?" I retort, narrowing my eyes at him. "By who? Mr. Khan? The Protectors? Your brother, the great Archangel Michael?"

He grimaces. "Things are so much more complex than you realize ... and so much simpler in some ways as well. You must prepare for excruciatingly dark times ahead. You will be so challenged, Jasmine." Reaching out, he brushes the hair off my forehead. It's been sticking uncomfortably to my skin. The heat in here is stifling due to the lack of ventilation and the overcrowding.

"How did they get me here? I mean, that guy — I really fought. How did he hold me?"

Raphael shakes his head. "Gabriel and I helped. You needed to be brought here. You needed to see the truth about what's happening. About what cruelty is happening."

"I'm so tired," I say, the words catching in my throat. A tear slips down my cheek. "There's so much suffering. The boats of refugees, Isabelle the dog, Penelope …"

Raphael nods. "Allow yourself to feel it. It's your burden. It's part of what you're meant to be." He takes my hand. "Close your eyes, Jasmine. Rest. You need to rest."

"Jasmine? There's someone here to see you."

I bolt up. How long have I been asleep?

Raphael's gone and Eva is standing over me.

"To see me?" My heart does a nervous somersault. I run a hand through my tangled hair. My fingers get stuck midway through.

"Noni is with them in her office. She wanted me to come and get you."

I slowly hoist myself off the mattress and to my feet. Exhaustion has left me feeling slightly shaky. Definitely not great if any threat should rear its ugly head.

"Where is this office?" I ask, following Eva as we weave our way in between the survivors, many of whom are stretched out on the floor, still asleep. They likely didn't get much rest during their time in the camp … or before that.

"Just through that door," Eva answers, pointing just ahead and to our left. It's where Noni, Raphael, and Gabe came out of last night when I first arrived at the CCT headquarters. "They're waiting for you."

I raise an eyebrow at her. "You're not coming?"

She shakes her head. "Craig and Noni want to talk to you alone. Well, along with the man who's come here with Craig."

"Craig?" I ask. "Is that someone I'm supposed to know?"

"Oh, I thought maybe you'd met him. His twin daughters attend the same grade as you at Beaconsfield. He and Noni have been studying us — the Seers — for a long time. They're pretty much the lead team of the CCT. If they want to speak to you privately, it's something pretty critical for sure." She stops talking and quickly looks me up and down. "You definitely have a lot of people paying close attention to you."

I ignore her comment. There's no need for me to read her mind. The jealousy in her voice is so strong, I can almost taste it.

"Okay, see you in a bit," I say with a shrug. I'm trying to seem unfazed by it all, but my curiosity has definitely been piqued.

There's a window beside the door to Noni's office, but the glass is the frosted kind that ensures privacy by allowing only the silhouettes of the people inside to be detected. I knock twice and wait. That little butterfly of nervousness unfurls itself again, even though I know the chances of Raphael being in there are next to nothing.

The door opens. Noni pokes her head out. "Jasmine. Good. We've been waiting for you."

She steps aside to let me in. I slip past her and into the room.

As soon as my eyes adjust to the brighter light, I see him. He gets up from his seat at the table as I enter.

"Mr. Khan!" I cry, running over and throwing my arms around him. He hugs me back tightly. Tears spring to my eyes. "How did you find me?"

His gaze travels to a tall, distinguished-looking man sitting at the table who looks even more like a teacher than Mr. Khan. "Craig … I mean Mr. Jakande brought me here. I'm so glad you're okay," he says, his voice shaking with emotion as he lets go of me.

Mr. Jakande stands up. He's much taller than Mr. Khan and built a bit like a professional football player. "It's a pleasure to finally meet you, Jasmine. I've heard a great deal about you from my daughters, Amara and Vivienne." He extends his hand toward me.

"You're Amara and Vivienne's dad?" I ask, shaking his hand.

He nods and pulls out a seat for me beside Mr. Khan's. "I am. These are interesting times to be the parent of Seers. I'm sure your mother would agree."

I sit down, lean back in the chair, and fold my arms across my chest. "My mom has no clue that my sister and I are Seers."

"Actually, she knows now," Mr. Khan says, his voice heavy with fatigue. As he takes his seat again beside me,

I notice that dark shadows ring his eyes. I imagine I look just as bad, if not worse.

"What?" I ask. "What do you mean she knows? How?"

"Long story," Mr. Khan says. "And we have more urgent things to discuss with Noni and Craig at the moment." He stops and stares hard at me. "Jasmine, I really need you to be open-minded about what's going to be suggested here. I'm not happy about it either, but it needs to be done."

I look around the table. "Okay," I say, slowly dragging out the word. I'm not loving Mr. Khan's implication that I can be closed-minded.

Mr. Jakande clears his throat. "Jasmine, Jamil tells me that you've actually been to the Place-in-Between. Twice. It's quite incredible that you've lived to tell him about it, don't you think?"

My eyes shoot daggers at Mr. Khan. *What's he doing telling people about this?* Suddenly, I feel so vulnerable, I might as well be sitting here completely naked.

"Yeah. I had help, though. Lily and Cassandra — they're these two other Seers — were with me. And Raphael. He goes to Beaconsfield as well." I watch for Noni's reaction. This is my chance to see what she knows about Raphael's true identity.

"We know Raphael well," Noni says. "His sister, Uriel, helped guide us to the fragments of the Dead Sea Scroll that contained a vast amount of information about the Daughters of Light and your powers as Seers. And Raphael helped guide us to you."

"The thing is, Jasmine," Mr. Jakande continues, "the world as we know it is changing, evolving … collapsing. Humankind is responsible for one part of that. Climate change, as you know, is a threat that has wiped out most of the Earth's species. Now the rest of the world's biodiversity is at risk of extinction — including homo sapiens. It has also triggered great intolerance and cruelty. Greater than any of the earlier genocides in our history."

"Well, I knew things weren't exactly upbeat, but I've always looked at the future through a kind of glass-half-full kind of lens. You know, being just a few months short of turning sixteen and everything, what you're talking about is a pretty big downer."

Mr. Jakande grimaces. "I was told you have a sharp wit. That very well might be an asset."

"Naw, you think I'm a smartass," I say with a smile. "And that I'm always thinking about some quick comeback, rather than listening like I should." I tap the side of my head. "Seer mind-reading talents."

"For god's sake, Jasmine," Mr. Khan interrupts. "I'll make this very clear. You need to go back to the Place-in-Between. The ring has to be put back in the Roman Wall where it belongs. Otherwise, not only will someone else be able to control the demons during the time of the Final Battle, but we'll also lose our safe space in the city of London. We need that space because it's the only way we can ensure sanctuary from the demons and any other dark forces during the battle.

You're one of the seven warriors for certain. One of the seven Daughters of Light who will fight in this battle. You have a lot resting on your cheeky little shoulders. The fate of humanity, in a nutshell." He stops and, hand shaking, wipes away a few drops of spittle near the corner of his mouth.

He's furious with me and physically exhausted. I don't need to read his mind to know he's near the breaking point.

"You've already been told you're the Chosen One. You're going to have to take the lead when the time comes to confront the darkness. The outcome of the upcoming time of conflict will determine what the next phase of the Earth's history looks like. It's time you stepped into the role. As your Protector, I suppose I need to have faith in you. But quite honestly, you have to prove to me — and fast — that the world's glass isn't half-empty with you in such an important position."

# JADE

Seth takes my hand as we walk, and despite the building heat and humidity, his skin stays cool and paper-dry to the touch. This doesn't help me at all, as the combination of the heat and my nervousness is turning my palm into a virtual waterfall.

"Are you okay to go to the Commons?" he asks. "I thought we could have a bit of …" He stops as a red flush springs up to connect his freckles. "Of a picnic. I brought some food and stuff with me. I hope that doesn't sound stupid."

"It's sweet. But how did you know I'd be out here walking?" I ask. Really, it doesn't matter what his answer is; I already know I want to hang out with him in Commons Park more than I've ever wanted anything in my entire life.

"I was going to go myself but thought I'd bring extra just in case. Call it a sixth sense." He gives my hand a gentle squeeze as we begin to walk in the direction of the Commons, even though I haven't agreed to go. Maybe he's sensed how much I want to do this as well.

We walk in silence for a few minutes, just drinking in the early morning birdsong around us. The sun is already pressing down, heating the dried grass and exposed earth in the front gardens of the townhouses we pass. The park itself is filled with succulents and shrubs and dotted here and there with trees that've managed to survive the drought. The remnants of a large splash pad sit, unused since water restrictions started, as a sad reminder of the park's past. A couple of old water fountains stand, pipes rusting, their water source having been shut off years ago. A faded sign above the fountains reads: *Don't waste a drop! Water is precious.*

I think about Mayor Smith's upcoming bottled water initiative and can't help but wonder if it is a precursor to turning off the city's taps — at least part of the time. It's already happened in so many other North American cities.

Seth spreads his towel on a patch of brown grass hidden in the middle of a group of bushes. It gives us nearly complete privacy. We sit down and he begins to unpack his knapsack, taking out food I haven't seen since before being abducted to the Place-in-Between. Large, ripe berries, slices of plump white chicken breast, and sunny, yellow wedges of lemon floating in glass bottles filled with water are spread out on the towel. It's like a mirage.

"Where did you get all of this?" I ask, saliva filling my mouth.

Seth holds up his right index finger to his lips. "Hush. I have my ways," he says playfully.

"But …"

*No one can get this kind of food anymore,* I want to say. *Unless you're someone like Mayor Smith or one of the other major city leaders, and even then …*

Seth picks up one of the blackberries and holds it to my lips. The purple flesh of the berry is warm from the sun.

"You're very special to me, Jade," he says, placing the berry between my open lips.

I bite down, and the warm, sweet juice trickles down the back of my throat. It's so delicious, I want to devour the entire container. I'd forgotten what berries even tasted like.

Somewhere in the distance, thunder rumbles. Storms don't usually start until early afternoon. The air is definitely shifting, though.

Seth leans forward and tilts my chin up with his hand. His eyes suddenly look very old.

Something's not right. I can see ancient deserts in his eyes.

He leans in to kiss me.

Suddenly, I don't want to be here at all.

"Jasmine might be the Chosen One," he whispers, "but I've chosen you."

I open my mouth to scream, to tell him to stop, but no words come out.

Then his lips meet mine, and images that I can only imagine are straight from Hell are unleashed into my mind. They are far worse than anything I ever saw in the Place-in-Between. My body collapses against his. I try to scream but am unable to move. I'm paralyzed.

*This is what the fly caught in the spider's web must feel like just before being devoured*, I think.

Then the world around me slips away.

# JASMINE

So I'm heading back to the Place-in-Between. Or at least I'm going to try to get there. After my telling off by Mr. Khan, I pretty much shut up. Even I'm not stupid enough to push things after someone has a go at me like that. And really, he's right. I've screwed up enough. But what they're proposing scares me to death. I mean, come on, if we're being really straight up here, there's a fifty-fifty chance it just might lead to my death.

At best.

And how many people would be clamouring to do something with odds like that?

The thing is, according to Noni and Mr. Jakande and the rest of the CCT's intelligence-gathering, not only does the ring need to be back in its rightful place in order to give us a chance at winning in the Final Battle, but Smith — and maybe even some of the other city-state leaders — are planning a little mini-apocalypse of their own. The CCT, which, Noni tells me, actually stands for

Climate-Change Transitioning, is just as hunted as we, the Seers. It's just that they're being hunted by Smith and the other governmental officials, rather than a bunch of scary-ass demonic creatures.

"You couldn't find another acronym?" I asked. "I mean, it was pretty easy for Smith to twist it to make you sound like a terrorist organization, don't you think?"

Noni leaned forward, elbows on the table, her slender, brown fingers intertwined. "Our mandate is to help humanity, as well as the creatures of the natural world, transition as equitably as possible during this time. There will be loss and suffering, but it needn't occur on the scale it is at the moment. Economic and political inequality deepened in the early years of climate change, as soon as those in power, the elites, saw that the Earth's resources could not sustain even half of us more than a few decades into the future. Our aim is to reverse that, to open the borders again, to try to expose governmental corruption and lies. We want a more socially just world as we transition into this new phase of the Earth's existence."

"Well, no offence, but that plan seems to have already backfired. Big time. So many countries are destroyed. You just need to look at all the survivors floating around the oceans. And here, at least in places like Los Angeles, your plan's been a colossal flop. I mean, a lot of innocent people died on those buses and on the LA Metro when you bombed them. Doesn't seem to make sense if you're are all about social justice."

I thought back to the footage of the riots in Los Angeles and the military presence called in by the mayor at the time. There were mass arrests and looting as people tried to take whatever they could, especially bottled water, in order to survive. California was one of the first regions in North America to really be hit by climate change, and those who weren't incredibly rich but could still get out had already had left the state. That meant Los Angeles was filled with only the very wealthy and the very poor. When bombings began on the Metro lines and buses, the only way for the working poor to get around the city, chaos ensued. The military gunned down crowds of poor inhabitants for simply trying to gather water from wherever they could find it. Fires raged through the urban landscape, crossing the long-dried-up basin of the Los Angeles river and zipping up the hills to the wealthy enclaves, destroying everything in their path. The wealthy dashed, many of them to second homes in New York City or here in Toronto, and so the poor were blamed and left to become ash, along with the rest of the city.

Then the executions of those arrested and charged with the bombings started. As active members of the CCT, they were convicted of treason without trial and immediately sentenced to death. Each death was broadcast live. A deterrent for others who might be contemplating joining the CCT, claimed the US president, the mayor of Los Angeles, and other politicians. Millions of people watched the executions.

Those executions were the entertainment event of the year. It was rumoured that some people brought out chairs and sofas to lounge on and ate popcorn while viewing them.

"We had nothing to do with those deaths, Jasmine," Mr. Jakande said, his voice quiet and calm. "We're responsible for things behind the scenes, so to speak. The hacking of political email accounts to reveal corruption, the redistribution of wealth from a trust fund to a struggling farmer, or changing the computerized schedule of electricity blackouts to ensure a lower socio-economic area gets its share of energy."

"I get your point," I said. "But if you're not behind the bombings and terror attacks, then who is? I mean, you've got people in all the major city states, don't you? The ones that still have some resources? Like New York, London, Copenhagen."

Noni and Mr. Jakande quickly looked at each other.

"We do have branches of the CCT in those cities and several others. We suspect the governments and the leaders of the world's largest and still-functioning city states are colluding to keep citizens fearful and thus suffer less questioning of their policies and procedures. And we think they're using vulnerable citizens, the ones who will do anything — even sacrifice themselves — to help with this. Of course, we know that Smith, with the help of Mr. Jawad, was able to recruit demonic souls to aid her. That was definitely not something we anticipated."

"But why are they doing this?" I ask, my voice shaking with anger. "Why would they be blowing up their own citizens, including children? I thought the whole idea was to keep other people, outsiders, climate-change refugees, *whatever they want to call them*, out of the cities. What the hell? It makes no sense."

"What their end goal is, we're not sure of … not yet, at any rate," Mr. Jakande answered.

"Jasmine," Noni said, leaning toward me. "Please let us worry about Smith and the political situation. Because if you don't get Solomon's Ring back to its rightful place, and soon, none of this will matter."

"Okay," I said, sitting back and trying to digest the whole thing for a moment. "But someone needs to explain to me how putting the ring back in the Roman Wall in the Place-in-Between is the same as putting it back in the wall in the real London … the London that's here and now. On Earth." My thoughts were getting jumbled. I was way too tired for this. "Because isn't the Place-in-Between a totally different place? And if it is, then it's not really London, right? I mean, how can it be, if London is here? The real city is here. Right?"

"Again, it's something we're still investigating, hypothesizing about, really," Mr. Jakande said. "But there seems to be a multidimensional aspect to it. Time is not linear in the Place-in-Between, but it seems, from all the textual evidence, that it is still London … in a manner of speaking."

I'm lost. Completely lost. At the best of times, I'm not a mathematical, science-geek kind of girl.

Noni must've sensed my feelings. "Think of the two Londons as imprints of the same picture. They're both the same, but not exactly the same ... like identical twins. Despite being from one egg and sharing the same DNA, there are genetic variances in twins of the same genome."

My head felt like it was going to blow apart. "What?" I asked, feeling like a complete idiot.

Noni smiled. "It means that twins' genes are virtually the same, but with some differences. For instance, one twin may develop breast cancer due to a genetic predisposition, while the other twin may not have that variance in her DNA."

"So you think putting the ring back to where it was hidden all those years ago, but doing it in the Place-in-Between, will be the same, or at least close enough, to putting it back in the wall here in London?"

Mr. Jakande folded his hands on the table. "We believe it will be," he said.

He and Noni exchanged another quick glance.

"At least we hope so," he added.

# JADE

Though it's Sunday, Mr. Khan has asked us to meet at Beaconsfield. So here we are, sitting in his classroom, the sun streaming in the windows. It feels strange to be here with the place so empty and quiet.

Everyone involved in what happened other night is here, except Fiona and Jennifer. That seems unfair, because I'm sure we're going to get the lecture of our lifetimes right now, and they were in on everything the other night as much as the rest of us. The funny thing is this new Seer, Eva, is with us.

I look over at her. She's sitting at a desk, looking out the window. I'm pretty sure she might be a year or two older than the rest of us. Her hair is tucked under a silk headscarf that she's carefully wrapped around her head. According to Jasmine, she's a climate-change refugee who lost her sister on the journey here. Now she's staying with Ms. Samson until a family can be found to take her in.

Mr. Khan clears his throat. The skin framing his eyes is dark purple. I've never seen him look so exhausted.

"What happened Friday night with regard to all of you, aside from Eva, breaking curfew and chancing your lives, is inexcusable," he says, his tired gaze stopping to rest on each of us. "But that's not why you've been brought here today." He pauses. "It seems a ring that's been in Mayor Smith's possession is being used to control the demons. The only way to get it back to where it belongs is either by crossing the Atlantic and somehow entering the UK, or..."

"Crossing the Atlantic?" Cassandra interrupts. "With who? The pirates that ferry the refugees around? If we even survived the voyage and got to land, which is totally unlikely, we'd just end up being turned away. Or worse."

Mr. Khan nods. "I realize that, which is why we need the seven of you to get to the Place-in-Between and leave the ring there."

My blood freezes. For a moment, the room spins around me.

"You want me to go back down there? Are you serious?" Vomit rises in my throat for the second time today, and I swallow it back down. It burns my insides. I fight the nausea that follows.

Mr. Khan nods, his face solemn and serious. "I'm so sorry, Jade. This is the last thing I want you to have to face. I can't imagine what it will be like for you..."

"No, you can't," I snap. "That's why I'm not doing it.

There's plenty of Seers who can do this with Jasmine. Seers who didn't lose years of their life in that place."

Jasmine glances over at me with a look of shock, but I think that's more her surprise at me talking back to Mr. Khan in front of her and everyone else, rather than my reaction. I know she felt — at least partly — what happened to me today. She asked me if I'd sensed anything really weird as soon as she arrived home with Mr. Khan.

I lied and said no. Stupid decision, because she knows I'm lying. I'm just not ready to tell anyone about what happened. Maybe that's because I'm not one hundred percent sure of what happened myself.

I got home minutes before Mom woke up. To say I was lucky is a huge understatement. My clothes were berry-stained, covered with dusty dirt and dried leaves, and my hair was a tangled mess. I'd just managed to shove my pole back underneath my bed and change my clothes when she came out of her bedroom.

"You're up early," she said with a sad smile. "Your body needs sleep, with everything going on."

"Couldn't sleep," I muttered, giving her a hug. What I wanted at that moment, more than anything else, was to rest my head against the warmth of her terry-clothed chest like a baby. If I could've had one wish at that moment, it would have been to turn back time, to turn it back to before the Earth was being destroyed, before I was taken, before Dad died….

Before whatever happened today.

A big part of me feels like it was my fault. I went out, alone, early in the morning, into a very secluded part of a pretty empty park with a boy I'd only met once before for a few minutes.

And I'd wanted — at least at first — to be with him. Then I didn't, though I can't remember why.

And though it felt like the images playing in my mind had lasted for hours, it turned out only minutes had passed when I came to.

I sat up, disoriented and alone, amongst squished berries that stained the towel like blood. My mind felt like I'd just been through some crazy shock therapy. I tried to piece together what had just happened to me.

Why had Seth left? Maybe I'd had some sort of seizure, something to do with the trauma of my abduction and my time in the Place-in-Between that was triggered by his kiss. Maybe that explained the strange visions.

If that was the case, I don't blame him for splitting. For all I know, I could've been foaming at the mouth, eyeballs rolled back into my head like two boiled eggs that had just been popped out of their shells … yet something tells me that wasn't really the way things played out.

"Jade?" It's Lily. She tucks a strand of her black hair behind her ear and leans toward me, her face a mask of concern. "Are you okay?"

"What?" I ask, quickly noticing that everyone is staring at me with the same worried expression.

"You totally zoned out on us," Jasmine answers. "You're so not okay." She turns to Mr. Khan. "How can we possibly try to get the ring back to the Place-in-Between tomorrow morning when she's like this?"

"How about we don't talk about *me* as though I'm not even in the room? Didn't you have more than enough time to do that when I was gone all those years?"

Jasmine's eyes widen with hurt. She opens her mouth and then swiftly closes it again.

"All right, all right. There's more than a few of us here who are exhausted beyond belief, so let's just be a little more civil," Mr. Khan says. "We have no choice but to do this tomorrow. If it were feasible, I'd say we try tonight. However, after the events of last night, you need to sleep. Especially Jasmine and Eva. We need to keep in mind that the longer we have the ring, the more dangerous it is. Remember, the demons are on this side, walking the Earth, and that means, ring or no ring, they will need to feed. With no one controlling their actions or their source of food, it could mean random attacks on people at any time — day or night. And predators always attack the weakest prey. That means children, babies, the physically disabled, the elderly …" He trails off. "You get the idea. Thus, tomorrow at the break of curfew in the morning, we meet at King Station. Sharp. Try to avoid being caught on camera by drones, if you are able to. I'm sending all seven of you and a guide."

He stops speaking and looks around at each of us.

The classroom door opens. Ms. Samson stands in the doorway for a moment, leaning on her cane, her painfully thin body silhouetted by the late afternoon light filtering down from the skylights in the hallway.

"And I don't think I need to remind you that under no circumstances do we want to lose a pair of twin Seers whilst you are down there," she says as she makes her way to stand beside Mr. Khan. Her lips are pressed tightly together, and concern radiates from her deeply lined face. "This needs to be done. I met with Noni and Mr. Jakande earlier today. I believe we can trust them. And truly, we have no other choice."

"Why seven of us?" Lily asks. "It seems like a lot."

Ms. Samson nods. "The number has power. Significance. We feel you're safer as Seers in that configuration at the moment. According to what we've learned over the last twenty-hours, the veil between the two worlds is thinning. The boundary between the Place-in-Between and our world has never been so weak. This is a very dangerous time."

The next half hour is spent showing us where the ring needs to go and how London's Roman Wall has changed over time. After all, we have no guarantee what time period we'll end up in … if we can get there.

As everyone's leaving, Mr. Khan calls me over. Jasmine stops in the doorway as well.

"Go on, Jasmine. Wait in the hall," he says. "This will be quick."

She gives Ms. Samson and Mr. Khan a curious look but steps into the hall and out of sight without another word. It's pretty unlike my sister not to have some sort of witty comeback or smartass remark, especially with Mr. Khan. She must really be exhausted.

I walk over and Mr. Khan pulls a chair out for me before taking a seat himself. Ms. Samson refuses his offer of a seat with a firm shake of her head.

"I'm going to make this short and sweet," he begins. Each word is clipped. He's tired and on edge, and his words are cold and hard — like diamonds on ice. "I'm sorry about what happened to you. I'm sorry you were abducted and spent those years away from Jasmine and your mother. Hell, I'm even sorry your father died before that, because you were just a kid. But make no mistake, you're going down there tomorrow. You're going down there because our world is spinning out of control, and you and I and the rest of the Seers might just have a chance to make things a tiny bit better. We need to ensure that Smith and Mr. Jawad can't keep using the demons for their own purposes. And we need to be sure no one else can either."

"I didn't mean what I said earlier," I whisper, my cheeks burning. A tear slides down my face. "I don't know what's gotten into me."

"Well, whatever it is, sort it out. Because your sister needs you. We all do," Ms. Samson says, leaning heavily on her cane. "Now go to her."

# JASMINE

Sleep. I don't think I've ever wanted or needed anything more, and yet it totally evades me. Every cell in my body screams with exhaustion, and yet I'm wired. My brain spins like a washing machine. I glance over at Jade's empty bed. It's only 5:00 p.m., so obviously I don't expect her to be in there, but the emptiness strikes me hard nevertheless. I blink back tears. Why do I feel something is tearing us apart, something dark and much bigger than both of us could ever imagine?

When I do fall asleep for a few brief and fitful moments, I have a strange dream about a black widow spider. I'm trying to save it as it dangles over a cliff, hanging on to a single thread from its web. Desperation fills my chest. The spider is screaming at me to save it from the wind that wants to snatch it and smash it against the rocks. And its screams sound incredibly human.

It sounds like Penelope.

I lean over the edge, the wind pushing at my back. For

a second I consider walking away, but then I remember that I'm a Seer. I'm super strong. I can do this. If I can fight demons, I can save a little spider. Sunlight glistens off its black shell of a body, shimmering and dancing out at me.

The wind picks up, and for a moment I'm thrown off balance, and the little spider screams louder as she twists on the thread, the red skull-like shape on her belly flashing at me. There's not much time, so I take a deep breath and reach out.

I've got her.

The spider's screaming stops. Tiny legs tickle the palm of my hand as I step backward, away from the cliff's edge.

"You're finally safe," I whisper.

And that's when the spider rears up and sinks her fangs deep into the flesh at the base of my thumb.

I bolt awake and look at the new video watch Mr. Jakande gave me. The fear was that Smith would be able to track me with mine and find both me and the watch, so Mr. Jakande vowed that he'd dispose of it in such a way that the watch, and the personal data I've got on it, won't be easily found. I hope he's right.

Seven thirty. Though still aching with fatigue, I'm also shaking and sweaty from the nightmare and need to move. I throw my bathrobe on over my pajamas and head down the hall to the living room. Jade's reading something on her tablet, and Mom's asleep, her head leaning back against the sofa.

Absently, I rub at the palm of my hand. Even though it was just a dream, I swear I can still feel the puncture wounds from the spider bite.

Jade looks up at me and gives me a tired smile. "Hey," she says, keeping her voice low for Mom's sake. "You should be sleeping."

I shrug and plop myself heavily down onto our velvet armchair. "Can't sleep. Guess there's too much on my mind with everything." I pause, biting at my bottom lip nervously. "Listen, I know you've taken a lot of shit because of some things I've done lately …"

"That's putting it mildly," Jade murmurs, though there's no real edge or anger in her tone.

"Yeah, well, I am sorry. Really sorry. I don't want all of this stuff Smith has me doing and my bad decisions to continue to affect you … and others. I'm super sorry you have to go tomorrow. In fact, I'm feeling pretty sorry for all of us who are heading there, but you most of all. I love you and wish there were some way Mr. Khan would just excuse you."

"Protector's orders. But you know and I know this is way out of Mr. Khan's hands. Guess I have to face my demons," Jade says with a bitter laugh. "Literally."

"What do you think about the fact that this Uriel chick is coming with us? To guide us?"

Jade raises an eyebrow at me. "You mean Raphael's sister?"

"Yeah. Why did Mr. Khan pick her? Do we even need a guide?"

Jade puts her tablet down, leans forward with her elbows resting on her quads, and gazes at me. "You mean why isn't Raphael coming with us again?"

"Well, that too." My face burns. She's read my mind.

Jade leans back in her chair and rests a hand on her stomach. "I don't know. Maybe he's busy. And we need a guide. My memories of the Place-in-Between are gone. Wiped clean. And I don't exactly think you, Jade, or Lily are experts on it. Raphael was a huge help. I suspect we need Uriel in the same way."

"Something's wrong," I say.

Jade sits back and places her hands across her belly. "In case you hadn't noticed, there's a ton of things wrong: climate change is destroying the world and our food supply; demons are roaming the city at night and actively hunting Seers; if the world's greatest cities aren't destroyed or in the process of being destroyed, their mayors are executing people and essentially establishing dictatorships. Yeah, I'd say there's a load the size of an elephant poo that's wrong."

"You know I don't mean all of that, though," I say. "There's something wrong with you. Or us. Physically. Something's different."

Jade shrugs. "I think we're both pretty exhausted after last night. And it scared everyone to death, especially Mom, when you were kidnapped. I mean, I've been irritable and feeling a bit fluish the last few hours. Probably just my period coming or something."

"Maybe," I say. "I'm going to head back to bed. God

only knows what we're going to have to face tomorrow." I don't remind her I know she's not due to have her period for at least another week.

"You've got the ring, right?" Jade asks.

I nod and fish a silver necklace out from under my pajama top. The ring hangs from the centre of it. Since we've been back in Toronto, it's felt like an ordinary ring.

"Let's hope the demons can go at least one night without feeding," Jade says. "Or that they feed on animals, rather than humans."

"I don't know if I believe in hope anymore," I whisper as I turn and walk back toward our room.

# JADE

We're not ever supposed to run the tap, but I can't think of any other way to mask the sound as I vomit over and over again into the toilet. I'm on my knees, clutching the cold rim of the bowl. This has to be the flu. Or my nerves going haywire. Whatever it is, I swear I just puked up a lung.

I stand, legs shaking like Bambi on ice, and flush the toilet. Then I brush my teeth and splash cold water on my face.

*How can I possibly do this today?*

Maybe Jasmine's right. I'm not okay. And I'm certainly not okay to face the dangers waiting for us in the Place-in-Between. But there's no way I'm going to let her, or Mr. Khan, or the other Seers know it.

I grab the side of the sink and look up at my reflection in the mirror. I'm definitely paler than normal. Maybe some chicory or mint tea will help.

Jasmine is up already. Her pole is propped against the wall beside the kitchen table. She's sitting, eating some dried toast, and she looks nervous, which makes me feel a little bit better.

She looks up at me and smiles. The skin around her lower eyes is puffy, and it makes me wonder how much sleep she actually got last night. "There's a pot of chicory on the stove. Are you feeling better?"

I nod. "A little. My stomach is still a bit off."

I manage to eat a bit of dry toast with my chicory. Both Jasmine and I are mostly silent during breakfast. Mom comes in about fifteen minutes after me, pours herself a mug of chicory, and then immediately bursts into tears.

"Why my girls? Why do you have to be given this burden of saving the world?" she says, slamming her mug down so hard that brown liquid spills over the edge and onto the worn countertop.

We both jump up to comfort her.

"It's going to be fine. We'll be back before you know it," Jasmine says. "I promise."

I raise an eyebrow at Jasmine from over Mom's shoulder. There's no way we can make that promise, and she knows it. I think we've deceived Mom enough in the past. It's time to be honest. We owe her that much. There's no guarantee we'll even make it back.

We finish eating, fill our water bottles, grab our poles, and head out the door after another bone-crushing hug from Mom. I didn't want to let her go and really hope she didn't sense the terror wracking my body when I did.

The morning air makes me feel like I've just stepped into a massive convection oven. My stomach somersaults uncomfortably, and for a moment I'm afraid I will puke all over the sidewalk.

The walk to King Station takes us about twenty minutes at a fast pace. More than a few times, tsunami-sized waves of nausea wash over me, and by the time we reach the others, I'm soaked in sweat and noticeably shaking again.

The others are already waiting when we arrive. Six sets of eyes regard me with concern and sympathy as we approach. No one says a word, though, likely due to my bitchiness yesterday.

Except one person wasn't with us yesterday. Uriel. She's incredibly tall and thin, with skin and hair so pale, it's practically translucent. I wonder how she can even be out in the sun without full body coverage.

She regards me coolly. "You're not well, Jade," she says. "We need to reconsider your joining us today."

I hate the way she says "we." *We're* not reconsidering anything. If I don't go, it'll be because I've decided it's not a good idea, not anyone else. Including Uriel. But she's just said exactly what everyone is thinking. I know it.

"I'm fine," I say. "It's just a bit of nerves. After all, no one else here has lost years of their life to this place. My reaction, I'd say, is pretty freaking normal." I raise my eyes defiantly to the others.

"Whatever. We need to get on with things," Cassandra says. "Mr. Khan wanted us to stay off the radar as much as possible this morning, so standing around isn't exactly the smartest move."

Jasmine looks at me as we turn to head down the subway steps. "I know what Mr. Khan said, but you don't need to do this," she whispers.

"Yeah, I do," I reply, grasping my pole tighter. "I need to do it for a lot of different reasons, the most important being that you'd be a lot weaker down there without me, and you know it. You went to the Place-in-Between once before to come and get me. It's my turn to face my fears and go down there for you."

# JASMINE

I watch the back of Uriel's head as we descend the first set of stairs toward the subway platform at King Station.

First impressions? Physically, she's very different than Raphael. Her white-blond hair shimmers, even though there's not much light down here, and I watch her long, thin, skinny jean-clad legs take the steps two at a time. Her personality seems to be nearly as cool as her dress sense. So far, I'm not impressed.

The ring hangs heavily from my neck this morning. It's as though I ate four dozen doughnuts last night and drank buckets of milkshakes. This heaviness is a new thing, and I have no idea what it might mean.

I look over at Eva. Her face is partially hidden by her hood. I'm pretty sure the others don't even know about her scars. If she's not wearing her hoodie up, she wraps her scalp in bright, colourful headscarves. I want to tell her it's okay, that we've all been through some pretty heavy stuff and will understand. She's also the only one of us without her twin. I wonder if that makes her think about her sister and what happened to her even more right now. She's staring intently down the subway tunnel, as if she's willing the train to arrive.

"Oh, my god," Vivienne says. I turn toward her and see she's staring at the massive computer screen on the wall, where a 3D holographic breaking news clip is playing. Red lettering flashes across the bottom of the image.

*Toronto is on high alert. Repeat. The city is on high alert.*

The news broadcaster is young and pretty, her gleaming white teeth offset by a hijab the colour of rubies. Beads of sweat dot the chestnut skin of her forehead. The perspiration betrays her emotional state; it's the only crack in her picture-perfect broadcasting facade.

But it doesn't take long to see why she's feeling more than a little apprehensive.

Images flash across the screen of bodies, dismembered with bloody, steaming intestines strewn across the sidewalk and onto the brown, dusty front lawns of several Toronto homes.

"Shit," Cassandra says. "It must be the demons."

I look at Uriel. She's here to guide us, isn't she?

*Toronto residents are advised to stay inside with their doors and windows secured. Initial eyewitness reports indicate that Mayor Smith's night workers, many dressed in their orange jumpsuits and wearing sunglasses to disguise their identities, are behind the savage attacks ...*

"What do we do?" I ask Uriel. "Either we need to get the ring back, or I have to use it to stop the demons from massacring half of Toronto. Right?"

*The mayor's office released an official statement just seconds ago: Based on very early intelligence-gathering, we believe the night crews were infiltrated by the CCT ...*

"If you used that ring now, it would be tantamount to suicide," Uriel replies. "You'd be hunted down as the mastermind behind the CCT or as some sort of witch. The government would find a way to make you disappear, and if you were lucky, it would be quiet and relatively pain-free. Then the ring would be back in the hands of those bent on using its power to destroy." She looks over her shoulder at the stairwell and escalator behind us. "The subway system is going to be shutting down, if it's not shut down already, but it doesn't mean you can't still get to the Place-in-Between." She's incredibly composed, considering everything that's happening. "Not only are we underground, but the worlds are collapsing, coming closer together ... getting thinner. It's easier now to flip between the two." She pauses. "And more dangerous."

*This latest act of barbarism demonstrates that they will use whatever means necessary to destroy this great city. They want us to be consumed by ashes, just like Los Angeles was ... and then the abundant, safe water supply of our city will be in the hands of those who support refugees and criminals ...*

"What's that?" Eva asks, cocking her head to one side and pointing farther along the darkened tracks.

"What's what? " Amara asks, coming up beside Eva. She follows her gaze into the tunnel.

And that's when I hear it. There's a low buzzing sound, and then a series of tiny lights that I'd thought were signals for oncoming trains grow increasingly larger. Drones.

"Grab hands," I say. "We need to get to the Place-in-Between."

Everyone secures their poles under their armpits and then links fingers. I make sure I'm hanging on to Jade with my right hand.

"Anyone who has been there, you need to visualize something you saw when we were there. Anything," I say, as I close my eyes. "Everyone else, try to clear your mind."

*Evacuate the station at once. Repeat. This is a Toronto and RCMP police announcement. A complete evacuation of all TTC vehicles and stations is in full effect immediately.*

I try to push the announcement out of my consciousness and focus on my memory of the Thames River instead. An image of the swirling water around our boat as the ferryman guided us toward London Bridge drifts into my mind. I hear the gulls and can almost smell the salt water, the fish, and wafts of human feces….

The buzz of the drones is getting louder. It's like we've angered a field full of wasps. They're coming toward us. We're on camera for certain now. Mr. Khan's not going to be happy about that….

I need to refocus, to force what's happening in the here and now, in real time, out of my mind. Pushing the drones out of my mind, I concentrate on my memories of the Place-in-Between, of London….

A wave of vertigo sweeps over me. I feel like I'm falling. It's that same sensation that sometimes happens just before sleep; just before I slam back awake on the safety net of my mattress.

Boots on stairs. Yelling. Chaos. It sounds far away. And yet I know it's happening in Toronto — in the station.

"There they are," a male voice shouts.

"You need to step away from each other," someone else says. There's a definite threatening tone to his words, but his voice is fading, being replaced by another sound: a sound that is almost soothing. Like tap-dancing, but slower, more rhythmic.

"What the hell…?" It's the first male. "Are you guys seeing this? Are you seeing what I'm seeing?"

"Let go of each other, or we shoot!" a different voice chimes in. "Drop your hands! This is your only warning."

"Back off!" Eva's shouting now. "Don't come near us." She's let go and stepped away from the circle. Though I wasn't holding her hand, I know she's gone because we've lost some of our focus, some of our power. Her voice reaches me from somewhere to our right now … I think she's moved toward the stairs.

"We need to stay touching," I say. "Think of London. Do not think of anything else."

*Like getting shot …*

There's another shout. The sound is guttural; it's the cry of a warrior. It's Eva.

A sudden pulling sensation makes me feel like a spider caught in the suction of a vacuum cleaner. The rhythmic tapping becomes louder as the air around me changes and shifts. It's colder, almost wet. I open my eyes, but everything is dark and hazy.

Slowly, the darkness shifts and my eyes begin to make out the shadowy figures standing with us in the alleyway.

One thing becomes very certain, very fast. We're not alone.

# JADE

We're in the Place-in-Between. Before even opening my eyes, I know I'm back. It's the damp that does it. The heavy, moist air closes in around me like a blanket, making my clothes feel clammy. I shiver uncontrollably. My legs are unsteady, even though I'm leaning against something solid. I reach behind my back. My fingers touch wet brick. There's a soft rain falling through the yellow haze of the dimly lit street about twenty feet in front of us.

Funny how I couldn't remember much about the Place-in-Between when I returned to Toronto, but as soon as I'm back here, it's as familiar as my own bed. Almost as if I never left.

I look down at my clothes. I'm in a long, wide skirt that skims the ground. I reach down. The edge of the fabric is wet. I'm also wearing boots that pinch at my feet and wool stockings.

"'Allo, gells. You all right?"

I snap my head to the left. It takes a few seconds for

my eyes to adjust and take in the figures walking toward us through the evening fog. There's three of them, the one who just spoke and two following closely behind. Problem is they're between us and the arched entrance of the alleyway. Behind us lies what looks like a closed-in cobblestoned area. If we go that way, we're trapped.

There's no choice. We move together toward the figures. It's clear all six of us are a bit disoriented, and the thick, yellow fingers of fog that wrap themselves around everything here aren't helping to clear things. I feel like I've just been jolted awake from a long nap and am still hovering in that place just between waking and sleeping. A place that's somewhere between reality and dreaming.

It's impossible to see their eyes. Impossible to know if these are lost spirits or demons. I take a deep breath. My nostrils take in a heavy stew of smells: human feces, the rotting carcasses of stray cats and dogs, and the stench of fish mingled with heavy pollution. The smell of death and blood hangs in the air like dirty laundry, but it doesn't seem to be coming from these men.

"You're not leaving us, are you?" the first man asks. "Not without giving us at least a peek at your strawberry creams?" He laughs, revealing a row of badly chipped yellow teeth.

I sigh with relief. He and his friends might be annoying and perhaps even drunk, but they're definitely not demons.

One of the other men slides in front. Droplets of precipitation glisten like tiny fairy lights in the thick, dark curls that frame his head. He winks in Cassandra's direction as he reaches into the inside pocket of his well-worn suit vest and pulls out a silver flask.

"Have a bit of a tipple with us, won't you? Then you can be off on your way." He takes a large swig from the flask, wipes the back of his hand across his lips, and then holds the silver container out toward Cassandra.

"No thanks," she replies, taking a couple of steps forward and to the side of them.

Jasmine walks up beside her. "Sorry, guys, but we need to get out of here. Things to do. Places to be, so if you'll just step aside…."

The first man sticks out his arm, effectively blocking Jasmine and Cassandra from moving forward.

"Listen, gell," he says, leaning in so that his face is only a few centimetres away from Jasmine's and his eyes level with hers, "you and your pretty mates will be giving us a kiss and a bit of a feel before going anywhere. Understand?"

The rest of us rush forward to stand behind Jasmine and Cassandra just as my sister reaches out, grabs the man's arm, and with the speed of a gazelle, twists it behind his back in one fluid movement.

"How's this for a little feel? Do you like that?" Jasmine asks, her eyes narrowing. "And by the way, you stink like a pile of rotting dog shit. Have you ever brushed those yellow stubs you try to pass off as teeth?"

The man roars in pain, his face contorting into a Halloween mask of fury. Her fingers sink into his flesh. He's a lost soul, which makes the molecular composition of his body much less dense than ours. It also makes Jasmine's grip on him weaker than it would be on a regular person. It's a bit like holding onto a sausage made of Playdough.

A look of confusion sweeps across his face as he struggles against her. The man's two friends spring into action, each of them grabbing one of Jasmine's shoulders to pull her off.

Lily and I leap at the men. I push one of them up against the alley wall and pin him against the damp brick while pressing my pole into the thick flesh of his doughy neck.

"We'll be leaving without you getting a feel or a peek at anything," I say, hoping each of my words sound as full of danger as the growl of a rabid animal. "By the way, if you make even the smallest move as we go, my pole will be shoved so far into your body, you'll be gagging on it."

His eyes widen. "I bet you lot are the Ripper," he says, spittle dropping from his lips into his beard. I can feel him shaking, though I don't know if it from actual fear or adrenaline-fuelled anger. "I reckon there's no madman — it's actually you and your deranged mates 'ere running amok around here, tearing those poor women to shreds and leaving their steaming insides all over the place. Otherwise you wouldn't be out here. Though travelling in a pack is safer than alone, that's for sure."

My grip on the man loosens for a moment. "What are you talking about?"

"See? Feigning ignorance. Makes me all the more suspicious of you. The murders have been all over the papers. As well as Jack the Ripper's letters to the rozzers."

"The rozzers?" Amara asks. "Don't you speak English in England?"

The man stares at us in disbelief. "The coppers, the rozzers. There's not a soul in London that doesn't know about it." His eyes narrow. "But no one's said it has to be a man murdering them women. It could be a woman … a strong woman or two … or six."

"Where are we and what is the date?" Lily asks. She's holding the man she grabbed by the neck. As she finishes the question, she tightens her grip on him, causing his eyes to bulge out from his reddened face like a goldfish that's been tossed from its bowl.

"Are you mad?" he sputters, his voice hoarse. "You're just off Miller's Court, Whitechapel. And this is the evening of November 9, 1888."

"London, right?" Lily asks, letting him go. He slides a few centimetres down the wall before regaining his balance and righting himself.

The man spits to the right of him, narrowly missing Jasmine. Wiping the back of his hand across his mouth, he stares at Lily. "Are you escaped from Bedlam? Made it across the river, did you? Mad as hatters, you lot are. Of course you are in London."

Harsh laughter erupts from the other men. "Be on your way. We won't be touching any of you, lest we catch your madness," one says, though I can read his mind. In reality, we terrify him. "Be forewarned, though, gells, you've just escaped one type of hell and come to another here in the East End."

# JASMINE

We emerge from the alleyway and into a busy street. The light is less dim here due to the flames that flicker and dance from within their glass cages. Soft rain continues to fall, covering everything with a layer of sooty moisture.

I look over at Jade. She's rubbing her left temple. Her face looks ghostly white in the lamplight. Something's wrong. A little worm of worry unfurls in my stomach. She's not well, and something tells me it's more than just your everyday flu.

"Are you okay?" I ask, walking up beside her and placing my hand on her arm. The fabric of her dress is heavy with moisture. "You did an amazing job with that lost soul guy back there. He was ready to pee himself. I guess there are sexist idiots literally *everywhere*." I throw her a lopsided smile, hoping to get one in return.

She smiles back weakly. "Thanks. I'm okay. Just a bit of a headache, that's all. Maybe I'm allergic to this hellhole of a place."

I want to tell her I know it's more than a headache. It feels like more than that to me. And I know it does to her as well. The pain is deeper, sharper. It's more a hammer to the thumb than a minor ache. I shouldn't have let her come.

"Do you think this might actually be hell?" Amara asks, looking around us, her gaze coming to rest on a pile of rotting garbage infested with rats the size of small dogs. As if understanding her, one of the largest rats rears up onto its hind legs and looks at her, its tiny eyes glistening scarlet in the light.

"It's limbo," I say. "The Place-in-Between. It's not paradise for sure, and I'd definitely say it's hellish for the lost souls down here who have to keep reliving tragedy and suffering, but I've never had anyone tell me it's actually hell. Not like the place some religions talk about."

Cassandra brushes a wet strand of hair away from her face and turns to look at Uriel. "Now what? Other than Jack the Ripper, this doesn't seem to be a very violent time in London's history." She looks around, wrinkling her nose in the direction of a group of drunk men. "Though the city stinks and is gross, that's for sure."

"We need to get the ring back to the Roman Wall," Uriel says. "The danger for us is the demons — they're sure to know we're here now. Also, your world and this one are so close together at the moment, they're almost overlapping. The beginning of time and the end of time are coming together. You're all able to move between the worlds more easily because of it, but so are the demons."

"I know this is the understatement of the year, but that really doesn't sound like a particularly good thing," I say. "So, let's just find this wall, put the ring there, and get out of here — ASAP. We need to get back to help Eva." I don't want to mention that it feels very different down here this time, more dangerous, and that I think we need to get my sister out of here as soon as possible.

The others nod. "I wonder what those bastards are doing to her," Lily says, her voice soft.

I can only imagine what is happening to Eva, if Smith needs to cover her ass. For all I know, she might try to make it seem like her little demonic crew is actually under the influence of the CCT while they feast on random Torontonians. Because now that I have the ring, there's going to be no one to stop them.

It also worries me that her terrorism goon squad saw us in transition. I have no idea what we looked like as we flip from our Toronto to the Place-in-Between, but I can guess it's pretty damn funky. Likely we fade like ghosts or something. Or maybe we become dancing molecules. Whatever happens, the drones were right there. Which means it's all on camera….

I'm not letting my mind go there. I need to focus on the here and now and not give in to any negative emotions. Especially fear. I know that will make the demons more powerful.

"You're right that it's not a good thing. And it seems that the dark powers, those of the Archons, are dominant down here because of it…." Uriel trails off, looking troubled. "We need to head down Commercial Street to Aldgate East to place the ring back in the Wall — as close to where Queen Boudicca put it as possible when she took her life. There's a church called Christ Church on Commercial Street. We can go use it to get back to your world after we put the ring in its proper spot."

Commercial Street is crowded and loud. Scattered amongst the boisterous drunken men and women are ragged beggar children. A few offer a shoeshine with cloths stiffened by layers of crusty dirt or try to sell other worthless trinkets. I bet most of them can pick pockets faster than a lightning strike.

Despite my walking quickly, the damp continues to chill me to my bones. I wish I had a warm jacket rather than the thin cloak that's wrapped around my head and upper shoulders. The entire place feels like a grave, like death.

"'Ello, gells," an older woman whispers as we pass by, her voice as raspy as a cheese grater. She's sitting on a wooden crate in front of a pub. The sound of smashing glass and off-key singing floats out of the pub windows.

Lily gives a half-hearted wave.

"Want a bit of a tipple?" the woman asks, holding a green glass bottle toward us with a shaky hand. "Fancy a bit of gin?"

There are a few men standing around her, leaning against the brick wall of the building. Most of them look completely drunk. One catches my eye. He's a lot younger than the rest, is slouched against the wall, and is so thin, his toothpick body looks like it could topple over in a strong breeze. A bridge of freckles covers his narrow nose and spills across his cheeks. The thing I notice immediately is the way he's watching Jade. Intensely. It's like she's the only person in the world. And it's creepy.

Lily, who's standing closest to the woman, wrinkles her nose. The woman reeks of alcohol. She better hope no one lights a match around her, or we'll be watching an instant human fireball.

"No thanks," Amara says, pulling Lily backward by the elbow.

"Too posh, are you?" the woman hisses, lifting the bottle to her shrivelled lips. Liquid spills down the sides of her chin as she swallows mouthful after mouthful of gin or whatever cheap liquor is in the bottle.

"Let's go," I say, turning on my heel.

"Jasmine," the woman says, her voice crackling like a campfire. "They're coming for you. We're all coming for you."

The words hit me like a fist to the gut. I gulp at the damp air, my chest tightening with fear. Though the intensity of the feeling lasts only a few moments, I know it's enough — especially since it's me feeling it and sending the vibes of terror and shock into the Place-in-Between.

The woman begins to laugh. Her laughter crackles like a campfire, fracturing the night air.

"Soon there will be nowhere to hide. You're the fox. They've got your scent."

*Is she a demon?*

As if in response, the ring begins to pulsate from the chain around my neck. It's a reminder that at least for now we're safe down here because of it. I can control the demons … until the ring goes back into the wall, that is.

*Is putting the ring back even a good idea? After all, how will it help us, the Seers, if we get rid of the one thing that can keep us safe — the one thing that can stop the monsters that are hunting us for our souls?*

"Ignore her. We need to keep going," Uriel says, interrupting my thoughts. She motions us to follow her with an abrupt wave. Her blue-grey eyes narrow as she glances over her shoulder, her gaze coming to rest for a brief moment on the skinny, freckled guy.

I check him out one last time. He looks like he's not more than a couple of years older than us at the most.

Jade. I want to keep her close to me. If her health declines any more, she's going to be in a huge amount of danger once this ring is put back.

*If I put it back. After all, how much do I know about Noni and Mr. Jakande? How much does Mr. Khan know?*

*And what if they can't be — or shouldn't be — trusted?*

I look over at my sister, and my heart leaps into my mouth. She's staring at the skinny guy like she's hypnotized. Or in love.

# JADE

My hair stands on end, electrified by the shock of seeing him. How can he be here — here in the Place-in-Between?

I take another look, and that's when he looks up, his eyes glistening with recognition when he sees me. That inviting smile dances across his lips again.

*He's not surprised to see me.*

How can he possibly be here? And more importantly, why isn't he having a heart attack from the shock of seeing me in this place?

After all, as far as I know, humans — the regular kind — can't survive here at all. Even Seers with souls will start to fade eventually. I believe the only reason I was able to survive for as long as I did was because my soul was still on Earth, in the Ibeji doll Lola owned.

I look over at Seth again. He's still staring at me. That familiar longing, the feeling of wanting — no, needing — to reach out and touch him floods my body. Then it hits me: if Seth is here, that means he's not human either. Especially considering the way he's casually hanging with the local lost souls and possible demonic entities … like he's right at home.

*He can't be a Seer because he's a boy. And he's not demonic, so …*

"Jasmine," the woman says. Her use of my sister's name jolts my attention from Seth.

*How can she possibly know Jasmine's name?*

She lifts her hand and points a bony finger at us. "They're coming for you. We're all coming for you," she says, her voice trailing off into a phlegmy giggle.

I look over at Jasmine. She's chalky white. Fear crosses her face like an Olympic sprinter for a moment before she regains her composure.

"Soon there will be nowhere to hide. You're the fox. They've got your scent."

There's a sharp intake of breath from Lily.

"Ignore her," Uriel says to Jasmine as she turns to walk away. But just before she does, her gaze falls on Seth. He returns her stare, the corners of his lips slowly reaching upward into a smile. It's not the teasing, flirtatious smile that he always gives me. Though it indicates familiarity, it's also cold and menacing. It's the smile of a snake.

Still, every cell of my body fights walking away from Seth. I want to stay on this dark and rainy street with him, even though my mind is screaming that the danger here is beyond anything I've encountered before.

"Come on." It's Jasmine. She's at my side, linking her arm through mine and steering me away, her face a mask of concern. "Weird question, but do you know that guy?"

Instinctively, I pull my arm out of hers. "I'm fine. I can walk myself. And I have no idea what you're talking about. What guy?" But even as the lie tumbles from my mouth, I'm not certain I've got the willpower to walk away from Seth.

Jasmine raises an eyebrow. She knows I'm not being honest. "We're all going to start to weaken here soon, just like last time. You know that, right? Which means you'll be even weaker than the rest of us." She pauses, looking thoughtful. "We also won't have the ring to protect us on our way back to the church. As soon as it's back in the Roman Wall, it's open season on Seers."

We're walking faster now, and I find myself digging my fingernails into the palm of my right hand in order to stop myself from turning around to get one more look at Seth. The tug-of-war between my body and brain is intensifying.

Vivienne moves beside us. She nods discreetly toward some of the people on the street. "How many of them do you think are demonic?" she asks, keeping her voice low.

Jasmine doesn't slow her pace but does take a long, lingering look at the street around us. There's a group of women gathered together on one of the corners, making clear attempts to get the attention of men passing by. I guess this area of London was pretty popular for prostitution.

"It's hard to tell," she says. "Some must be, but the demons might also be hiding from us. I don't know about you, but this time down here feels different. Like it's more dangerous, more alive … though that sounds weird, I know, because nothing in this place is actually alive. Other than us."

She stops speaking as a couple of men pass by. One is dressed much better than the other. A sleek top hat is perched on his head, and a long, dark cape swirls dramatically around him. He stands out like a sore thumb from the poverty and grime of the street. The other man is walking directly behind him, his hands stuffed in his pockets, a cap pulled so low down on his forehead, it nearly rests on his eyebrows. Beneath his wide jaw sit shoulders that are nearly as wide as he is tall. He looks over at us with a dark scowl. Though he's certainly not a demon, deep hatred is reflected in his eyes.

"Look away," Jasmine says, grabbing my arm again. This time I don't resist. My headache is back and worsening with every step. Tiny lights dance into my line of vision like fireflies.

The man continues to look at us. He even makes a point of turning to watch over his shoulder as the distance grows between us. Eventually the yellow fog swallows him up into the shadows.

"I don't think he was demonic," Vivienne says, relief flooding her voice. "His eyes weren't like theirs."

Jasmine shakes her head. "No, he wasn't a demon. He was the Ripper. I heard his thoughts. He was imagining which of us he'd like to mutilate."

# JASMINE

"Oh my god," Vivienne says. "Jack the Ripper's *just* a lost soul? It seems to me that he's almost as evil as the demons themselves."

She's got a point. It confuses me that a soul like the one that just passed us, one that was so full of hate and violence, his energy nearly knocking the oxygen out of my lungs, could just be biding time in the Place-in-Between. But he is, and that means that the souls of some of the most violent, hateful figures from history might be walking around down here as well.

"I don't know," I reply. "Uriel mentioned something about darker places. Maybe there is another place where souls like that are supposed to be. If the barrier between our world and here is thinning, maybe the same thing is happening between here and that place."

Uriel turns onto a new street, her long skirt swishing behind her as she moves. It's just as busy and poor as the last one. She stops and motions all of us to come together. We huddle around her. Tendrils of yellow fog wrap around the dirty hems of our long skirts. It seems to be thickening around us like overcooked pudding.

"We're getting closer," she says, her pale face glowing otherworldly. "Once the ring is back in the wall, you will be safe in Hawksmoor's sanctuaries and able to return to Toronto. However, you'll need to make it back to Christ Church on Commercial Street. It's the closest sanctuary. You'll no longer be able to control the demons on the way there, and I believe they know that."

The ring is pulsating around my neck again like a beating heart. I look over at Uriel. Yeah, she's supposed to be our guide, but then Raphael was supposedly my guide and guardian as well, and he's pretty much completely ditched me. I don't care what excuse he uses. It wouldn't matter if someone told me to stay away from him — I still wouldn't. If I've really been somehow specially chosen for something, maybe I need to be a little more careful in who I trust.

"How could they possibly know that?" I ask, placing a hand protectively over the ring. We've been down here long enough that we should've seen some demonic presence. But there's been nothing.

"Just as we can guide you, there are beings that can do the same with the demons. They are the creators of the demons. The Archons." Uriel pauses. "And at least one is down here, amongst us, right now."

My heart skips a beat. "The Archons?" I say. "I've heard of them. Aren't they like the flip side of you guys?"

Uriel raises an eyebrow at me. "Flip side?" she asks, confusion edging into her voice. "A more accurate description would be that the Archons are our balance. Between the two groups we were supposed to ensure harmony prevailed on Earth: a balance of good and evil, if you like."

"Well, that obviously didn't happen," I interject.

"No, it didn't. And that's because the temptation to get involved with human beings is strong. For Angels as well as Archons." She stares hard at me. "I believe the demons here are being gathered to try to prevent your return home. You need to be very careful after the ring is returned."

"Do we really need to put it back? It seems like suicide if what you're telling me is true," I say.

"The ring's power is too great for any mortal to resist. Power corrupts. Mortals are too weak to resist using the ring for their own personal gain." She stops and looks at me. "You understand what it's like to desire something you know is forbidden … something that, should it come to fruition, would cause irreversible damage and destruction. Don't you, Jasmine? You know that's why I'm here with you right now, and not my brother."

My face burns. There's no cattiness in her voice. She's just saying it like it is. Which means what happened between Raphael and I is not a secret. I wonder if Uriel knows he visited me in the hospital and at the CCT warehouse. Was Uriel the one who told him to ignore me? Is she the reason he acted like I didn't exist when we were with the CCT?

We walk in silence for the next few minutes. Even the swishing of our skirts seems to echo through the fog that hangs around us like a curtain. It's now so dense, it's nearly opaque. Anything could emerge out of it and be nearly within touching distance of us before being fully visible.

Lily grabs my hand. Her flesh is clammy, and I can feel her fear seeping through the pores of her skin.

"I've got the ring," I whisper to her. "We're safe."

*For now.*

She leans over to me. "I just have this really bad feeling," she says, her voice cracking with emotion. "I'm trying not to be scared. I am. But I can't shake this feeling that we're in so much more danger than ever before."

# JADE

I catch pieces of the conversation between Jasmine and Uriel through the haze of pain I'm dealing with. Every time my feet hit the cobblestoned street, it feels like shards of glass are being rubbed into my brain, leaving little blood-filled cuts behind.

I can barely walk.

My sister wants to keep the ring. I know Uriel senses this as well. But it's their discussion about another type of supernatural being down here with us that sticks in my mind.

*Archon.* I've never heard the word before, yet somehow it sounds familiar. Seth isn't a demon, yet he can't be down here if he's not a Seer or a lost soul. And he's not a lost soul, because I've touched him. His flesh felt like mine.

*Which means he has to be something else. Something not human.*

"We're here," Uriel says, breaking into my thoughts.

She stops walking. A wall of grey stone sits in front of us, rising out of the fog to tower above us like a giant.

"Now what?" Cassandra asks, wrapping a threadbare shawl around her long, dark hair. "We leave the ring and just hoof it?" She looks around at us, her eyes serious. "Does anyone feel like it's suddenly become too quiet?"

I hadn't noticed, but she's right. I've been so busy just trying to function, to stay upright with this pounding headache, that I didn't notice how the people, the rhythmic noise of the horse-drawn carriages, and the bustle of conversation had all but disappeared.

"We need to get back as soon as we can," Uriel says, her voice full of urgency. She glances behind her shoulder into the fog that's closed in around us. "Jasmine, you need to go place the ring between the rocks. Look for a crack or crevice and be sure to place it as deep within the wall as possible."

Jasmine hesitates. It's only for a few seconds, but it's noticeable — at least to me. Then she walks toward the wall, her hands moving to the nape of her neck to unclasp the chain that holds the ring.

Amara leans over to me. "How are we even going to find our way back to this place with all the smog?" she whispers.

"Uriel will guide us back. That's what she's here to do." My voice is hoarse. Each word catches drily in my throat. The effort to speak makes me feel even weaker.

Amara frowns at me. "You're feeling a lot worse, aren't you?"

I open my mouth to answer just as Jasmine turns and begins walking back to us.

Something whizzes to the right of me in my peripheral vision. Amara's head turns in the same direction, her eyes following mine.

"What was that?" she asks, her voice trembling ever so slightly.

The words have barely left her lips when a black shadow emerges from the fog behind us.

Vivienne screams. Her pole clatters onto the slick skin of the cobblestones. Amara leaps blindly toward her sister, pole ready, her face contorting into a mask of fear.

It was impossible to see the demon until it was nearly on top of us.

And now it's hanging off Vivienne, its arms encircling her neck like a boa constrictor, fangs bared in a grim caricature of a smile.

Amara pauses. The demon lowers its head closer to the back of Vivienne's neck. There's no way Amara can attempt to decapitate the demon without seriously injuring, or worse, delivering a deadly blow to Vivienne as well.

Vivienne's eyes are wide with fear.

Jasmine runs to Amara's side. "Don't be afraid," she says. "Your fear will only —"

The sentence is cut short as the demon sinks its teeth into Vivienne's right shoulder. Her screams cut through the dense fog like a machete. A dark stain slowly spreads from under the demon's chin as Vivienne's blood seeps through the fabric of her dress.

The air around us is electric with fear. My head begins to thrum with pain once more.

"Get off of her," Amara screams. She drops her pole, leaps onto the demon's back, and begins pounding at its head with closed fists.

The demon doesn't react. Amara's blows appear to be doing nothing. It's strong. Stronger than any of the creatures we've encountered before.

Vivienne's head slumps onto her left shoulder. The whites of her eyes glow eerily out at us, boiled egg-like and vulnerable.

"The wall," Lily shouts. "They're on the wall!"

I look up. There are several black silhouettes running along the top of the wall, as well as at least one climbing through one of the holes in the small archways that I assume were placed there as windows of some sort. The first of the demons leaps to the ground with the grace of a cat and begins to gallop toward us.

And that's when I see him. He's standing just to the side at the wall, leaning against it in a way that seems almost relaxed. His slender frame is unmistakable. He smiles at me as he tilts his head to one side, taking in the action like it's nothing more than an entertaining movie with popcorn.

He waves at me.

There's no denying it. He's beckoning me to come to him.

# JASMINE

We're under attack.

"Let go. You're not helping her," I say to Amara as I grab around the waist. I pull her off the demon. She collapses against me, tears streaming down her face. She can't do this. There's too much fear. It's coming off her in waves. She knows Vivienne's life is draining away. But her fear and the Seer blood the demon is consuming is like a super protein shake for the creature. It's gaining power by the second.

I'm not even certain I can defeat it on my own now. But I'm not going to let Vivienne die without a fight.

"The wall!" Lily shouts. "They're on the wall!"

With one fluid movement, I slide my pole between the demon's chest and Vivienne's back and pull with every ounce of strength I have.

Out of the corner of my eye, I see Amara dive to retrieve her pole as another black figure races toward us, but I force myself to focus back on the demon in front of me.

My pole bends like a ballerina's spine as the demon resists. I know there will be a breaking point, and my first instinct is to give in, to salvage my pole.

There's a sucking sound like a boot being pulled out of thick mud as the demon releases its teeth from Vivienne's shoulder.

It twists to face me, two crimson lines trickling down from the corners of its cracked lips to its chin. Its flat black eyes glare at me.

The demon leaps, fangs bared. I'm knocked off balance as I scuttle out of the way but manage to hang on to my pole. My right hand slams onto the cobblestones, sending bolts of pain up my wrist and into my arm.

From somewhere to the right and just behind me I hear Cassandra shout, followed by the all-too-familiar wet tearing sound of a pole travelling through flesh.

I leap back to my feet just as the head of a demon rolls past. The acrid smell of copper fills my nostrils.

*How many of them are there?*

I've got no time to even look around to attempt a guess because the demon lunges at me again. This time it manages to grab my left arm, twisting it behind my back in one fluid motion. An audible snap, like a tree branch breaking in a strong wind, reaches my ears just seconds after the blinding pain shoots through my wrist. I yelp like a wounded puppy, tears flooding my eyes.

It's my left arm. But I still have my pole firmly in my right hand, which means I can fight…. I take a deep breath, wincing against the pain.

*But it's so strong. Stronger than any demon I've ever fought.*

I push down the internal voice that's encouraging my fear and swing at the demon with my pole. But with my left arm hanging like a limp balloon at my side, the result is beyond pathetic. My aim is completely off, and the pole collides somewhere around the demon's collarbone. It's enough to cause the demon to roar, but not enough to cause any damage.

Cassandra's suddenly beside me, her dress covered with bits of jelly-like demon flesh and deep red bloodstains. Beads of sweat glisten on her face, and her skin is red from exertion, despite the damp night air. She glances at my broken arm, her eyes widening with concern, just before she rushes forward to take a swing at the demon.

Her pole connects perfectly but sinks only a few centimetres into its neck.

With an audible grunt, Cassandra frees her pole. She turns her head toward me. "Stand behind me," she says, her words as rapid as gunshots. "You're too hurt."

The demon takes advantage of the moment and grabs at Cassandra's pole. She lets out a surprised cry before managing to close her hands around the end of it.

"We've got to get to Christ Church," Uriel yells from somewhere behind us.

*No kidding,* I think. But how are we supposed to go anywhere with Vivienne so injured, and when we're about to be the main course in a demonic feast?

I move in front of Cassandra and clasp her pole with my good hand just above where she's holding it. We're in a tug-of-war with a demon that clearly has the upper hand. Its pull is much stronger than our combined force.

Just as my fingers are loosening and about to give up their hold, there's a wet, squelching sound, and the demon's head topples over onto its right shoulder. Its grip slackens and Cassandra and I stumble backward before losing our balance completely and falling on top of each other on the cobblestones. The demon collapses on top of our legs a moment later, its head hanging like a yo-yo by one stringy bit of ligament.

With a disgusted grunt, Cassandra flips the corpse off us.

Wincing, I look up. Lily's standing above us, her pole slick with blood, one hand extended toward me.

"That's the last one, as far as I can tell ... for now," she says with a grimace as she helps me to my feet. The slightest movement makes my broken arm feel like it's on fire. "Uriel said we don't have much time to get to the church."

"Where's Jade?" I ask. In all the confusion, I've lost track of her. I try to push down my growing panic. The last thing I want is to strengthen any demons that might be lurking in the fog, waiting to pounce on us like a cat on a mouse.

"Right here. I'm okay," Jade says, emerging to the left of us from the fog. She spots my arm and rushes to my side. "What happened?"

I notice that her pole is clean, and she's remarkably calm, considering what just occurred here.

"The demon that attacked Vivienne managed to grab me…. Where is she?"

"With Amara," Lily says, her voice quiet. We walk together to where we left Vivienne after the attack.

Amara's cradling her sister in her arms as though she were a newborn. Tears stream down her face. The front of her dress is smeared red. Vivienne's eyes are closed, and her skin is as grey as the moon. Uriel stands beside them, her face a mask of concern.

"We need to go," she says. "NOW."

"I heard," I say. I crouch down beside Amara, taking my time. My balance is completely off because of my arm.

I touch Amara on the shoulder. "How is she?" I ask. I don't want to ask if she's still alive, but that's exactly what I'm wondering, and then I realize Amara's able to read my thoughts anyway.

"She's still got a heartbeat. It's really faint, but it's there," Amara replies, her voice barely a whisper. "I can feel that she's still here with us, but …" her voice cracks with emotion. "She's lost a lot of blood … I feel that she's going to let go soon."

"She's not," I say. "She's going to be fine. We'll get her back through, get her to the hospital…."

"No, we need to leave her and go," Uriel says, breaking into the conversation.

"We're not leaving her," I snap. "Where's your brother?"

I raise my head up to meet her gaze. Never before in my life have I wanted to slap someone like I want to slap this pathetic excuse of an angel.

She stares back at me, unflinching and silent. Her blue eyes are like emotionless chips of ice.

Anger surges through me. "Because you know what? He'd be able to help us. Which is a lot more than I can say for you. What use are you to us right now?"

"I speak the truth. I provide wisdom," she answers flatly. "My brother can't be here because of you. Could he have saved Vivienne? Perhaps. But that doesn't matter now. We need to go immediately, or all of you may perish."

Blood rushes to my face. It feels like everyone's eyes are boring into me now. Really, did Uriel pretty much just accuse me of causing Vivienne's death? She might as well have just called me a murderer.

I look back at Amara. "I can't carry her," I say, my face burning with a mixture of shame and anger. "My arm."

"That's okay. I'll do it. We can swap if she gets too heavy," Cassandra says, stepping forward. She takes a black elastic off her wrist and twists her long black hair into a loose bun. Squatting down, legs apart for stability, she motions to Amara. "Put her on my upper back," she says. "And then let's get out of here."

# JADE

Carrying Vivienne is definitely slowing us down. We're staying as close together as possible as we hurry along Commercial Street, both for safety and because of the dense fog. The street is still busy, but many of the lost souls seem more interested in drinking, singing, and arguing than paying any attention to us. It still feels odd being here, knowing I spent so many years of my life here and yet having virtually no memory of that time.

Uriel leads the way, her shorn, pale hair making it easy to follow her. She turns back every few minutes like a mother duck, making sure we're still behind her and out of danger. Impatience and confusion are etched into her face. We haven't seen — at least to our knowledge — any more demons since leaving the area of the wall. I think that's confusing her.

"How much farther is it? I think I'll need somebody to take Vivienne soon," Cassandra says, her face red with exertion. Streaks of sweat line her face, and the neck of her dress is drenched to the skin.

"We're nearly there. It's only about two blocks away," Uriel says, throwing the words over her shoulder without slowing her pace. Her manner is brusque, businesslike.

Cassandra stops, dropping onto one knee. "I said I need someone to take Vivienne," she says, annoyance edging her voice. This isn't directed at any of the Seers — instead she keeps her eyes fixed on Uriel, who ignores her.

"I'll take Viv," Amara says, her voice heavy with sadness. "I should've done that in the first place."

Cassandra looks away from Uriel and nods. "Are you sure? This has been hard enough on you."

"Yeah, I'm sure," Amara replies, bending down and gently brushing a hand along Vivienne's cheek. She draws her hand away suddenly, as though she's just touched a boiling hot stove. Her mouth opens, lips curving to form words, but no sound emerges.

"Are you okay?" Jasmine asks, putting her good hand on Amara's shoulder.

Nodding, Amara leans in close to Vivienne and puts three fingers to the side of her sister's pale throat. Tears well up in the corners of her eyes. Shaking, she crouches down.

"Put her on my back," she says as the tears spill through the dark lashes of her lower eyelids and down onto her face.

Cassandra raises an eyebrow questioningly at Jasmine as they place Vivienne onto Amara's back. She's clearly uncomfortable giving Amara this task when she's so emotional, but I think it would be cruel not to let her carry her sister.

Out of the corner of my eye, I notice that Uriel's already walking again. There's now about a ten-foot gap between us and her. She's definitely not making any Seer friends on this trip. Not that she seems to care, anyhow. As we hurry to catch up with her, I make sure to keep an eye on Amara. The strain of being down here is showing on all our faces, and I'm worried carrying Vivienne is going to be too much for her, both physically and emotionally. We're all ghostly pale now, and dark circles are beginning to stain the skin around our eyes. Uriel's right about one thing — we definitely need to get back.

It doesn't take long for Christ Church to become visible just ahead of us. The spire of the building towers above us, pointing toward the night sky like a giant's index finger out of the yellow glow of the fog.

"Vivienne's coming to," Lily says excitedly. She moves beside Amara.

"Wait!" Jasmine shouts as Lily reaches out for Vivienne's hand to support her.

And then I see why Jasmine shouted the warning. Vivienne's sitting up, her body moving as stiffly as a geriatric patient that hasn't walked in three months. Then she turns her head toward me, her eyes opening wide. There's not a glimmer of recognition in them, just a flat, deep darkness.

Vivienne's gone.

Lily turns her head toward Jasmine. It's only for a second, but it's enough.

"Get away from her!" I yell. "Amara, drop her! Put her down!"

The demon takes advantage of Lily being momentarily distracted to clamp its hand tightly around her wrist. Lily yelps in surprise as the creature leaps off Amara's back and lunges at her with the grace and fluidity of a wildcat. Both the demon and Lily tumble to the cobblestones in a frenzied heap.

Amara straightens and swivels around. Confusion sweeps across her face.

Cassandra grabs her. "She's gone. Vivienne's gone," she says, wrapping her arms around Amara's shoulders in a gesture that is likely intended to restrain as much as to comfort.

Jasmine steps forward, holding her pole above her head with her good arm, ready to strike. Her thoughts are easy for me to read. She's terrified, totally unsure of what to do, knowing she can't deliver a fatal blow to the demon without possibly killing Lily. And she's remembering Jamie Linnekar and how his energy or something was still present enough that she was able to connect with him before beheading him the night we were attacked. She's afraid Vivienne will experience some of the pain and be still aware enough, like a coma patient, to realize it's Jasmine dealing the fatal blow.

The thing is, we don't know how to expel demons

from the newly possessed. We've only been taught how to destroy the body.

The demon sinks its fangs into the fleshy part of Lily's upper arm. She shrieks with pain.

"Kill it!" Cassandra screams. "Don't let it take Lily as well!"

Jasmine glances up at all of us, her eyes wild with panic, then back down at the demon and Lily. She bites at the corner of her bottom lip and swings her pole.

The demon rolls out of the way fractions of a second before the pole crashes into the cobblestones beside its head, sending shards of bamboo flying. Lifting its mouth from Lily's arm, the creature roars in defiance.

Amara's face contorts with pain. Her mouth opens and closes soundlessly, tears spilling down her face. I can't imagine the feelings she's struggling with right now. The thing is, every one of those emotions is definitely going to be making this demon — a demon with half a Seer soul — stronger right now.

It's clear this isn't going to be an easy battle. The demon was already incredibly strong before it fully possessed Vivienne's half-soul. And yet I'm not scared. Reaching into my pocket, I fold the palm of my hand around the ring. It feels surprisingly warm against my skin. I won't use it unless I have to.

I rush forward to move beside Jasmine as the demon leaps up and grabs at her. There's no way she can do this with only one good arm. She quickly slides backward, just outside its reach.

"Run to the church!" I yell toward the rest of the Seers.

Lily manages to get to her feet, though she's unsteady. The sleeve of her dress is bloodied and torn.

"Vivienne!" Amara sobs as Cassandra leads her away by the shoulders. "Fight it, Vivienne." The words are full of hollow hope, though. She knows her twin is gone. There's an emptiness within the very core of Amara's being now. And that's because half her soul has been torn away. It makes me wonder what Jasmine felt when I was trapped down here and my soul was captive in an Ibeji doll.

"Get her out of here!" Jasmine shouts. She doesn't want Amara to see Vivienne's body being decapitated. But most of all, we can't chance this demon getting its hands on her. On it getting the shared soul of two Seers.

The demon draws its lips back into an ugly sneer. I spot the half-moon-shaped chip that Vivienne knocked out of the bottom of her left front tooth last year. We were in class and laughing so hard at some random joke that she hit her mouth on the glass bottle she was drinking from. Tears well up in my eyes. But this thing in front of me isn't Vivienne….

*I need to remind myself of this.*

And as if to confirm the thought, it charges at us again with the ferocity of a rabid dog. This time Jasmine connects with its neck. Her pole rebounds toward her, and though it knocks the demon back a foot or two, it leaves only a superficial red mark on its skin.

Jasmine looks at me, her face awash with panic. "I'm

not going to be able to do this," she says. "My arm … I don't have the strength or the aim."

I nod, grabbing the ring out of my pocket and cradling it securely in my fist. "Let me take care of it," I say. "Stand behind me."

# JASMINE

We should just run, just try to outrun this demon that's taken Vivienne's soul and is inhabiting her body. That way we'd at least have a chance at getting back to the others. There's strength in numbers, and being split means we're all at greater risk. It would definitely be the smarter decision, and unlike me, Jade is usually sensible.

That's why I can't figure out why she wants to stay and fight. Me, well, I want to get that demon out of Vivienne's body, even if she's still in there. But I'm well aware that my first instinct is often not the best course of action. Though the demon hasn't possessed her for long, Vivienne's lost a lot of blood. A lot more than I think anyone can survive losing, but I'm no doctor. She likely won't live, even if we find a way to drive out the demon without decapitating it. I just don't like the idea of some demon using her body as a house down here for the next few decades. And I don't think Vivienne would've liked that either.

The demon lunges at us again, and Jade slices through the air with my pole, using it like a baseball bat to catch the creature squarely across its abdomen.

*What is she doing?*

"Decapitate it," I say. She knows this is the only way to make the demon leave the body and to render it harmless. Why isn't she going for its neck?

Jade holds the pole up across her chest like a barrier as the demon swipes at it.

"Stop," she says. Though her tone is firm, it's calm — incredibly calm. Just like it was when we were at the wall.

The creature immediately freezes in place and tilts its head toward us as though waiting for the next command. I know that look. I've seen it happen with Mayor Smith's work crews and when I was in the climate-change refugee camp.

I turn to Jade. "You've got the ring," I say, my voice thick with accusation and disbelief. "Why would you take it? How could you do that when we've risked everything — and lost Vivienne — to come here and put it back?"

"I'll explain everything later. You questioned whether putting it back was right decision, too," she replies matter-of-factly. "Now stand back."

Before I have time to say a word, Jade walks up to the demon, holding my pole like she's a major league slugger in the last inning of the World Series. "Get out of her," she says through gritted teeth as she swings. The pole connects with the inert creature at the front of its throat, tearing open the skin and exposing what was once Vivienne's spine. A horrible cry rises from deep within the demon moments before Jade takes a second swing. This one cleanly severs the head, leaving it to thump to the wet surface of the cobblestones, closely followed by the body crumpling beside it in a lifeless heap.

I walk over to the head. Dark curls, damp from the effort of the fight, frame the ashy brown skin of the face. Vivienne's face. Her eyes are open and stare, unseeing, at London's night sky. The demon is gone.

Crouching down, I gently push closed her upper eyelids. "Rest in peace," I whisper. It feels so wrong to leave her body here, even if Mr. Jakande does know about the Place-in-Between and the risk we were taking coming here. My heart twists at the thought of telling him what happened down here.

Jade comes and stands over me. I straighten and stare hard at her. She's my twin, but suddenly I feel like there are things about her that I don't know at all.

"You could have saved her," I say, the words tumbling out of my mouth. "You could've commanded the demon to leave the body and her alone. She didn't need to be fatally wounded."

# JADE

"We need to get to the others. I really hope you did the right thing. Because I know what it's like to have blood on your hands," Jasmine says as she stands up.

I get it. My taking the ring must seem like a huge betrayal, like I've gone behind her back. And she's right that I could've told the demon to vacate Vivienne's body. The honest truth was that I didn't think of that in the midst of all the chaos, but I doubt that Vivienne could've survived, considering the amount of blood she'd lost. I know Jasmine is angrier with me than she's ever been, but there's no way I can tell her everything right now. The right time to explain everything will come.

The church is cavernous and silent as we enter. For a moment, I wonder if everyone else made it here safely. After all, they didn't have the security of the ring.

Then I hear a low whistle from somewhere at the front, near the altar. We scurry around the perimeter of the building, making our way toward the sound.

A second whistle. "Over here." The voice is unmistakably Cassandra's.

We reach the four of them within a few seconds. Everyone's huddled behind the altar. There's a low candle burning beside them.

"Is Vivienne…?" Amara asks, her voice quavering with emotion before she has the chance to finish the question.

Jasmine nods. "She's at peace," she says quietly.

"A demon attacked us when we first got in here, and Cassandra and I were barely able to fight it off," Amara says. "I think we're weakening with each loss and injury or something…." Her voice cracks again as tears spill down her cheek. She stares silently down at her hands.

"We need to get back. Period," Cassandra says, her voice thick with urgency. She's leaning against the altar, cradling Lily in her arms. "I'm not losing her. Not here. Not now. And not like this."

Jasmine and I quickly take a seat. "Let's do this, then," she says. Her worried eyes slip back to Lily. I know what she's thinking: Lily was conscious and walking when we left her.

Uriel holds her hand up, palm forward. "Not so fast. Things aren't the way they're supposed to be," she says, keeping her voice low. Her brows draw together in a frown. "The demon shouldn't have been able to come in here. All of Hawksmoor's churches should've been places of sanctuary from the demonic forces as soon as the ring was returned back to the wall."

Jasmine's eyes practically burn holes into me. She suspects the ring being taken from the wall has altered things. Maybe — but I don't believe that the bad guys and good guys are as neatly defined in all of this as she does. And with good reason.

"I'm not sure what it means," Uriel continues, "but getting back might not be as simple or straightforward as it should be. The membrane between worlds is very thin right now, which already made everything dangerous enough before this eventuality. All of you will need to really focus and stay unified in your vision when you shift through."

"I thought you said you were the wise one," Jasmine mutters.

"Can we just do this?" Cassandra snaps. "So we have a chance to save my sister."

She's right. We've lost enough — too much — on this journey down here.

We move until we're sitting in a circle. The cold stone floor of the church chills me to the bone. Cassandra lifts Lily's head so that it's resting on her shoulder. Lily's dark hair spills around her still face like a halo. Cassandra gently takes her hand.

"If we're all touching, we'll all get back together, right?" she says to no one in particular.

Uriel presses her lips together tightly but offers no answer.

"Close your eyes and think of Toronto and nothing else," Jasmine says to all of us as she takes my hand.

# JASMINE

I hear the demon just as the familiar, funky feeling of transitioning begins to hit me. I'm imagining Toronto, the skyline with the CN Tower jutting out from the surrounding buildings, our apartment in Regent Park, the water of Lake Ontario. My body begins to feel like it's floating. I'm no longer fully in either place....

Shuffling. A strange shuffling from somewhere in the middle section of the church reaches my ears. Panic floods my body. It could be a lost soul, but chances are ... I need to focus on Toronto. We need to get back.

*What happens if we stop shifting midway through?*

Will we all make it together? Or will the molecules in our bodies get scrambled like some science experiment gone horribly wrong?

*Maybe we can make it through.*

*Maybe not.*

More shuffling. It's closer but taking its time getting to us. Why?

Jade is the first one to break our chain of contact. I think she's going into the pocket of her dress for the ring. It's hard for me to tell because her thoughts are muddied ... which shouldn't happen to me as a twin.

Hopefully she's still holding on to Amara with her other hand.

# JADE

The ring. I need to get the ring out.

It's buried in a pocket in the skirt of this dress, which means breaking the circle to get to it. But it's that or possibly have a demon attack us while we're transitioning and weak from being down here too long.

The pocket is on my right side, which means I need to let go of Jasmine's hand to get to it. I'm going to make the time we're not touching as short as possible but still, I have no idea what breaking the circle will do as we shift back to Toronto. Hopefully nothing, or next to nothing….

The demon is getting closer, though it's taking its time. This strikes me as really weird, as it could've easily been on top of us by now and have taken total advantage of the fact that Lily is injured.

We're beginning to transition. I think about Toronto as the cavernous space around me suddenly feels like it's turning upside down, taking me for a ride with it.

I slip my fingers from Jasmine's and read her immediate surprise and concern.

Closing my hand around the ring, I begin pulling it out of my pocket when the entire place lurches to one side like a drunken elephant. Amara squeezes my hand tighter.

The air fills with a loud squealing that pierces my ears like a knife. There's a sudden stop to our movement and my head snaps forward and then back like I'm some kind of rag doll.

Then there's light. And noise. I look up and see the interactive plasma screen showing that we're on Line 1 between Union and King Station.

We're back in Toronto. Or at least Amara and I are. I don't see the others. Passengers are murmuring all around us. It seems we've come to a sudden stop in one of the tunnels, and people seem a bit more freaked out about it than usual.

"What's going on?" Amara asks from beside me. I look over at her. She's wearing the outfit she had on when we left: grey tank, ripped jeans, black high-top sneakers.

A middle-aged woman with wiry blond hair sitting on the other side of Amara stares intently at us. She leans over in our direction.

"Likely another security sweep. The police are still looking for the rest of them terrorists from yesterday," she says, her voice barely a whisper. She stares hard at Amara. "They'll be coming through this car any minute. Just to let you know."

"What terrorists?" Amara asks, confused.

The woman raises an unkept eyebrow at us knowingly. "Them teenaged girls … the ones that poisoned the first batches of water in the city and helped kill all them people." She pauses. "You know … the ones that looked a lot like youse and some of your friends," she says. "Your photos have been all over the news."

My heart leaps into my throat as the subway car doors slide open at the other end of train and a group of at least five heavily armed police officers in riot gear storm onboard, guns drawn.

# JASMINE

When I open my eyes, I'm greeted by an unfamiliar landscape. We're sitting on the edge of an elevated subway platform, but not like any I've seen in Toronto. For a moment I wonder if it's just a TTC station I haven't been to before, though that seems pretty unlikely.

The area around us is framed by tall buildings, and the platform itself is jammed full of people. All of them seem pretty interested in something happening on the train that's stopped, doors open, directly in front of us. It's painted red and blue with the letters DLR on it, not the colours found on any TTC transport or Toronto train. There's a river below us that is definitely not Lake Ontario, unless it suddenly narrowed while we've been away.

Cassandra is sitting on a bench just off to the side and behind me, still cradling Lily in her arms. Lily's softly groaning now and moving slightly. She's clearly coming to and in pain. I need to get her medical help but have no idea how.

A holographic display appears just above and to the left of the train. A slim woman with long, black hair and dark, almond-shaped eyes that seem almost too large for her delicate face begins to speak. She's got an English accent.

"Due to an incident at Canary Wharf station, there is congestion on the track, causing significant delays on the Docklands Light Railway trains to Cannon Street Station. We advise travellers to take alternate routes." She turns to face the other side of the tracks, the flowers on her long dress swirling with her. "A reminder that the current threat level for international terrorism in the UK is SEVERE." Turning back our way, she smiles, revealing a row of perfectly straight, paper-white teeth. "And as always, please mind the gap between the platform and the train."

A shared sigh of frustration ripples through the crowd.

An older man in a blue suit taps me on the shoulder. "I've already called 999, and I'm sure the transport police have as well," he says, the skin around his grey-blue eyes crinkling with concern. "Your friend must've hit something really sharp when the train stopped." He removes his tie. "You can use this as a tourniquet on her arm to stem the bleeding, if necessary."

I don't know much about men's ties, but it looks like a pretty expensive piece of cloth. "Thanks," I say as he passes it to me. "And for calling and stuff, too. Do you know what's happening?"

The man shakes his head. "No information's being given yet. Could be as simple as a jumper or as serious as a bombing or the threat of one." He cocks his head toward the two heavily armed police officers who are beginning to direct passengers toward the stairs at the end of the platform. "They clearly don't want us using the lifts, though," he says, his eyes drawing into a frown. "Guess it could be more serious than someone jumping somewhere along the line."

"Well, thanks again," I say. Taking the tie, I turn to go help Cassandra and Lily.

I see him at once. He's bent over Lily, his dark hair falling forward to partially cover his eyes as he examines her. There's something achingly familiar in the curve of his back, the way he nods as he speaks with Cassandra.

I'm suddenly shaking with trepidation, nervous to the point of nausea that Raphael will blow me off again. After all, being around me is breaking whatever orders he's been given. My focus should just be on Lily and why we're not back in Toronto, and finding out where Jade, Amara, and Uriel have ended up.

But it's not. Not fully — not the way it should be.

"Someone gave me this," I say to Cassandra, clearing my throat and sitting down beside her, all the while trying to avoid looking at directly at Raphael. "To help stem the bleeding."

"We need to try to get out of here," Raphael says. "She's still losing blood, but I need to help her without drawing too much attention. It's critical that we avoid detection here as much as possible. You don't have the proper identification." He glances around at the armed police officers, as well as a few drones flying back and forth.

"Where exactly is *here*?" I ask. I might as well find out now if Raphael is going to acknowledge that I exist.

He looks up at me, his eyes shifting from deep brown to a vibrant green. There's a softness in his gaze. Despite trying to push down my feelings, that familiar desire to touch him rises in me.

"We're in London, 2032. You've come through to here rather than Toronto," he replies. He keeps his voice low, I suspect, so that the commuters still left on the platform don't overhear us.

"We're back in our time, but not in Toronto? How could that have happened?" I ask. "And where are Jade, Uriel, and Amara?"

"In Toronto, I reckon," Raphael replies flatly. He glances at the officers again. At the moment they seem busy with a couple of drunken guys in their twenties who are refusing to hand over oversized cans of beer.

Raphael lays his hands gingerly over Lily's injured arm. She moans as his fingers touch her wound. Through the rip in the sleeve of her dress I can see the bloody gashes in her arm where the demon gnawed away at her flesh.

"I think know how it happened … how we came here," Cassandra says. "Lily was dreaming about London when she was unconscious. Her thoughts kept pouring into mine. They were so strong. Maybe because she thought it was the last place she was going to … to ever remember." Her voice wavers with emotion. "She kept thinking about Greenwich when we were last here. And I tried to push her thoughts down, but it was hard because I knew she was still with me because of them ... I guess I must've had London in my mind more than Toronto because of that as well."

"It doesn't matter what happened," I say. "We're here now and need to figure out how to get back." I stop and look at Raphael. "What were you talking about when you said we don't have proper identification?"

"Every Londoner needed to get microchipped at some point during the last six months as a means to keep climate-change refugees from sneaking into the city." He nods toward the drones and the police officers. "These guys are equipped with chip-detecting scanners, as are the drones."

I look over at the drones buzzing by us like hungry wasps. Lily is beginning to sit up. The colour is back in her cheeks, and her eyes are bright. Glancing down at the rip in her sleeve, I'm not surprised to see the skin underneath is perfectly intact and scarless, as if nothing happened.

"And if we don't have microchips?" I ask, not sure I want to hear the answer.

"You'll be taken to a Metropolitan police station and then likely to a detention centre on the coast. And those are pretty dreadful places," Raphael replies. "However..." He pauses, his eyes darkening.

"However what?" I ask.

"You were captured on video by the drones as you transitioned from Toronto. At the same time, several attacks took place in the city — including an attack on the water supply Smith distributed that day."

My blood turns to ice. "What does that mean?" I ask. "Because we obviously weren't responsible for any of that."

Raphael stares at me solemnly. "The truth can be manipulated, Jazz," he says quietly. "It can be manufactured. And Smith's forces obtained a confession from Eva. Under complete duress, of course."

"Duress?" I ask.

"She was tortured. Badly. But it means all of you are wanted as terrorists and for mass murder. The story has hit the international news. None of you are safe anywhere at the moment."

I stare at him. Clearly it's no longer just demons hunting us. I've witnessed Smith's plans on how to deal with anyone she perceives as a threat to her government. If we've been identified as terrorists, it's open season.

"Okay," I say. "What do we do now?"

Raphael looks around. "Get ready for the Final Battle. Get ready to fight and sacrifice in ways you never imagined possible."

# ACKNOWLEDGEMENTS

I'd like to acknowledge the generosity and financial support of the Ontario Arts Council in the completion of *Solomon's Ring*. I'd also like to thank everyone at Dundurn for helping this book come to life. A huge thank-you to my editor, Allister Thompson, and my agent, Amy Tompkins, for their hard work and dedication to this project. I'd be remiss if I didn't send a massive thank-you to my partner and best friend, Robert Stewart, who patiently puts up with my mad writing schedule.

**In the second book of the Daughters of Light series, the demon-hunted Seers are in a race against time return a stolen ring.**

Twin sisters Jade and Jasmine are finally together after a five-separation, but there's no time to enjoy the reunion. As Seers, sisters are being hunted by demons spilling through the rift, and the is on high alert against terrorist threats. The Protectors at Beacons have gathered as many Seers as possible, as the countries that have been destroyed by climate change are starting to close their bor On top of it all, Jasmine discovers that someone has stolen a ring the power to control the demons, and the Final Battle between Daughters of Light and the forces of darkness is approaching n quickly than anyone predicted.

**Mary Jennifer Payne** is the author of *Finding Jade*, book on the Daughters of Light Series, the YA novels *Since You've Been Gone Enough*, and several YA graphic stories. She lives in Toronto.

🏛 **DUNDURN**

$12.99 | £8.99

ISBN: 9781459737839

9 781459 737839